Scarlet

OTHER BOOKS AND AUDIOBOOKS
BY JEN GEIGLE JOHNSON:

The Nobleman's Daughter

Scarlet

a novel

jen geigle johnson

Covenant Communications, Inc.

Cover image: Arch of Marius-Illustration © duncan1890 courtesy of Istockphoto
Brunette Vintage Woman with Flowers in Hair © Dorota Gorecka / Trevillion Images

Cover design by Hannah Bischoff
Cover design copyright © 2018 by Covenant Communications, Inc.

Published by Covenant Communications, Inc.
American Fork, Utah

Printed in the United States of America
First Printing: May 2018

24 23 22 21 20 19 18   10 9 8 7 6 5 4 3 2 1

ISBN: 978-1-52440-468-0

To Sarah, who has her own love of performance and costume and who also cares for those who cannot care for themselves.

Acknowledgments

I AM BLESSED WITH VERY talented and helpful friends. Kimberly Vanderhorst's edits and beautiful way with words guided me early on. Dustin, John, and Adrienne Burger; Amy Wilson; Mindy Strunk; Didi Lawson; and Kristy Johnson all read early drafts. My weekly critique partners: Lisa Fenley, Jennifer Looft, Stacey Wells, Nuha Said, and my Latter-day Saint group: Matt Sullivan, Jessica Bell, David Christiansen, Reese Legara, and Cheryl Callison all added helpful guidance. I love working with Kami Hancock at Covenant. My family remains ever supportive. And of course, I must acknowledge the brains behind the original, the brilliant Baroness Orczy, who created the character of the Scarlet Pimpernel. All similarities to her story are my attempt at a nod in her direction.

Chapter One

Paris, France—1793

THE YOUNG URCHIN'S SHARP GAZE flitted through the crowd as if he knew things he shouldn't. Scarlet stood next to him, strangers pressed together by the mass gathering for the executions. Baked between the stone walls by the heat of the afternoon sun, Scarlet's neck beaded with sweat under her wig, and she longed to scratch her head.

"Kill the aristos!" a woman shrieked at them.

Scarlet jumped, hand at her heart, swallowing.

The woman's eyes bulged in their sockets, veins protruding along her neck. Her hand shook as she lifted a stained and wrinkled finger, pointing upward.

The last blade of the day rose by inches to the top of the guillotine. The angry woman, like everyone around her, willed it to drop, her expression full of yearning, nostrils flared wide to catch the scent of blood.

"Don't watch. She is deranged." Scarlet shielded the eyes of the young urchin standing at her side. His friends, also milling about them, far too young to witness, called him Abelino.

He did avert his eyes at first, but his neck turned, stretching out of her reach, until he found the woman again.

Moving farther away and dragging Abelino with her, Scarlet tried to place as many beating hearts between them and the crazed lady as she could.

Her body jostled a man to their left. He did not notice, chanting and rubbing his hands together with a feverish intensity. Evidence of bloodlust haunted the air, the cobblestone, the platform itself. People bumped up against Scarlet and Abelino, reshuffling the group; a great movement from behind rushed forward toward the guillotine. And they found themselves staring once again into the face of the woman. She worked herself into such a feverish frenzy, wringing her hands and rocking from foot to foot, that a line of drool traveled down her chin.

Scarlet and Abelino didn't watch the moment of death, but the grating sound of the sliding metal and the final thump at the end reached their ears. Abelino shivered. Deep regret filled Scarlet that she couldn't spare him from hearing it. A weight on her chest restricted her breathing, and she sorrowed for the loss of innocence and life.

But the woman showed no sorrow. She and her compatriots—a surging, seething, gruesome crowd of beings, human in name only—gave an exultant cheer and turned their attentions from *Madame La Guillotine* toward the west barricade.[1]

With a sigh, Scarlet squeezed Abelino's shoulder. "Off with you."

By all appearances, she was an older woman herself; at least, she hoped everyone viewed her as such, that she had hidden all mannerisms ingrained by her governess. She left the boy to fend for himself in the crowd and limped around the side of her cart, directing that the remaining coffins be filled.

She grabbed the arm of the nearest guard.

"And the heads, mind you. I need an extra bag for me heads."

Long strands of white-gray hair fell in her line of sight. She brushed them away when they tickled her nose. Her tongue moved around inside her mouth as if she had no teeth, coming forward at times, visible between her lips. She knew if she exaggerated ugly details that made people uncomfortable, they would not stare at her too closely.

A man in torn and tattered clothing watched as they loaded the last coffin on top of the others then climbed in behind them. She tossed the guards a bag of coins and then climbed up on her perch in the cart, reins in hand.

"Thank you, citizens. The doctor has a bit of work to do on 'em, to be sure."

One guard grimaced. "We don't want to be knowing, now do we?"

"Cut off the toes last week, he did." She leaned forward with a loud whisper. "Doing an experiment."

The guard slapped her donkey on the rump. "Shut yer trap, ye old hag. Just take your bodies and go."

She pulled on the reins to quiet the donkey. "Eh, now. Me papers. You forgot to sign me papers."

"Oh, blast and nonsense. Who'd confuse you for an aristocrat?" Laughing a bit too long at his own joke, he snatched the papers from her hand. "Give it 'ere now." The guard scribbled his signature, permission for Scarlet and her companion, known by the English nobility as Lord Simon Devereaux, to leave through Paris's barricaded gates.

---

1 This phrase is similar to one on the first page of *The Scarlet Pimpernel* (Baroness Emmuska Orczy, *The Scarlet Pimpernel Anthology*, vol. I [WilliamsBookseller.com, 2014], 1).

"To Bibot!" The crowd sought new entertainment, as they did every evening.

Cheers echoed off the walls of the square in anticipation of desperate aristocratic flights from the city. Any nobles not yet denounced sought to escape Paris before the committee accused them, but the barricades around the city had gone up weeks ago, and if the guards caught nobles leaving without the proper papers, they went straight to the Bastille, accused or no. The *sansculottes*, the poor, of France enjoyed these captures almost as much as they enjoyed the executions.

Bibot, the gatekeeper, a sharp-witted brute of a man intent upon guarding Paris's west gate, loved the aristos with a twisted obsession that increased the more he caught.

Though some had escaped in other ways, as of yet, not a single aristocrat had left Paris through the west barricade.

Scarlet hoped today would change Bibot's perfect record. Their lives depended on it.

The cart pulled up, next in line.

"Papers!" Bibot shouted, and the crowd cheered.

She handed them over, willing her hands to steady themselves, and said, "Carrying out the bodies, citizen."

Suspicious as always, the burly Bibot eyed the coffins in her cart. "Search them."

"Oh, not the bags, monsieur." Her voice took on a pleading tone, diverting his attention. She held her breath.

Bibot bristled, and his thick eyebrows raised and lowered several times in consternation. "Oh no? You there, toss me that bag!"

Relief warmed her, and she bit back a smile.

Lord Simon Devereaux, her ever-loyal partner and dear friend, dressed in ragged and filthy clothing, cradled the bag for a moment and then swung it over the side of the cart. It dented the earth where it landed and fell open to reveal what everyone nearby recognized as a mound of human hair. But Bibot reached down without looking, grabbed a handful, and held the head up.

The crowd cheered.

She watched his eyes, waiting for the moment of realization. Not even Bibot could countenance the lifeless appendage in his hand, she hoped. His reaction would either reward or doom them all.

The corner of his gaze caught human features in his tight grip, and he dropped the whole mess, cursing. Wiping a smear of blood across his shirt, he shoved the papers back into the cart. "Move out! Move out, I say!"

Lord Devereaux's face twisted and contorted, turning a bit pink. Then he let out the wail of a greatly disturbed man, maybe a little slow in his thinking. "Mine." He reached for the bag.

Exultant inside but outwardly incensed in all her actions, Scarlet clenched her fists. "Me heads!" she shrieked. "He's stolen our heads!" She caught Lord Devereaux's eye and nearly smiled, turning away before she could.

Bibot fumbled with the bag and tried to toss it back to her, but it fell short, hitting the edge of the cart only, and spilled its contents, which bounced across the stony ground before rolling to a stop.

She stood, waving her arms about, entreating the crowd. "Me heads! Thief! Give me back me heads!"

Lord Devereaux increased the volume of his own wailing, their discordant notes clashing together in such a jarring sound Bibot was sure to bless their departure. The cart began to pull away at a quicker pace.

Grumbling from the crowd surprised her.

A man called out, "Here man, it's her property, now, isn't it?"

Would they support her when challenging their hero, Bibot?

The man himself chased after, tossing heads inside until they had all been returned, and Scarlet reclaimed her seat and her taciturn demeanor. She brushed off her torn clothing, a cloud of dust rising from it. Lord Devereaux too resumed his seat, legs dangling off the back of the cart.

The impenetrable Bibot shivered in disgust, wiping his hands over and over down the front of his trousers.

Abelino waited up ahead at the side of the path, clutching his side and laughing as though he couldn't stop, full tears on his face. As the cart approached him, she looked down into his bright countenance and winked. He grinned even wider and ran off into the darkening streets of Paris.

***

Familiar landmarks encouraged her in their race to escape as dusk turned to night. Dark old trees, gnarled but cheery, welcomed their cart to the journey's end. She sighed. "Lord Devereaux, my scalp itches; my very brain tingles. This wig is reaching the point of unbearable." Lady Scarlet Cavendish pressed one delicate finger against the back of her head while holding the reins in her other hand.

He climbed over the tops of eight coffins to sit beside her in the front.

"I'm weeping in sympathy, my lady."

She scowled and pushed the donkey faster as their rickety cart lumbered along the old country roads.

"I could do without your sarcasm, sir."

They rode in silence for a moment. Scarlet knew he bit his tongue, stopping his response, but only just.

She goaded him. "I see your smirk, you know."

He laughed. "Can I not even smirk without your knowledge?"

"Certainly not." She brought the donkey to a walk, concern for the others reminding her to avoid a large pothole. "I hope our passengers did not get too jostled going at the speed we did."

Lord Devereaux ran a hand over his face. "I'll be happy when we reach Dover."

She turned to him and placed her hand on his arm. "I do hope you care for yourself while we are home. Rest, Simon. Go to a ball. Visit Penelope."

He nodded. "It's Franny."

"Is it?" she asked.

"Her name is Franny."

She frowned. "Find yourself a nice Penelope."

He shook his head and grinned. "What, precisely, is *wrong* with Franny?"

She waved her hands. "Penelope just has such a nice *ring* to it. Penelope. See?"

They pulled deep into a copse of trees where members of their league waited. Lord Andrew Hastings and two others started opening coffins and helping the five members of the de Molier family climb out, legs shaking beneath them, onto the soft earth beside the cart.

Moonlight lit the area immediately around them, and a path to their front led down a hill to the edge of water, visible only to the keen eye.

Scarlet breathed out in satisfaction.

Stepping forward to the group, Lord Hastings said, "Come with us, please." He held his arm out for the young lady, the de Molier's eighteen-year-old daughter, Suzanne, to take. She smiled weakly up at him, her blonde curls softly bouncing on her shoulders, and allowed his escort down the small path toward a waiting jolly boat.

The smell of damp earth, welcome after the pungent odors of Paris, mixed with the salt of the sea. Twilight had grown dark, the trees above them merely shadows against the starlit sky. But the sound of low waves, lapping against a boat, directed their footsteps.

Scarlet slapped her reins, shouting to her donkey. The cart pulled away from the group as if she were returning to Paris, but she left the donkey tied to a tree and circled back by foot.

Nimble fingers worked through her change of apparel. Bless her modiste for the modifications she had made to Scarlet's various costumes. Scarlet had hidden a satchel in the hole of a tree, and she was now closer to the group than any realized as she retrieved it.

Suzanne's voice carried to her. "So she works for the Pimpernel, then? I do wish we could have thanked her, even though she is a bit frightening to gaze upon."

Scarlet peered through the trees.

Andrew patted Suzanne's hand still on his arm. "The Pimpernel and his accomplices wish to remain anonymous. We function with the utmost secrecy and hope you will help us maintain it."

Suzanne nodded vigorously, and her father, a portly gentleman with graying hair, responded, "We will never speak of it. Please express to the wonderful man how grateful we are."

"To think we could have been beheaded by morning." The Comtesse de Molier lost her composure to tears. "Bless him. Oh, bless the man."

The comte pulled her into his arms.

Their daughter cleared her throat. "Well, I for one should like to join him. It's appalling what this dreaded committee has done to our beautiful France." Suzanne's lower lip protruded ever so slightly, and Scarlet smiled at her bravado.

Lord Hastings cleared his throat. "Such fine sentiments, and brave ones too." He leaned nearer to Suzanne, lowering his voice. "I feel the same—all those on the league do—which is why we step in to aid the Pimpernel when we can." He took hold of her small hand and held it in his own, eyes searching her face until she blushed and stared at her slippers.

Lord Devereaux gestured toward the water. "I will pass along your gratitude to the Pimpernel. Now, if you could hurry and step into this modest conveyance, we have one more passenger, and we will be on our way."

"One more? But who?" Suzanne craned her neck to see into the trees around them.

Lord Devereaux fell back into the shadows.

Out from the trees stepped Lady Scarlet Cavendish. "Never fear, my dear Lord Devereaux. I am here. Oh yes, my dears! I have arrived!"

Completely transformed, she prayed she looked resplendent, distractingly so, in her latest gown. Her hair was tied back in a modest and simple low bun and her cheeks, no doubt still rosy, the only evidence of her rapid ride through the countryside. All sign of age and dirt wiped from her youthful and glowing face, she hoped she looked to be no more than her true age of five and twenty.

She practically glided toward them, hands reaching out to all, greeting each in turn. She allowed Andrew Hastings, a dear member of her league, to help lift her above the water and place her in the dinghy with the others.

"Thank you, my dear Lord Hastings."

Lord Devereaux came out from the shadows, and he too had transformed, free of mud streaks and grime, dressed in shiny hessians, a jacket, and a tied cravat.

He approached Lord Hastings. "Showing off a bit, are we?" Lord Devereaux muttered. "Tied the oriental?"

Lord Hastings raised his chin to show off his immaculate neckcloth. "At least I'm not wearing my wig. Tut, man! Did you bring the powder as well?"

When both men paused at the same time and eyed Suzanne, who watched their exchange with large open eyes, Lady Scarlet Cavendish smiled in amusement.

Lord Hastings straightened his shoulders.

"Boys, gentlemen. Let us make haste. Our boat awaits!" Lady Cavendish called to them as she pointed out into the darkness, the light from the moon illuminating only the shimmering water to their front. The men jumped in and took up oars, and the jolly boat floated out from shore, making its way into the darkness of open water.

Suzanne said, "Lady Cavendish, it is good to see you again, but I do not understand. You are coming with us?"

"Oui. I find I am tired of French shores and long for my beautifully *English* homeland."

Suzanne's face wrinkled. "But how did you come to be here?"

The comtesse chastened, "Suzanne."

The young lady bowed her head. "I did not mean to pry."

Lady Cavendish smiled indulgently at her. "You will find, *ma fleur*, since the passing of my dear Rupert, may he rest in peace, most things I do are a bit eccentric; but I am harmless, I assure you."

Andrew and Simon coughed into their sleeves.

She narrowed her eyes. "You see, I was here visiting France, but my dear friends were in need of transportation, so I asked the staff to arrange it, and here we are. Now, shall we be off, then?"

The passengers turned to see where she pointed. The side of a ship, with a rope ladder dangling down, appeared out of the darkness. Their small craft sidled up to it, and Lord Devereaux helped each person grab hold of the rungs and make their way up the side of the boat.

As soon as all other passengers and Simon were up and over the top, Lady Cavendish stepped nimbly onto the ladder and, with a great shove of her foot, pushed their jolly boat away, toward shore. She knew that someone would be along to collect it and anchor it once again amongst the trees. Then, hoisting her skirts with one hand and flinging them over her shoulder, she climbed up the ladder herself and onto the deck. As she breathed in the ocean air with great satisfaction, a smug smile found its way to her lips.

"Thinking of Bibot?" Simon arrived at her side.

"How did you know?"

"The first aristos to sneak past his eminence. This deserves a celebration."

Lady Cavendish smiled. "I saw the boy again."

Simon's gaze sharpened. "Did he recognize you?"

"I think he did. He looked right at me and grinned his impish smile."

Simon shook his head, staring out at the dark rolling water. "How does he do it?"

She shrugged delicately. "He is observant."

"He is dangerous."

Lady Cavendish clucked her tongue. "Nonsense. He is a dear child. They call him Abelino."

"Well, he has me worried. It is uncanny how he can find you in a crowd no matter what you look like. Your own mother wouldn't recognize you in one of your disguises, but this child can. How old is he?"

She thought for a moment. "He can't be more than nine or ten. But there is nothing for you to worry about in him. Spend time instead helping me think of more creative ways to save our dear brothers and sisters in France. We must get word of the denouncements earlier. We save all we can, but news of many of the condemned reaches our ears too late."

Simon eyed her for a moment and then nodded. "Certainly." He bowed to her then paused. "No one could possibly save them all. You take so much upon yourself. Be happy with the ones we do bring to safety." Turning, he moved across the deck and down the stairs below.

Lady Cavendish watched him go, more grateful than ever for such a capable team. Finally alone, she let out a long breath. The east and south barricades were closed, which had left the west barricade as their only option today, and the risks had weighed on her. The ship tilted, and she reached out with shaking hands to steady herself. She willed her shoulders to loosen, her jaw to relax. It might take their entire journey across the channel for her to calm, but thoughts of the sprawling grounds of her estate soothed her.

"Captain!" she called.
"Aye, my lady."
"Let's go home."

Chapter Two

THE CHEERFUL YELLOW OF THE walls and the teal and orange in the curtains of her favorite morning room did little to lighten Scarlet's angst. She clutched a recent letter in her fist, and her foot tapped the floor.

"There is nothing for it but to go back."

Pulling out a new sheet of white paper and dipping her quill in ink, she began to write. She was so intent upon her missive that, at first, she did not hear Buckley, her butler, clearing his throat and announcing a caller.

He cleared his throat again. "Excuse me, my lady. The Honorable Baroness Lady Pinckney to see you."

Jarred from her missive, tension gathered around her eyes, the frustration at being interrupted and by such a distasteful visitor intensifying her growing angst. But she said only, "Show her into the front parlor, Buckley, and could you ask for some tea?"

"Very good, my lady."

She sat back in her chair for one indulgent minute, squeezing the bridge of her nose and closing her eyes. Lady Pinckney. Had the woman no one else to harangue with that tongue of hers? She breathed in deeply. Ridiculous, what this woman reduced her to. Bibot troubled Scarlet only half as much.

She stood, squared her shoulders, and marched, knees up and head high, down the hall to the front parlor. The footman raised his eyebrows, but she returned his gaze with a wink, nodding for him to open the doors.

Lady Pinckney stood immediately and rushed forward, kissing both of Scarlet's cheeks and gushing over her gown. Smiling stiffly, Scarlet thanked her politely. While Scarlet poured tea, Lady Pinckney relayed all the uncomfortable and disadvantageous things she had heard or seen throughout the week.

"And you will not believe what I tell you of Lord Panning. No! He was caught retying his cravat while leaving the pantry. There are those who claim a maid has recently been dismissed from their employ . . ."

If Lady Pinckney were to be believed, the whole town was in an uproar and everyone unhappy.

"What a to-do! You will be pleased to hear the musicale was splendid, simply angelic. Our lovely debutantes showed their talents quite well, but did you hear that new Italian woman's selection? She sang a piece from the opera! The opera . . ."

Scarlet listened politely and nodded her head whenever Lady Pinckney looked her way. Maybe she would forebear her personal attacks, and Scarlet herself would be spared.

Forbearance not her strong suit, the baroness said next, "Oh, my dear, how lucky you are your husband is dead."

"Oh. Hmm." Scarlet felt the familiar stab of loneliness. Dear Rupert had been gone only these past two years, and thoughts of him were tinged with ache.

Lady Pinckney had married the Baron Lord Michael Pinckney, yet she appeared to loathe him. "You have all the best luck, Lady Cavendish. When you marry a man for position and title as you obviously must have done, and then you have to endure his presence in your life for only, what, three years?" She sipped her tea, watching Scarlet over the rim of her cup, eyes calculating.

"Two and a half," Scarlet replied.

Lady Pinckney fanned herself. "Like I said, all the best luck. And now, here you sit, the wealthiest woman in London, and a widow at that." Lady Pinckney clucked her tongue. "Though if I were in such a position, to be sure, I would make much better use of all that had been given me."

Scarlet limited her response to raised eyebrows. Maybe the woman would stop.

"Oh yes, indeed. Have you considered how much good your substantial wealth could accomplish? How much the League of Orphans could use your support?" She shook her head in disappointment and bit the edge of her sandwich.

Scarlet stared absentmindedly out the window, the crux of her frustration so aptly demonstrated by the annoying Lady Pinckney. At times, desire bubbled up inside to share with someone, to worry jointly with another human, or at least to know that someone at home worried and waited for her return. But Lady Pinckney would never be that someone, and so she pursed her lips.

Searching for a distraction on the lawn, she sat up abruptly in her chair. Two familiar riders approached down the front lane.

Lady Pinckney must leave, and now.

Scarlet stood up. "Ah, my dear Lady Pinckney." The odious woman looked up in surprise as Scarlet stood over her. "I am terribly sorry I may no longer be the brunt of your dull wit this morning."

Lady Pinckney began to demur and then paused and frowned.

Lady Scarlet continued. "Yes, very dull; you don't mind me mentioning it, I am certain. But if the baron would deign to engage in some lengthy conversation with you for any stretch of days, he could sharpen you up again. Why, he's as droll as any I daresay, and you are to be commended. Married above yourself. Quite a catch, that one. Bravo, my dear." Scarlet clapped her hands together in gentle applause, looking hopefully at Lady Pinckney.

Her guest's normally creamy complexion turned a shade of red so dark, it reminisced of purple. Sputtering, she rose from her chair, and Scarlet breathed a sigh of relief. The woman was leaving.

Scarlet motioned toward the parlor entryway. "I shall ask Buckley to show you out through our back gardens. They are quite lovely this time of year. I feel the walk will aid in your constitution. Looking a bit peaky today. Your color is off, my dear. Perhaps more, dare I say, romance might aid in that department. Nothing like love's fresh bloom on a lady's cheeks. How well I remember my first months of marriage: bliss, I tell you."

She stared off across the room with such an expression of rapture that Lady Pinckney stormed from the room, Buckley directing the way toward the back of the house. Scarlet fell back into the nearest chair with a huff.

Moments later, Andrew and Simon walked through the front door, visible from her front parlor. She craned her neck down the hallway, ensuring the complete exit of Lady Pinckney. They bowed synchronously, and Andrew said, "You summoned?" His eyebrow rose to extreme heights on his forehead.

Lady Scarlet could not help but laugh. "Oh, Andrew. Do control that thing. Soon it will be up in your hairline, and we will lose sight of it altogether."

"Oh, but Lady Cavendish," he protested. "All the truly roguish lords have mastered the look. The ladies are overcome. Near swoons in my presence with the simple raise of an eyebrow and my lips just so." He paused to show them.

Simon grunted. "You look ridiculous, and that's the truth. Perhaps if you improved your wardrobe instead?" He raised his quizzing glass to take a closer look at Andrew's breeches. "Use some color, man. A goat would be more interesting to gaze upon."

"Perhaps if we could set aside our ridiculous focus on fashion when no one else is around . . ." Scarlet stood and gestured for them to follow her into her study. Once inside she explained, "Lady Pinckney is here about the place somewhere."

With an extra dose of theatrics, the men gasped and checked the hallway, which inspired a grateful laugh from Scarlet.

"We sent her out by way of the rear gardens, but she will be none too pleased when she finally sorts her way out of there, and I hope the two of you are long gone or safely ensconced in here before then."

"Relieved to avoid the encounter, naturally." Simon shuddered.

If Lady Pinckney were to get a whiff of their presence, she would never leave. She sought male attention wherever it could be found. And worse, the neighborhood would soon be made aware of her suspicions as to the men's motivations for visiting Scarlet.

Scarlet indicated that they all be seated and rang for some more tea. Looking into the faces of her dear friends, a lump formed in her throat and she almost couldn't speak her next words. "We must go back to France at the soonest tide. Tonight, if possible with a team of six."

Simon and Andrew both sharpened their gaze and, without hesitation, nodded.

Scarlet eyed them both. "You are either the bravest and most loyal men in all of England or the most smitten with me. Which is it?"

Simon smiled gently and then quirked his brow. "Well, it isn't your manner of dressing that attracts us, I assure you." He waved his quizzing glass over her person. "Lavender, my lady, to be sure. With red. No, I cannot possibly be smitten with that." He reached for her hand. "I know not if it is bravery or insanity, but we have pledged to serve thee and our league. If there is a need for us in France, then it is to France we will go."

Scarlet's eyes misted over, and she looked questioningly at Andrew.

He swallowed and nodded. "I would not miss an adventure with the lot of you, not for all the balls and lovely smiles in London."

Scarlet breathed out in relief and nodded.

The butler entered. "Lord Courtenay, Marquis of Exeter, to see Lord Devereaux, my lady."

Scarlet nearly choked on her tea. "How can he know you are here?"

Simon rose his eyes to the ceiling. "I cannot fathom how, but he is almost as persistent as you, Lady Cavendish. The man wants to be involved."

"Of course he's involved. Does he not remember our recent escape with the de Molier family?"

Andrew brushed his jacket. "He wants to know the Pimpernel. We've had a devil of a time dissuading him. I feared he would take to following us around." He indicated the direction of the front door as evidence.

Scarlet eyed them both. Her heartbeat sped up as it did every time she let another into her confidence. "I see no need to tell him . . ." She let her voice trail away. The man could be trusted. He had been remarkably brave and selfless on all their missions.

Her friends watched her, waiting.

"Should we include him?"

Andrew nodded, but Simon hesitated.

"Do you not trust him, Simon?"

He adjusted his quizzing glass. "I do trust him to safeguard this knowledge with his life. I just don't know how he will respond."

"Respond?"

"You are a bit much to take in at first glance." Andrew's eyes twinkled, but she could see his sincerity there as well.

She was used to people doubting her. She relied on most of her disguises eliciting that very sentiment to save her life. "Oh, he will recover. It is decided. Let him in."

Her butler nodded and turned from the room.

Lord Courtenay entered, his broad frame and commanding presence filling the small study. He bowed to them, eyes flitting from one to the other, obvious disappointment written in his lowered mouth and wrinkled brow.

Rising from her curtsy, Scarlet offered her hand. "To what do I owe this pleasure?" She smiled when embarrassment clouded his eyes.

He looked from Andrew to Simon, who offered only bland expressions, and then returned a helpless response to Scarlet. "I have come to call on you, my lady."

Andrew raised both brows high on his forehead. "Have you?"

He scowled. "And to have a word with Simon here."

Scarlet grinned. "Well, don't let me stand in your way. Have at him."

"Pardon me?"

"Have your word. He frustrates all and sundry at times. I too understand the need for a word with Simon now and again."

Lord Courtenay cleared his throat, uncomfortable.

Scarlet almost had pity on him. "Come now, my lord. What is it you have to say? You did say you wished to call on me as well. Shall we have a bit of tea? Sit, I will pour."

Lord Courtenay sat where she indicated and accepted tea from her hands. He cleared his throat again. "How have you been, Lady Cavendish?"

She bit her cheek. "Very well, and yourself? Have you been travelling of late? I heard of a recent voyage, I believe."

He looked to Andrew again. "I—well, as you know—travelled on your ship back over from France."

"Oh, too true! We were together, were we not? Though we did not converse much—seemed not the thing at the time; rescues going on and other such things." She waved her hand about as if rescues were the ordinary topic over tea. "Do you often travel to France? Are you in league with my friends here, skitting about across the channel, risking lives and my ship?"

He returned his cup to its saucer. "I do enjoy a good game of cards with them, if that's what you mean." His eyes flashed.

She would have thought him handsome if he had not been so often a guest of her late husband. Much like a brother now, she could only tease. But she tired of niggling him and stood, walking to the other side of the room.

"Men, give him our next assignment."

Simon turned to him. "We are to return to France tonight. We have only—"

"Wait, what are you doing, man?" Lord Courtenay looked meaningfully at Scarlet.

"Following orders. Now listen closely."

Lord Courtenay's eyes widened. He swallowed a couple of times.

"We will leave with the tide," Simon continued. "Please prepare yourself and call in two of the others. We will need a smaller team, just the four of us here and two more."

"The four . . ." He kept glancing at Scarlet but did not address her. She found this amusing.

"Lord Courtenay, is there a problem?" She raised an eyebrow.

"No—well, I don't think so. I was not aware of your knowledge of the league plans."

She nodded her head and sat behind her desk, opened a drawer, and pulled out her ring. "You are not aware of a great many things." She held out her ring, motioning for him to take a look.

He did and his eyes widened. "How did you get that?"

Andrew snorted, turning his head to smile at the wall.

"It has been in my family for nearly a century; grew the little red pimpernel flower all over our northern estate. This ring belonged to my father and his before him."

Lord Courtenay's blank stare would have amused Scarlet, but the time grew short now, and their sport at his expense was over.

He smacked his hands together. "Lord Cavendish! Why did I not see it? Of course he would be involved."

She opened her mouth and closed it again. "No, my dear Lord Courtenay. He passed away before the Pimpernel came to be. I fear this will come as a bit of shock to you, even with evidence right before your eyes, but I am the Pimpernel. Me."

His blank stare continued.

"But we are losing time. As Simon explained, we go out with the tide. Which, we learned on our last trip from Calais, waits for no one. Gather the men. We will convene on the ship tonight." She stood as if to dismiss them, and the men rose. "And, Lord Courtenay, we guard this secret closest of all. Every life depends upon my identity remaining a secret."

He nodded, following Andrew and Simon to the door, and then he paused, his back stiff. "I will not do it."

The men stopped.

"You are a woman! Our very lives, as you said, are in your hands."

"And capable ones they are, let us remind you." Simon's eyes held a sharp glint.

Lord Courtenay shook his head. "It is by miracle alone we have survived thus far."

Scarlet let out a long breath. "You may choose to step away, of course. We have no room on our league for any but the most loyal. But let me ask you: Are you willing to sacrifice for those who cannot help themselves? Place your very life at risk to save another?"

"Of course."

"Then nothing has changed. You are a great addition to our league."

Simon clapped him on the back. "Come, man. It takes some getting used to. If it would help, you may continue to think of her as a man."

He harrumphed. "That I could never do." Then he turned a deep shade of red. "I mean, you are lovely, Lady Cavendish, dear Rupert's marchioness."

Simon opened the door.

"Wait." She hated to stall their departure, but they must know the purpose of their hurried voyage.

She paused, eyeing them. "We are going after Comte Matteo Durand."

Lord Simon dropped his quizzing glass and stepped back inside the study. "Lady Cavendish, forgive me, but you cannot be serious. He is practically a revolutionary! Childhood friends with Éléonore Duplay." He waited for her reaction. Seeing none, he added, "Robespierre's mistress."

"I know who she is, Simon," Scarlet continued. "But, I assure you, Comte Durand is most definitely not a Jacobin or anything of the like. He has become dissatisfied with the violent turn of the Revolution. He cannot help the misfortune of a childhood acquaintance."

"A possible lover." Simon's eyebrows furrowed. He opened his mouth to continue, but Scarlet held up her hand.

"I have it on the highest authority that he is loyal to the *dauphin*, the rightful king of France." *Were he but recognized by his own citizens*, she thought.

The injustice of the dear child's situation weighed on Scarlet, and she longed for the day when he would be free.

Her voice lowered, and she narrowed her eyes. "Comte Durand has, on occasion, also been a loyal aid to the Pimpernel." She noted their surprised expressions with satisfaction. "Someone has denounced him to Robespierre himself, having discovered a supposed hidden lineage. Whether or not it is true no one can say, but he is accused of being a prince *legitime*."

"The literal bloodline of a prince? How can that be possible?" Simon frowned.

"It matters not how possible it is. Says Robespierre, 'Matteo Durand is almost as aristo as the *dauphin* himself.'" Scarlet shook her head. "And we all know his accusation is enough." She frowned, frustrated again at the abhorrent timing. "They tried to get word to us while we were still in France, but the messenger arrived too late. The comte himself will discover his new patronage when the Committee of Public Safety shows up at his door ready to haul him off to meet *La Guillotine*."

Andrew began pacing. "A friend of the Pimpernel . . . Matteo Durand. I am all amazement."

Her eyes followed his movement. "I have never met him. But he has been invaluable, yes."

Lord Courtenay's eyes widened. "You really are the Pimpernel?"

She ignored him. "His parents died when he was young, and he was raised by a wealthy uncle who has since deceased. A sad childhood. His uncle was said to be senile and the comte left much to himself, an occasional neighbor stepping in at times to set him right—raised mostly by the staff—and now that the uncle has passed, the Pimpernel might well be his only friend. And his only hope for escape."

Chapter Three

SOMETHING IN MATTEO'S BEDROOM CHANGED, as if the air shimmered differently around him. Hair on the back of his neck prickled. A quick look around the room showed nothing different from moments before, but a bead of sweat rolled down his temple. He slowed his breathing, softening his own movement, listening. A creak, unfamiliar, fingers sliding along a wall, a thump could be his imagination, so subtle and soft the sound. Behind his wall, another thump turned his head, and a shuffle at the servants' panel. And then the slow sliding of wood sounded behind him.

His skin crawled with the sensation of eyes watching, but he remained standing at his table, flipping through pages of a book as if nothing were amiss. The soft padding of feet moved closer. He shifted his weight forward to the balls of his feet while the intruder drew nearer behind him. Then he spun, grabbing an unlit candlestick. He swung it furiously in a great arc outward but stopped his arm before it connected with her face. "Éléonore. What are you doing here?" Stumbling from the stopped momentum, he retreated two steps, his breath catching. He ran a hand through his hair.

The corner of her mouth turned up, and she sashayed toward him, wearing a thin chemise. When she was close enough that he could smell the soap she used in her hair, their bodies almost touching, she said, "I missed you. I am alone tonight and wish I weren't."

Matteo frowned. "How did you get in here?"

She raised her eyebrows. "The servants' entrance, of course. Do you think I forgot all our games as youth, running through these halls?" She chuckled a low, throaty laugh. "Oh, Matteo. There is nothing about you that I have forgotten."

He folded his arms across his broad chest, the muscles tightening.

"You cannot be in here. Come back tomorrow through the front entrance, and fully dressed." He walked toward his bedroom door, swinging it open.

More and more, he regretted his childhood days, running at her side, fishing, climbing trees, the lot of it. She'd grown into a dangerous and powerful woman, and he could not be rid of her.

She pouted. "Don't send me out. Not yet. It's Robespierre," she whispered. "I am afraid." Her body trembled. "I need you, Matteo. You are my other half, the one my soul longs for." Reaching for him, she placed a hand on his arm. "He is too much. Too vicious. I am trapped." Pleading, she stepped closer, pressing herself against him, resting her head on his chest.

He stiffened, holding his hands out to his side, away from her. But for a flicker of thought, he hesitated, reacting to the raw fear in her face. A part of him felt drawn to the role he had always played in her life: protector, friend. When the other children of the aristocracy in his neighborhood had made fun of his awkward social habits, acquired from his recluse of an uncle, she'd stepped in as his friend. But, a commoner, she would have been bullied and shunned if not for his intervention. While they ridiculed, he was still a comte, which carried much more clout than any of them could boast.

He reviewed possibilities. If he could help her leave Paris, she could start over, free from the constant snare of her life. Cautiously he returned her embrace, considering further. He ran his hands up and down her back; then he stilled, remembering other hands that had held her thus. Pulling away, he searched her face. Before she could hide it, cunning—a shadow of Robespierre's own expression—reflected back.

Shaking his head, he moved away. "You don't need me. All doors are open for you. Leave on the next ship."

She widened her eyes. "But what of us? I need *you*, Matteo. It has always been you and I. We were made to be together." She ran her fingers up his arm.

All his hairs stood on end, and he stepped farther away from her. "You should leave."

Her lips thinned into a tight line and then, relaxing them, she pouted. "What is it? Am I no longer beautiful?" She held her arms out and turned in a slow circle.

Matteo shook his head. "It is what you have become that is no longer beautiful."

Her eyes bulged, and she slapped his face, a line of red filling the fresh white scratch along his cheek. Her sultry voice suddenly shrill, she shouted, "I had no choice. When the committee came for me, I did whatever I could to stay alive. How can you blame me for that? When you, you wouldn't take me!" Her words choked her and pain pinched her face, but her eyes flashed venom.

"Throwing yourself at Robespierre, using your . . . beauty to stay alive is . . . would be a torture worse than death. But worse even than that, you joined them, didn't you? Denounced innocents!" He pulled a handkerchief from his pocket, dabbing the blood from his cheek. "*You* are the reason the Dampierre family is dead. Even their children, sent to the guillotine. We grew up with them. How could you do that?" Hurt flashed through him as it had the day he'd heard the news, the day he'd come too late to save them.

"They were traitors. Guilty aristos who deserved *La Guillotine* for their crimes. How many died of hunger not one hundred feet from their estate? They earned their fate, as does every other wealthy noble." She sneered, and her face twisted into a new ugliness he did not recognize.

Matteo turned and reached for the bell pull.

Éléonore sneered. "Kick me out, will you? Force me from your home?" Her eyes narrowed into snakelike slits. "Your concern for these traitors is suspect. Perhaps you have turned your loyalties. What will happen, *Comte* Durand, when I withdraw my protection? Do you think Robespierre will sit for long and allow your filthy blood to pollute the streets of Paris?"

"I no longer care. I refuse to live under the thumb of your goodwill another moment. Be gone from my home and my life."

She whirled on her toes and strode out into the hallway. He followed her to the balustrade and watched her fume all the way down the stairs and out the front door.

Potier, his butler and friend, appeared at his side. "Was that . . . ?"

Matteo nodded. "Éléonore. I am afraid it was, and she did not leave pleased."

Potier's face showed concern, lines in his forehead deeper than usual. "Perhaps I should alert the staff and pack a few items?"

Matteo considered him for a long moment. "I think it would be best if we closed up the house. No one will be safe here for long. Please take any valuables as a gift for your family, except the family heirlooms. Don't risk your life for them, but if there is a place in some attic or cellar or other, I would be much obliged."

"Of course, Micho."

Matteo's eyes widened at Potier's use of his childhood endearment, and he gripped his shoulders in an embrace.

Potier's eyes shining, he said, "You are the best of men, my son. Go with God. But go. You are no longer safe here. We will be together again."

Matteo pulled him closer and held him, held on to his childhood, the cookies from Chef, the gentle encouragement from the man in his arms, and the relative safety of his home. Potier's family in the country would keep him safe for now. Matteo looked one last time into the tired old man's face, memorizing the laugh lines, now drawn with worry, and then he rushed back to his bedroom, pulled out his valise, and began throwing in items as quickly as he could.

Potier put a hand on his arm, staying his movement. "Allow me to do this. You go to your study and clear out everything you will need from the safe."

Matteo nodded and hurried down the stairs.

***

One week later, Matteo stood at the window of his new apartment on one of the most populated streets in Paris. Now that he had rid himself of Éléonore, the potential excited him. He made contact with old friends, and the beginnings of a team was in place. Finally, he felt free, able to make right all of his terrible wrongs. Already an enemy to France, what could he lose if he were to fight against the new Committee of Public Safety, fight against Éléonore and her precious Robespierre?

How nice it felt to be free of her ever-present threats and accusations. She always promised them, balanced with an ongoing conditional protection. That rolling tide of uncertainty and distrust had all but ruined his peace and threatened his sanity.

Not for the first time, he wished the tide of the Revolution had not spun so drastically out of control. He had labored for its beginnings, worked to turn the minds of the nobility to a more favorable, representative government. Even quietly supported the storming of the Bastille, until it had turned bloody, until he stood back in horror as he watched humanity's worst cajole each other into heinous behavior. He should have known on that day in July, the fourteenth, that it would worsen, should have recognized its beginnings when they stabbed de Launay, the director of the prison, multiple times and then paraded about with his severed head on a staff. Who but the most depraved souls would participate in such a crime? The prison had been taken at the time, with a paltry seven prisoners freed. And yet, the hungry crowd had sought to inflict suffering, had gloried in it.

Matteo could still see his own vomit in the street. As the violence had worsened, his dread had increased, and he'd spent many a torturous week, month, working feverishly and in secret to halt what he had helped ignite.

Matteo pulled a shirt over his head, stretching it across the tired muscles of his back. His arms ached from the exercise and exertion of the morning, his efforts to calm the agitation constantly pounding in his heart; but he felt at peace. When the Pimpernel once again had need of his services, he and his team would be ready.

Searching the street below, noting nothing out of the ordinary, he raised his eyes to the rooftops of Paris. He had chosen this apartment as a hideout because of the easy street visibility and because it had two entrances, one of which led down a set of stairs and into an alley.

A loud banging on the back door interrupted his thoughts. "Comte Durand. Open up for the citizens of France." The door rattled with persistent pounding.

No.

His senses immediately sharpened, his heart skipping beats in its rush to pound blood through his system. He grabbed his valise and ran to the front door. Swinging it open, he jerked to a halt. Éléonore stood in front of him, flanked by a squadron of guards. His mind raced through possibilities, palms sweating.

She stared at him, ice in her gaze. "Good. I see you are packed and ready. Guards."

She gestured with her hand. They rushed at him, wrenched the valise from his hand, twisted his arms behind his back, and tied his hands together.

Éléonore indicated the bag. "Although, you will have no need for that where you are going. The Bastille prisoners do not stay for long."

She cackled and walked away. The guards followed in her wake, jerking him along with them. They threw him onto the carriage floor, hands still tied.

Pressing his cheek into the floor, he inched up and twisted so that he sat on the bench. His mind scrambled for some sort of solution, some avenue of escape.

"Leave us." Éléonore joined him inside, her small frame sitting on the bench opposite.

The guard bowed his head and backed out of the carriage.

Her posture perfect, her chin high, she straightened her skirts and crossed her ankles, all the while grinning in such a manner he was sure her cheeks ached from the effort. Then she grew serious, and she stared at Matteo for a long moment.

Finally, she spoke. "Tell me. How does it feel to be utterly powerless? I wonder how you will react. Will you beg?" She watched him a moment longer. Then she gave the command to their driver to be off. "I could give you the same choices Robespierre gave me." She cleared her throat. "You can be my plaything. Come when I call, attend me when I need it, and in all things be at my side. Or . . . you can die a terrible death under the knife of *La Guillotine* tomorrow." She shook her head. "But I give you, Matteo, no such choice. You will be locked in the Bastille tonight and lose your head in the morning." She flicked a piece of lint off her dress.

Terror rose inside and threatened to black out his ability to think. He swallowed the lump in his throat and commanded himself to calm. Matteo studied her. He had one opportunity to convince her, one last hope to draw upon. "Remember when we climbed high into that tree? No one could find us. All day long they searched. It was just you and me."

She shrugged one shoulder, a slight lift he almost missed.

"We made a promise to each other. Do you remember it?"

Éléonore snapped, "To free France."

Matteo shook his head sadly. "No. To free France *together*. We saw before most people even noticed that France needed a new direction. It was you and me. We knew from the beginning."

Éléonore's face pinched in pain.

"We can still do that." He leaned forward. "This madness run by the committee is not what we hoped for. *Our* plans would have given our country peace, prosperity, happiness. We can escape, climb a new tree, get out of this nightmare, hide together until it's over. Please, Éléonore. Don't do this. Come away with me." He locked her with his gaze, eyes boring into hers. She hesitated. He saw the inner struggle. And then, in a matter of seconds, it was gone.

She shook her head, "*Non, mon ami*. It is too late for that. I find I am quite . . . happy with my arrangement. You must recall that last night was not the first time I have offered myself to you. I remember well your words: 'Éléonore, there can never be anything between us. I must marry the nobility, and you—you are the carpenter's daughter.'"

His head dropped, knowing his fate was sealed. If he could take back those words, spoken in the arrogance and naivety of youth, he would have, a hundred times. And now they had cursed him to his death.

"You see, I *am* freeing France, darling." Matteo shook his head, but she held up her hand. "Yes. I am purifying our homeland, washing her with the blood of all the wealthy and entitled aristos like yourself. And when she is free, when France is cleansed of your treachery, she will be ready for a new rule, for her destiny as a free nation." Éléonore's eyes shone as she spoke. "Besides. I have power, Matteo. Power like I've never had before. I find that I like it."

He looked back up into her face. "Until Robespierre summons. Where is your power then?"

Éléonore reached out and slapped his face again, the second time in a week. She was about to say something, but their carriage lurched violently to the side, throwing her onto the floor. Matteo used his feet to brace himself and remained upright. He kicked at the door. With any luck, the wheel had fallen off the axle altogether.

He bent his knees, ready to kick the door again when he was stopped by a pair of emerald-green eyes.

A face filled the small carriage window, raven curls spilling from a hat that tried to contain them, but all he noticed were the eyes. They met his, and he felt his response to her in the center of his chest. She stared back at him, unmoving for several seconds. Then she blinked and quickly opened the door, motioning to someone behind her.

A man entered the carriage and untied his arms. Éléonore in turn had her mouth gagged and arms and legs tied by men entering on her side of the carriage. He called over his shoulder, "Goodbye, Éléonore. I would say it has been a pleasure . . ."

His rescuers had subdued the guards, footmen, and driver.

Impressive.

He glanced around, looking from face to face until he saw one he recognized: a young boy he knew as a messenger for the Pimpernel. The lad winked at him, and Matteo smiled.

Saved.

One of the men said, "We must hurry. We are in no way out of danger yet." As soon as he finished his warning, a group of soldiers, part of Éléonore's own men following the path of the carriage back to the prison, rounded a corner toward them.

"Split up. Meet at point number one," the green-eyed woman shouted. Everyone broke off, running in different directions.

Four men flanked Matteo, two at each side. He burst into a sprint. "I don't need a cocoon. I need speed." He laughed at the exhilaration he felt at a full run. The others kept up, smiling too, although their faces, tense and pinched, bespoke the direness of their situation.

After dodging through alleys and across streets, they stopped in front of a beautiful home with flowers in the front beds. Their group of five rushed up the back stairs. Once at the upper landing, Matteo bounced on his toes, searching up and down the back alleyway while someone used a key to enter the door.

Already inside, the other members of the team waited.

For the first time, Matteo noticed that the green-eyed, raven-haired beauty was dressed as a man, wearing trousers and a loose white shirt. She wore a hat on her head, and she covered her face with linen, wrapped so that only her eyes were visible.

Immediately, she took command of the group. "We have little time. We will not lose them for long, and the gatekeepers will never grant our leave if we are pursued by soldiers. We must move faster than news can travel. With our change of plans, I say goodbye to you all. Andrew, please help Comte Durand into his new clothing."

Andrew approached Matteo and said, "Comte Durand? I am Andrew Hastings, at your service. If you will follow me?" They shook hands, and after another look at the strange woman who stood in the doorway at the back of the house ready to leave, Matteo followed him into a back bedroom.

Faster than the quickest valet, Andrew had Matteo dressed and primped as a fine French gentleman. As they hurried down the stairs to prepare to leave again, Matteo said, "What a fine house. To whom do I owe gratitude for such a beautiful place of refuge?"

A new woman entered, as captivating as the one who'd just left. "Do you like it, my dear? I purchased it several years ago, before this awful madness struck Paris. It was in a lovely part of town at the time." She sighed in an exaggerated fashion and then came toward them, hand outstretched.

Andrew reached for her hand and led her to Matteo. "Lady Scarlet Cavendish, this is Comte Matteo Durand."

Matteo's voice caught and then he cleared his throat; taking her hand in his, he bowed over it, kissing her knuckles while looking up into her face. "A pleasure." Matteo hoped he sounded more gallant than he felt. The beauty of the woman now standing in front of him was unmatched in any of his acquaintance. His thoughts whirled around him, not stopping long enough to be recognized. A thrilling tightness spread across his chest. Her dark hair complemented her lovely creamy skin, of which he had an ample view down her flawless neck and across her neckline. Diverting his eyes, he grinned into her face.

Lady Scarlet Cavendish opened her mouth and closed it, a blush heightening her color. Then she laughed—a beautiful musical sound—and said, "This will be a much more delightful assignment than I imagined."

Matteo frowned. "Assignment?"

One side of Andrew's mouth lifted and his eyes twinkled. "Yes, Lady Cavendish has agreed to ride with you in her carriage out the gates of Paris. We hope our planned deception will distract long enough for escape. You are destined for a picnic in the country with your newfound love." With his head, Andrew indicated Lady Cavendish.

She clasped her hands in front of her body and rocked back and forth on her feet. "Yes, well, as I said, a delightful assignment." Her eyes sought Matteo's, searching their depths. He felt his heart speed up as he sensed his soul bare to her. He wondered what she saw and hoped she approved.

After a moment, she said only, "Shall we?"

Was she married? He thought he remembered mention of a Rupert Cavendish, an obscenely wealthy lord or other in England. She must be his wife, but she wore no ring.

Although dangerously enticing, one thing disturbed him about the arrangement.

"I cannot allow you to aid in this manner, my lady. Perhaps you do not understand. Your life will be at great risk . . ."

Andrew coughed, covering his mouth with his hand and turning away.

Lady Cavendish's eyes sparkled up at Matteo. "I find I do not mind. But I do believe we must be off. The carriage is here waiting." And she gestured toward the front door.

He sat beside his new lovely accomplice and marveled at her courage. She appeared completely unruffled. "Why are you doing this?" he asked her profile.

She turned to him, and he was struck by the brilliance of her eyes, another pair of green eyes. Hers twinkled with fun and the strength of her kindness. She smiled up at him, and his brain clouded over.

Her voice, a golden timbre, soothed him. "Andrew is a close family friend. I help whenever I can. You dear French—what a horror you are experiencing." She placed a hand on her heart. "It is my daily prayer it will all end, and soon."

Matteo nodded. "I will not leave until our people are safe. Day and night I will work to bring a stop to Robespierre and his horrific reign."

Lady Cavendish looked out her window, her voice quiet but firm. "Comte Durand, you must leave France."

His body stiffened next to hers. "I cannot. Is that where we are headed? To England? Because if so, I must leave this carriage at once."

Lady Cavendish turned to him, her voice urgent. "You must not. The west barricade is upon us. Bibot is at this very moment hungry for aristocratic blood. We only hope we have won in our race to get here before the news of your downfall has reached his ears. Now, please, for all that is good and holy in France, do your part and play along, or we all die."

The carriage pulled to a stop. They had indeed reached the west barricade and were now a part of the line of people attempting to leave the gates of Paris.

"I cannot desert my homeland. There is much good I can do here. The Pimpernel. I could assist him. I could hide people. I must do something. I cannot simply leave."

Lady Cavendish moved closer to him and placed her hand on his arm, her body leaning suggestively into his. She reached her other hand to palm the side of his face. He noticed people in the crowds looking curiously, some venomously, into their carriage. Remembering their ruse, he smiled down at her and wrapped his arm around her shoulders, pulling her closer to him.

She said, "You will not be deserting them if you leave. If you stay, you will die, and then you will truly have deserted them forever. Robespierre is under the impression that your concealed bloodline has now been revealed and that you are, in fact, a prince *legitime* of France." She reached up and curled a lock of his hair around her finger.

Matteo's eyes widened in disbelief. "She wouldn't."

Lady Cavendish nodded. "I assume you are referring to Éléonore Duplay? She did. And now in France, your life is worth only the amount of enjoyment these lovely citizens will reap from your swift meeting with *La Guillotine*. Please, Comte Durand. You could do much good from the safe shores of England."

Her eyes implored him, wide and pleading. He didn't know how any man ever refused this woman. He nodded. He would leave, for now. But he would not desert France, even if he must help from afar.

"Kiss me!" Lady Cavendish pulled at his neck.

His eyes widened in surprise, but his body yielded almost without thinking. His lips bumbled a moment, searching, until he found hers. Awkwardly at first, his mouth pressed into hers, unsure of the expectation. Then her lips softened and responded to his touch. All thought flew from his mind. Her supple, full mouth was delicious. All he could think was how to devour her lips over and over again. He pulled her closer, deepening their kiss, maddeningly lost to the soldiers at their doors, to their driver who was explaining the outing.

At length, somewhere out of his body, he felt a hand shake his shoulder. Then Lady Cavendish stiffened. He pulled away and immediately sharpened his focus. Soldiers gestured from the opened carriage door, urging him to exit immediately.

Lady Cavendish laughed, her face still inches from his own, sitting on her bench. She called out to the soldiers, "What is it, men? Oh Bib-bot! Where is Bib-bot?"

Still heady from the feel of her lips, the exaggerated mispronunciation of Bibot's name caused Matteo to stifle a coughed laugh, turning his head to the side.

The soldiers parted for the man himself, who, when he saw her, stopped short. "Oh, my Lady Cavendish! I didn't know it was you in here."

She laughed again, and her tinkling sounds made even a few of the soldiers smile in return. "Well, of course you didn't, Bib-bot, you old dear. But I bring you a treat. Tell me that you recognize one of France's most loyal citizens? A personal friend of Éléonore Duplay herself?"

Bibot's eyes widened in concern. He looked at Matteo, who tried to appear as arrogant as possible.

"This, my good citizen Bib-bot, is Matteo Durand." She let that sink in for a moment. If they had never heard of him before, they were at least pretending to take her seriously. "And we are late for our droll little picnic in the country. If you would be so kind . . ." She gestured toward the gate at their front.

Bibot hesitated for only a moment before calling to the soldiers in their path, "Let them pass."

The men shut their carriage doors, and Lady Cavendish called out, "Ta ta, citizens! See you in a few hours!" She blew kisses to some in the crowd as they went by.

Matteo shook his head and moved a respectable distance away but kept to the same bench. This beautiful woman tucked more courage inside her little body than anyone he knew.

When they passed the gate, both relaxed their shoulders in great relief. "We beat the news of your treachery, but my guess is only by a hair." Lady Cavendish looked back behind them. "We must continue at this slow pace for just a few feet more until we are out of sight."

They turned a bend. Letting out another relieved breath, she said quietly, "Now." Seemingly of the same mind, the horses burst into speed, tearing down the old dirt road as if chased by the devil himself.

She turned to him, eyes sparkling. "You were brilliant. Thank you for playing along."

His mind sputtered at her smile. Was she referring to his kiss? He moved closer to her and raised his eyebrow. "What was it you said about this assignment being much more pleasant than you had originally planned?"

She blushed and looked at her hands.

Matteo asked, "Is there a Lord Cavendish waiting for you somewhere? Might he call me out upon our arrival?" He teased but watched her face closely.

A flash of sadness crossed her eyes. "I am a widow, you see. Lord Cavendish has been gone nearly three years now."

Matteo reached for her hand. "I am sorry." With his eyes, he tried to portray the sympathy he felt for this brave woman. Her hand found his lips before he realized it was his own effort that had brought it to him. He had never met anyone like her. Shaking his head and grinning, he considered her. She ignited all his protective instincts at once while at the same time emanating such an aura of adventure that he felt like discovering a new land at her side.

"What is it?" she asked.

He leaned closer and looked into her expressive eyes. "I find I have discovered a happy nugget to the sad tale of my exile to England."

"Oh? And what is that?"

His thumb rubbed circles across the back of her glove. "I do hope that my time in England will allow me to call on you? That is, if *you* will allow?"

She raised her eyebrows, eyes twinkling. "I think your time will allow. It is my understanding that you will be staying on the Cavendish estate, in the dowager cottage. My brother-in-law and his Lady Cavendish are seldom in residence but have come to stay for a time. And you are naturally welcome to take all your meals with us, if you'd like." She looked up shyly into his face. "But yes, I would much enjoy it if you were to call on me."

Matteo's grin stretched larger than he would have liked, but it could not be helped. Living in the near proximity to this enchanting woman while she was amenable to him calling on her, taking dinner with her—yes, this would be an enjoyable distraction indeed. And while he was there, he would immediately begin corresponding to France in hopes of his eventual return.

They felt the change in speed immediately as the horses slowed to a stop. "I will see you in Calais, my darling French prince." Lady Cavendish waved airily to him.

Andrew opened the carriage door and gestured for him to hurry. They rushed him to a donkey cart. He got in and they threw a blanket over his body. Sandwiched between piles of old cabbage, he hardly noticed the stale air under his blanket, his mind and heart alight with thoughts of Lady Cavendish.

Andrew called, "Sorry about the bumpy ride you are about to have. Don't say a word, and stay covered."

Matteo jerked his head up. "And what of Lady Cavendish? Who is caring for her?"

Andrew eyed him for a moment before responding. "We are. She will arrive safely."

Matteo nodded and pulled the blanket back over his head, lying on his side in a ball on the floor of a cabbage cart. He had never felt more alive or free. Gone was the ever-present overbearing thought that he survived under the thumb and goodwill of Éléonore. He felt exhilarated and empowered. Perhaps Lady Cavendish was correct: perhaps he would be of better use in England.

Chapter Four

THE CARRIAGE FELT EMPTY, BEREFT, as soon as Comte Durand exited. He carried all his confidence and fire and courage out the door, and Scarlet immediately missed him. She had leaned on his strength in their charade, more than she had with others.

And that kiss. She leaned back against her carriage bench, slumping in her seat. She blushed thinking about it. He'd made it desperately difficult to concentrate. Everything about him exuded masculine charm. She felt a new vulnerability, responsive to his excellent cut and the tightness across the breadth of the shoulders and chest of his well-fitting jacket. His dark hair, thick and wavy, had fought to fall across his forehead. Chocolate-brown eyes had searched hers with an intensity she had not felt in a long time.

Her response to him was no charade. And his lips had not been merely acting their part, either, she hoped. A hint of insecurity niggled at her. Surely Comte Durand was not toying with her; he could not possibly have deepened their kiss in such a way, not at the west barricade in Paris while their lives were in danger. No. He had likely been as affected as she.

And he had asked to call on her. How lovely and innocent. She hadn't felt the luxury of such a simple enjoyment in many months. She smiled, and the carriage took off at the same breakneck speed as before.

The driver opened up a hatch from above, and Simon peered down at her. "Dreaming of your new man?" He winked and raised his eyebrows as the carriage swayed and bumped along, moving ever faster.

She opened her mouth in exasperation. "Is that really what you want to ask me at this moment?"

He laughed, the noise lost to the wind outside, but she saw his face and imagined the sound. When Simon laughed, everyone joined him, so infectious was the sound.

"They are in pursuit, my lady. But we are only minutes from Calais. We will lose them there, rendezvous with your new French *amour*, and be off to Dover in no time."

Scarlet took a deep breath, ignoring the *amour* comment. Her eyes sharpened, and she said, "Perhaps we should allow them to stop us. I find I might enjoy a bit of conversation with Mademoiselle Éléonore Duplay."

Simon frowned. "Do you think she is with them?"

Scarlet nodded. "I have no doubt. Yes, Simon, let's have a bit of fun with this one, shall we?"

Simon raised his eyebrow and smiled wickedly down at her. Then he closed the hatch. As Éléonore became more of an opponent, Scarlet sought to understand her, wanted to see what rattled the woman. The carriage sped up, and the countryside whirled past them. They closed the last quarter of a mile in record time.

Calais spread out before them in a beautiful array of colors. Scarlet noticed all the usual sellers out on the streets, offering their wares. Rows of flowers perfumed the air next to fishermen, twine, and netting. The fishmongers provided their own aromas on the other side of the market, near the butcher's carts. Sellers of fruit, sailors' trinkets, folds of fabric, and exotic spices filled stalls and tables. Often, Calais gifted her with a sense of adventure but today, only the urging to return home.

Their carriage weaved through rows of carts and up and down thoroughfares. When they turned onto the busiest street in all of Calais, they were forced to a walk and were flanked by carriages, hacks, and donkey carts, all come to the seaside town for leisure or business or both. She turned, peering out the back window above her seat. Their pursuers followed, four carriages back. She smiled in anticipation. Then she startled as her own door opened, and Comte Durand stepped inside. Her mouth opened in shock, and she waited for him to explain himself.

"I saw your carriage, so I vacated my cabbage cart, as fine an equipage as it was, and returned to you."

She closed her eyes. "*Comte* Durand."

Eyebrows raised, he opened his mouth in question.

It was possible her tone held hints of her exasperation. "We are being pursued."

Eyes opened wider, he said, "Pursued? Here?"

She nodded slowly.

His forehead wrinkled in concern, and he whipped his head around to search the carriages around them.

She appraised him and then rapped on the roof.

Simon opened up the hatch. "Blast, man! What are you doing here?"

Opening his mouth to respond, Comte Durand paused and then shrugged. "Apparently not my brightest idea."

"Oh, never mind." Simon shut the hatch. Scarlet knew his mind had already begun sorting through their limited options.

Scarlet clasped her hands gently in her lap and bit the inside of her cheek. She couldn't be angry with the comte. Of a truth, he behaved as she would have done.

Éléonore caught up to Scarlet, and, one carriage behind the other, their speed picked up on the side roads and alleys.

For a citizen of Calais looking curiously on, as many of them were doing, the two carriages appeared to be seeking a bit of recreation on a sunny summer day.

Almost at the last possible moment, Lady Cavendish's equipage leaned precariously to the side, turning sharply to the left. They careened down a narrow side alley. Clutching the window frame to remain upright, Scarlet peered out the back window. Her lips turned upward as Éléonore's two wheels left the ground when they rounded the corner in pursuit.

Both passed an enormous pile of the ripest smelling garbage Simon could locate, she was sure. Scarlet held a handkerchief up to her nose and braced her body against the next sharp turn, a right onto a much wider street with cleaner air. Simon slowed their horses, allowing Éléonore to pull up alongside. Their equipages bumped and scraped one another until Simon signaled their horses to slow further.

Before either vehicle had come to a complete stop, soldiers surrounded Scarlet, muskets raised at her and all her men.

A voice carried over the group. "Wait. I want to do the honors." Scarlet's carriage door flung open to reveal a young woman, with dark hair and pale skin, blinking to adjust from the brightness of the sun.

Scarlet looked at her expectantly with a wide smile on her face. "Oh, my dear! How lovely to have some company! Won't you join me?"

Squinting eyes scanned the carriage. "Where is he?"

Confusion warred with amusement on Scarlet's face, and she stuck her lip out in a bit of a pout. "I'm sorry, who?"

"You know very well who." Éléonore's scowl might create permanent wrinkles, the lines ran so deep. "Now, where is he?"

Laughter filled the carriage. "Oh, my dear. Do come in here and join me. Such wit, such a clever girl. I must become acquainted with you, post haste." Scarlet waved her hand, gesturing to the seat opposite in the carriage.

Grumbling, Éléonore obliged.

"There now, we will have a chat. I am Lady Scarlet Cavendish, emissary of Prince George himself, come on a peace mission to France. And you are?"

Éléonore opened her mouth and then closed it. She swallowed and said, "Lady Cavendish. I am Éléonore Duplay, personal assistant to Maximilien Robespierre." She paused. "Did you say emissary?"

Adjusting her skirts, Scarlet said, "Oh my, yes, my dear. I've been touring, getting a taste of France, as it were. What luck that I should stumble upon you right before we set sail."

Éléonore mumbled, "Yes, luck." She tilted her head in confusion. "For Prince George, you say?"

Scarlet nodded, shaking her curls in her exuberance, and leaned forward. "France is a delight. A delight, I tell you." She checked the tops of her fingernails, holding her hands out in front of her to examine them. "But your fashion, my dear." She indicated the dress Éléonore wore. "Where are your beautiful gowns? Your glorious head pieces, your bonnets and slippers!" She gestured wildly over Éléonore's body, demonstrating her disappointment. "I had such dear hopes of starting a new trend when I returned to England, but no." Her pout enlarged, and she cast her eyes to the floor. Looking back up into Éléonore's face with the light of a dreadful realization, she asked, "Did you lock up all your lovely finery when you imprisoned dear Marie Antoinette?"

Scarlet sat back in her seat and fanned her face in horror at the thought. Her expression turned contemplative. Then she leaned forward again. "Your dress, for example. I am sure it is not your best. You are in a carriage pursuit, after all, but it highlights your worst features." She scrutinized Éléonore's face. "And your hair. Have you no lady's maid?"

Éléonore seemed to snap out of her surprise-filled daze and said, "I care not for your opinion on my manner of dress—"

"Oh, but you should, my dear, you should. I am, after all, somewhat of an expert. People seek me out for this kind of advice." Leaning in conspiratorially, Scarlet said, "Your influence will last only as long as your beauty. Surely you understand that." She eyed her with exaggerated closeness. "And might I say, just between us, you are letting some things slip—sagging a bit, maybe? A tighter corset, perhaps? They have a new design that pulls you in just so." With her hands encircling her own tiny waist to demonstrate, she watched Éléonore's face drain of color. "Well, no matter. I am sure you are the cream—a veritable diamond, my dear. How could you not be, Maximilien's personal assistant, yes?"

Éléonore Duplay clenched her fists, knuckles turning white. "Lady Cavendish, you were seen with a traitor to France only moments ago inside this carriage."

"A traitor to France? Where? Here?" Scarlet looked around innocently, picking up a blanket to glance underneath. "As you can see, there is no one here but me. And glad I am that you came for a visit too. It has been rather dull."

"Where is Matteo Durand?"

Scarlet threw her hands up to her mouth. "Matteo Durand? *The* Matteo Durand? Newly discovered prince *legitime* of France? Why, Éléonore, he is all the rage in London. All the talk. What lady wouldn't give anything for just the sight of him. Is he as handsome as they say?" Scarlet began fanning herself exuberantly.

Éléonore rolled her eyes. "Those of us who have more important thoughts filling our heads have failed to notice whether or not the man is handsome."

"Well! That I do not believe. If you speak the truth, then you have likely missed a most opportune moment to view a truly beautiful man."

Talk of Matteo with this woman sapped all the fun their verbal engagement promised. And all at once, the whole situation grew tiresome. She made an exaggerated view of her timepiece and then narrowed her eyes. "Mademoiselle Duplay, and now I am afraid we are through, you and I, for today at least. Must catch the tide, you know." She waved her hand in the direction of the sea.

"I'll tell you, before I go, something I have discovered—a secret, if you will." She leaned forward as though to whisper. "Two types of people live in the world with us." She nodded, indicating Éléonore lean closer, which she refused to do. "Those who build and those who destroy. On this latest trip to France, I have seen all I ever care to see of the second lot. You and your committee of public danger have done enough evil for one day. And I have a dreadful ache in my head. Now, if you could, please exit my carriage and be on your way. As lovely as Paris is this time of year, I tire of your France and all its citizens as well. My report to the prince will not be favorable in every aspect, no. Which reminds me"—she gestured for Éléonore to stay—"before you go . . . have you considered, my dear Éléonore, what will happen when every person of substance and education is executed? Who will rise to rule?"

Éléonore straightened her back and lifted her chin. "We will elevate the commoner, the working classes, the tailors, the chefs. They will rule."

Scarlet clucked her tongue. "Pity." And she shook her head sadly.

Éléonore asked through clenched teeth, "Why a pity?"

"If your chefs are busy ruling France, who will make your delectable pastries, I ask you? Chefs passing laws. No one baking. *What* will become of you?"

Red in the face, veins protruding at her temples, Éléonore exited the carriage and whirled around to glare at Scarlet. "He cannot escape me. I will have his head. One day his blood will spill at the base of her majesty, *La Guillotine*. I will see to it myself." With that, she summoned her guards and left Scarlet alone.

Simon opened the hatch and eyed Scarlet. "That went well."

She smiled weakly up at him. "It wasn't nearly as fun as I imagined. What a horrible woman."

Simon said, "Aye, that she is."

"Did you see if Comte Durand made it?"

Simon nodded. "He did. Rolled out right into that delicious pile of garbage as we went past, no one the wiser."

Relief warmed her insides. "See that he gets a bath, will you?"

Simon frowned. "With great pleasure. I'll throw him overboard myself after his stupidity. He's brash, brazen, doesn't follow directions . . ."

Scarlet smiled. She was thinking some of the exact same things, only her thoughts were more pleasurably inclined.

Simon added, "And therefore dangerous."

Her eyes sharpened, and then she shrugged. She felt too tired to care. "Let us be off, Simon. England beckons."

Chapter Five

MATTEO HELD A PIECE OF chocolate between two fingers. "You must try this, my lady. It is delectable."

Scarlet and Matteo enjoyed a moment of leisure on the back terrace of her estate before Scarlet's other house guests descended. They shared a table and breakfast while going through their correspondence or, in Matteo's case, wishing he had correspondence. Thoughts of Potier and his other staff plagued him, moments alone with Scarlet his only solace.

The estate sat within an easy distance of London but was far enough away that Scarlet could enjoy a bit of land and gardens. Most relations would have asked her to move immediately into the dowager cottage, but her brother-in-law, knowing it to be her favorite, had insisted she maintain her residence in the home. Though Matteo enjoyed their company, he was grateful the marquess and marchioness lingered in their chamber during the morning hours.

Bored, he tried to distract her again. "You will never taste anything as delicious as this bite, right here."

Lady Cavendish looked up from her reading, into his eyes. "Oh?"

"Yes." Matteo moved his chair closer to hers. "Prince George had these delivered for you today. They are from my own France. I promise this will not disappoint." He quirked up his eyebrow. She closed her eyes and then slowly parted her lips. Matteo swallowed. *Steady, man.* He placed the chocolate inside on the flat of her tongue, brushing her bottom lip with his fingers as he pulled away. She closed her mouth and then groaned in pleasure.

"Mmmm. Comte Durand." She opened her eyes. "I am overcome." After an exaggerated sigh of pure ecstasy, she lifted her eyebrows a couple of times, teasing. Sitting up taller in her chair, she said, "And your delivery of that little morsel was almost better than the chocolate itself." She blushed. "Really, you are too much."

Matteo sat back in his chair and laughed. "You, my lady, are delightfully candid." His eyes memorized her features one more time. "I have discovered in my short stay here that beautiful truisms roll off your tongue night and day. I find I am quite captivated by them."

Leaning back into the pillows on her chair, her eyes searched his own. "And I find that you are quite distracting."

"Distracting? In what manner am I distracting?"

Lady Cavendish blushed again.

Matteo adored unsettling her. He raised his eyebrows, waiting for her answer. "Hmm?"

She opened and then closed her mouth, grinning. "You would ask me such a question and expect a response, Matteo." Her hand rose to her mouth. "Comte Durand."

"I love the sound of my name on your lips. Please, call me Matteo."

She nodded. "And you may call me Your Highness."

He opened his mouth and then shut it again, narrowing his eyes at her.

She burst into the beautiful song that was her laughter, waving her hands around in a most unladylike manner. "I cannot help it, what with you being a new prince and everything. If we are to pass out royal lineage to all and sundry, then I would like to also benefit." She paused and looked at him through her lashes. "Although, the title is much more fitting for you."

He stood up and reached for her hand. "I am no more prince than Buckley the butler is, and you know it as should anyone else with any sense. The Durand bloodline is centuries old." Secretly amused that she received so much enjoyment from teasing him, he pulled her to her feet. "Now come, let us go for a walk. I am getting restless."

"As you wish, my Prince *Legitime*."

He groaned. "Can I not dissuade you?"

She shook her head. "I'm afraid not. Word will leak out, and we will soon be overcome with visitors of the female variety, all hoping to win themselves a handsome French prince."

"Handsome?" He raised his eyebrows a couple of times. "So, I'm handsome?" He tucked her hand into his arm as they began to walk. "Am I charming also? Well-spoken?"

She sighed, her eyes bewildered and almost . . . sad. "You are everything a man should be."

He tilted his head to the side. "Why the forlorn sigh?"

She met his eyes, and for a moment, he thought she might express something hidden in their depths. The secret flickered and lingered there in the vibrant green, but then she blinked it away, closing him out. Instead, she stopped and put her hands on her hips, a coy smile on her face. "Well."

He grinned, facing the rarity before him, taking in her stance—refreshing, distinctive. She emanated a vibrancy that crackled in the air around them. "Yes?"

"I just don't know what to do with you, that is all."

"I can think of a few things."

She blushed again. "Sir, have you no sense of propriety?"

"To what are you referring, my fair lady? I was thinking of draughts and a stirring game of croquet."

She laughed and put her hand again on his arm. They began walking through her rose garden. "Look at us. It has been but a week with you living here on the estate and here we are, the most comfortable pair, taking breakfast together. We argue over who gets to read the post."

Matteo's heart began to pound. "It's the most natural thing in the world living here with you." He stopped.

Scarlet turned to face him. "As I said, I just don't know what to do with you. With all the servants everywhere, and the marquess and his wife, we are certainly well-chaperoned, but the neighborhood will talk." She looked up into his eyes, and he saw a hint of wariness. She was a widow, he knew, but he didn't know anything about her previous relationship or how she felt about her late husband.

He tried for a change of subject, something that had been weighing on him anyway. "Let's think on this, shall we? Two wonderfully engaging and attractive people, forced together on this lovely estate, with nothing to do except to save France and stare into each other's eyes . . . oh and again, did I mention, save France?"

Scarlet grinned. She squeezed his arm and moved closer, leaning her head on him, just below his shoulder. "Fair enough," she said. "Let's save France."

Matteo grinned down at her. "Can we stare into each other's eyes as well? There will be time for that and for a bite of chocolate now and then." He tried to overexaggerate his expression with the hope Scarlet would laugh again.

"Yes, I'll save a few minutes for that. Oh! And for attending balls. Did I mention Prince George's ball tonight?"

"I don't want to talk about the ball just yet."

"You don't?"

Matteo pulled her closer to him and wrapped her in his arms. She fit perfectly under his chin. "I could stay just like this for a very long time. It scares me."

"Am I so fearsome?"

"Terrifying—blindingly so. I hold you just like this, and even France does not need me so dearly. My own stomach does not require food. Sleep is far from my thoughts. The world has shrunk to a very small area of only you and me, standing in your back garden."

"It is lovely, is it not?" Scarlet sighed. "And yet . . ."

Matteo stepped back slightly so that he could look down into her face. "Say it not, fair lady. Allow me a moment of delusion." He paused dramatically, eyes closed. "There, it is done. Before we move on to what we must, let me just express my gratitude."

Scarlet wrinkled her nose, and Matteo held up his hand. "Hardly scintillating, but necessary. Thank you,"—he paused—"Scarlet, for bringing me here to England." Her name flowed from his tongue in a sweetness he wanted to taste again.

"I do believe the Pimpernel was also involved."

He narrowed his eyes in frustration. "Yes, of course."

"Now, why this face?"

"No one will tell me how to reach him, how to speak with his league. I cannot even communicate with Lord Devereaux. Lord Hastings refuses to give me anything but bland platitudes. I have sent numerous requests for his attention. I might die before I can even offer my assistance to the man."

Scarlet reached her hand up to his face and with her finger smoothed the stress lines on his forehead and then around each eye. "Do you wish so badly to rush into danger?"

Matteo took her hand in his own and kissed her knuckles before placing it back on his forearm. He stepped forward on their path. Then he ran his free hand through his hair in frustration. "No, it is not that. But I cannot simply do nothing. And with a good disguise, I do not see what would be wrong with me playing some small part. I could wait at the docks. I could help man the ship. I could acquire lodging. Anything at all would be preferable to nothing." He paused and with a sheepish lift of his shoulders said, "You see? You are no longer in my embrace, and all the troubles return."

Scarlet shook her head and pulled gently on his arm. "Come, let us finish taking our turn about the gardens."

He allowed himself to be led down another path toward a pond and gazebo, his mind still racing. As much as he was drawn to this beauty by his side, he felt equally agitated by the state of his brothers in France. More could be dying by the day, and he knew nothing about it. He hadn't yet heard from Potier to know of his safety or to hear how the rest of the staff fared, despite his many inquiries.

After his own denouncement, he knew several other families of his and Éléonore's acquaintance could be next on her list. He had written letters to warn each one of them as well but had heard nothing in return.

Scarlet interrupted his thoughts. "We really do need to discuss Prince George's ball."

He groaned again.

Pulling away, she led him to a bench. "Come now, it won't be so bad. You do like to dance, do you not?"

Matteo smirked. "I am French, am I not?"

Laughing, she leaned closer. "You are most definitely French." She rested her hand on his arm as they sat, turned toward each other on a bench overlooking the pond. "The prince himself is most anxious to make your acquaintance. It is my hope that you two can become friends of sorts. He is in need of a reliable confidante, and I can think of no better advisor on the affairs in France than you yourself would be."

He felt the lead in his chest lighten. "I might be of some assistance, yes. I could help him understand the best ways to attempt any sort of negotiation with Robespierre."

Scarlet nodded. "You are also acting on a sort of goodwill mission with all the nobles here in England. The more of their affections you win, the better chance we have of aiding the French." She paused, her grin suddenly wicked. "Especially among the ladies. You must woo them all."

He puffed out his chest. "Perhaps they will find me beguiling, captivating, at best interesting?"

She giggled. "And the lords need to respect you."

"I will do my best. Tell me about a few of the noble families I need to impress." He sat up higher on the bench and tilted his head so that his nose was high in the air. "I do believe I know how to put on airs with the best of them." And he sniffed with a perfected air of disapproval.

Scarlet imitated him and, with her nose even higher than his, said, "Sir, in England, we do it this way." She burst into a fit of giggles at the nonsense, and Matteo's heart felt even lighter. A diplomatic emissary—he understood better what his task could be in an effort to aid France. Surely he could do some good from England after all.

Chapter Six

Scarlet's slippered feet touched the top stair that led down to the front entrance of her home. As each toe stretched forward to the next step, the purple layer at the bottom of her gown pulled back just enough to accent the lovely yellow of her slippers. Another layer of skirts provided a band of orange that circled her gown. Many folds of fabric billowed down from her waist to the floor in embroidered, accented teal and gold. The sparkle of gems reflected bursts of light all throughout the folds. Satisfied that she would make an impression, she picked up her feet and hurried faster. As she rounded the curve in the staircase, her eyes fell on Matteo waiting at the bottom.

Oh, how natural it felt to see him there. She tried to show in her smile what she had not been able to express with her words. She loved his courage, his kindness. She loved his loyalty and sense of duty. She loved the way she felt at his side. And suddenly she could not approach him quickly enough.

When he saw her, his mouth fell open, and he made a real effort to swallow.

Her lips turned, joyfully acknowledging that, in some way, she affected him too. He rushed up the remaining stairs and held her hand, descending with her.

His eyes captured her own. "You have stolen my breath and my words this evening, my lady. I have never seen such a stunning creature as yourself."

"A bit improved from our gardening this afternoon, I gather?"

"Oh, not improved, no. A gardener does not look stunning, no. A marchioness on her way to the prince's ball, when her name is Lady Cavendish—*she* looks stunning. But let us not overlook the charms of Lady Cavendish the gardener; she is something altogether more appealing." He stepped closer to her at the bottom of the stairs and looked down into her eyes. "Earthy, real, bare."

She blushed and looked down. "Matteo, honestly."

He tilted his head. "Perhaps *bare* is a bit inappropriate, is it not? I mean only the French understanding, *au naturel*. I find you are loveliest without a single adornment."

"Then all this effort for nothing, *Comte*?" She turned in a circle, arms out.

"Oh *non, mon amie*. For nothing? No. You have made a good Frenchman's blood simmer and his heart pound. Surely, that is not for nothing." He waggled his eyebrows at her, and she laughed again.

"And you, Matteo, are as handsome as I have ever seen you."

He held his arm out to her. "Will you accompany me to the prince's ball, my lady?"

"I would be delighted."

In the carriage, Scarlet squirmed in her seat. She wrung her hands. She swung her feet.

Matteo reached forward and lifted her hand to his mouth. "What is troubling you?"

She sighed. How would she explain this? "Matteo, I also have a part to play in London at these events—an act of sorts."

Matteo's eyebrow raised. "And what is your act?"

Staring out the window at the passing darkness, she remembered why she had avoided becoming close to many people. What could she say to Matteo? He deserved to know more, but most of the reasons for her carefully protected façade she could not reveal, ever aware of the lives protected through her guarded secret.

When she turned back to him, her lips quirked in a crooked smile. "I will leave you to guess. But be prepared." She squeezed his hand, suddenly anxious and hoping to please him. "Please understand that the person you have come to know is more the real core of who I am than the one you will see tonight. She is . . ." Scarlet blushed and looked into Matteo's warm chocolate eyes. "She is something else entirely."

Confusion flitted across his face, but he said, "So I should play along—as you say—help you with your deception?"

Her free hand reached forward. "You can, or at least do not appear overly shocked by it. Remember, I am helping France too, in my own way."

Tilting his head to the side, he regarded her for a moment before shrugging. "I hope to be entertained as well as useful this evening, then. Would you do me the honor of saving me the first dance?"

"The second." A tender smile graced her lips. "The first is already engaged. Prince George and I will be opening the ball."

Eyes opened wider, Matteo goaded, "Ah, two princes battling for your lovely hand?" He sat up straighter in his seat and inflated his chest. "I feel I am up for the challenge."

She tapped him lightly on the shoulder with her fan. "It is nothing like that at all. Remember, you are to be the prince's new friend, his confidante. We must earn his trust."

Chuckling, he said, "Of that, I am fully aware. Never fear, dear maiden. I will not neglect my duty." He frowned. "My other duty is not so pleasant. I am to—what was it you said—charm and woo the ladies." His eyes showed his disbelief and distaste for such a task.

Scarlet tipped her head. "You will see that the most popular lords and nobles tend to have the most power. Let us win them all this evening, and then you must be prepared, for they will disturb our peace from this point on with their incessant morning calls and visits and invitations."

Matteo moaned. "For France."

Scarlet nodded. "For France."

The carriage rolled to a stop, and Matteo exited first so that he could help Scarlet down. In the moment she had alone, she closed her eyes, breathing deeply. The part she was about to play had never felt so bothersome as it did today. A week of the refreshing sincerity Matteo offered and expected had quite spoiled her for the facetious, ever-rolling tide of the *ton*.

He held out his hand. As she placed hers in his palm, she realized just how comfortable it felt right there.

She ducked her head lower than usual to make room for her rather tall headdress. Even so, several of her tallest plumes bent as she exited.

He chuckled. "You are almost as tall as I with that monstrosity on your head."

Gasping, with a hand to her throat, she said, "Why, Matteo, do you not love them? They are all the rage. After today, you will see many a lady with similar colors, I assure you." She turned her head to one side and then the other so that he could get the best view of her purple and yellow feathers tipped in gold.

He grinned. "Hmm. Shall I? More's the pity."

Scarlet's laughter began low and appreciative, but as they neared the entrance, it raised in intensity and volume until Matteo watched her in surprise. She nudged him with her fingers, which were resting on his arm. He immediately joined in with her, laughing louder and throwing his head back in abandon.

Through his teeth he asked, "Just what are we still laughing about, Lady Cavendish?"

She leaned in and whispered, "Absolutely nothing. Well done. You will do just fine tonight."

Matteo eyed her, his expression small parts amusement and distrust.

But Scarlet breathed a small sigh of relief. At least Matteo wouldn't give her away with his incredulity. They began their ascent up the entryway stairs. Her hand still rested on his arm, but she began to regret her extra-large bustles at the sides of her gown. She almost couldn't reach him, and her arm ached. She could turn her body slightly to angle closer, but that was awkward while climbing stairs.

She had asked Annabeth to cinch her waist extra tight, and her tiny waist benefitted, but her diaphragm could not expand to give her much-needed air. These very trifling details, for some reason, felt particularly bothersome this evening.

Pausing to catch her breath, she said, "I tire of the entrance to Carlton House. Must we make a whole journey of our visit? I feel that before we even reach His Highness, we have gone to France and back ourselves."

"Would it be so." Matteo's eyes pinched, and he looked away.

She immediately regretted her callousness.

After their ascent up the front stairs, they entered the home into a grand foyer.

Indicating a set of ornate double doors off to their left, Scarlet said, "The prince keeps his private rooms on this floor in that direction."

"Interesting choice." His voice had lost some of its timbre, sounding flat.

She nodded. "Yes. You will see that most of the receiving rooms and banquet halls are on the lower floor. We will reach the next set of stairs to descend just up ahead."

Brilliant gold chandeliers hung from the ceiling, flames flickering with the movement of air in the room. As they approached the main hall, the backs of a line of people queuing up to enter came into view.

"He said it would be a small affair." Scarlet sighed and slowed their steps.

Matching her pace, Matteo chuckled. "From what I understand, this *is* a smaller affair by Prince George's standards." He pointed along the upper walls, where murals lined the large receiving room. "Stunning bit of artwork though, is it not?"

Scarlet nodded. "Yes. Truly beautiful. He has more than two hundred pieces—several Rembrandt—and he acquires more all the time. I believe some of these were gifts from your own France."

"I recognize some of the artists, yes." He stopped in front of one titled *White-Tailed Gnus.*[2] "This one by Jacques-Laurent Agasse—he was Swiss-born, but my father had one of his in our own gallery in France."

---

2 This painting was likely part of the prince's actual collection in Carlton House (see Allison Lee Palmer, *Historic Dictionary of Romantic Art and Architecture* [Lanham, Maryland: Scarecrow Press, 2011], 19).

"I would love to see it one day."

"If it is still there." The muscles on his arm flexed and tensed under her fingers. His fist clenched. "I hope the staff were able to escape; with any luck, they have some of the family heirlooms with them, but I care mostly for my staff." He looked off to the right for a moment and then turned to her, face tight. "I have heard nothing from Potier. Nothing. I know not if I still have a home at all. Did the staff reach safety? I know nothing!" His jaw worked as he no doubt ground his teeth, and his fists clenched tighter.

Guests in front of them noticed their approach and began to turn in anticipation of an introduction. The sound of chatter approached behind them. Somehow she must diffuse the intensity. Overly loud, she called to him, "Matteo, my darling prince—"

"Don't. I cannot abide this inane frivolity, not when—"

Leaning into him as if to whisper in his ear, she said, "Shh. Now is not the time for a self-indulging display."

Matteo's eyes widened in anger. "Self-indulging? How can you—"

"Yes. Put those thoughts aside. We are nearly to the prince, and nursing sorrows right now is a luxury we cannot afford."

His eyes lost their light and he searched her face. "How can you be so unfeeling? When you sit here in safety in all of your wealth and comfort? What thought have you given to those who are suffering not two hours from your shores?"

The sounds of people approaching behind them grew louder. Scarlet's eyes closed. Tipping her head back slightly, she lowered her voice further. "Matteo, please. Trust me when I tell you our work here tonight is important."

Just as they entered the next room, octagon in shape, they were both interrupted by the shrill voice of Lady Pinckney. "Lady Cavendish! Oh, Lady Cavendish I hoped that was you!" Her bustling red face all too soon appeared, overly close, in front of them, with her husband close behind. "Oh, but those stairs." Fanning her face, she breathed heavily for a moment longer, exaggerating the heaving of her chest and moving closer to Matteo. She looked meaningfully at Scarlet. "I heard you have a guest." Her eyes moved from Scarlet's to Matteo's and back.

Scarlet sighed. "Comte Matteo Durand, might I present Baroness Lady Claudia and Baron Lord Michael Pinckney."

Matteo bowed smartly to the baron and extended his hand. "My lord." Then he kissed Lady Pinckney's, cradling it for a moment. "My lady, I am enchanted."

Her eyes widened, and she swallowed quickly before fluttering her eyelids at him and repeating her deep curtsy. "The pleasure is all mine, I assure you.

We heard you were here for a visit. We must have you over to the house. It is simply indecent of us as neighbors to leave you all alone in that dowager house for this long. We will have a neighborhood party in your honor. It is time you leave the utter solitude at the Cavendish estate and enter our society."

"I find I am quite comfortable in my lovely dowager cottage." Matteo tipped his head in her direction. "But I would be delighted to further our acquaintance. It is a great kindness you offer me, and I thank you."

"Oh, it is no great kindness, my lord." The baron smirked. "She is going to primp and prance to all the ladies with this piece of news, I can assure you. Do, sir, back out now, while you still can."

"You will attend as well, will you not, Baron?" Matteo smiled at him. "Offer up some sustaining beverage now and again when the need arises?"

He patted Matteo on the back and motioned for him to walk with him farther into the room. "Certainly I will be there. We will suffer through it together, I daresay."

That left Scarlet no option but to accompany the baroness through the room to the right and down the remaining stairs to the lower level.

Delicately clearing her throat, Lady Pinckney said, "I've no doubt what has been keeping you so sheltered off from us the past week. What a delicious-looking Frenchman."

Scarlet blushed. "You misunderstand, I assure you."

Lady Pinckney eyed her for a moment. "No, I don't believe I do, but never fear, your secret is safe with me."

Scarlet almost scoffed at that. No secret was safe with Lady Pinckney. "As dear as Comte Durand is, I am sure he will soon be dear to us all. He is far too concerned with his homeland to become overly distracted by any one of us, I am afraid." She fanned her face in mock disappointment.

Lady Pinckney clucked her tongue. "Not to worry. Even if *you* have failed to do so, I am sure there will be those of us willing and able to distract him."

Matteo glanced over his shoulder and winked at Scarlet. She smiled in relief. He was not angry anymore. She still felt a bit stunned by the direction of their earlier conversation. He seemed, of a truth, disdainful of her and her lifestyle. Well, it could not be helped. She felt disdainful of it as well. But she could not tell him her greatest secret. There would be no stopping him from marching straight back to France and to certain death the minute she again left England's shores.

At length, they descended the last staircase, and Matteo returned to Scarlet's side so the baron and his wife could enter together.

The master of ceremonies announced, "Lord and Lady Pinckney."

Lady Pinckney whispered over her shoulder, "Ta ta, Comte Durand. I will see you in but a few moments."

The baron shook his head good-naturedly. "She will not rest until she has claimed you as her own showpiece amongst the *ton*."

Matteo grimaced through his smile and then shuddered as the couple moved forward and into the ballroom to greet the prince.

Laughing, Scarlet placed a hand again on his arm. "You will not have to try overly hard to win her over, I'm afraid."

"What a horrible creature. Did she really slight you, or did I misunderstand?"

Scarlet sighed. "You understood. She is mostly harmless. People see her for what she is and don't pay her much mind." She reached for his arm, to feel his strength. "But she does rankle every now and again."

They stood at the entrance to one of the larger rooms on this level. Opened doors and hallways extended to their right and left in one long corridor of connecting rooms. To their front, out the back door, a series of tents increased the living area and continued onto the lawn, decorated in all manner of flowers and greenery.

Matteo rested his hand along Scarlet's lower back. "I apologize for my words earlier. I spoke in haste and in anger. It is not you at all who causes the weight of my worries. Of a truth, you are my only balm." His eyes communicated such a tender regard that she swallowed the growing lump in her throat and blinked back moisture.

They stepped forward, and Scarlet pointed to their names on the master of ceremonies' paper. "Not to worry, Comte Durand. As you will very soon discover, there is much in England to cause such feelings to surface now and again. The best we can do is paint our most cheerful, smiling faces and enjoy the ridiculous when we come across it." She winked at him.

The footman read their names. "Lady Scarlet Cavendish, wife of the former Rupert Cavendish, Marquess of Whitmore, accompanied by His Royal Highness, Matteo Durand, Prince *Legitime* of France."

Matteo faltered. "What have you done?"

"Smile, Your Highness. Your kingdom awaits."

Prince George always asked the footmen to make mention of Rupert in all her introductions at Carlton House, and for the first time she felt impatient at his continued insistence. But she couldn't suppress her grin at Matteo's new title.

Matteo's steps were slow in starting, and his hand tightened on the fabric at the back of her dress. "We will have much to discuss this evening, then." His eyes flashed briefly into hers, and then he raised his hand to give a wave with a brilliant smile to many curious eyes. They entered together to meet a growing crowd at the center of the room, all turned expectantly toward them.

Scarlet's laugh rang out across the group. "Oh, look! How droll! You have a welcome party, Your Highness. Tut tut! We must be about meeting them all."

Matteo's mouth opened as he turned to watch her face. His eyes narrowed slightly and then opened again. In resignation, he whispered, "For France." And then he raised an eyebrow to her and responded, "You must introduce me, my lady, for I fear I have the greatest desire to become intimately acquainted with the whole of your English court."

At his words, those ladies nearest him fluttered their eyelashes, and they curtsied as he passed. Scarlet hid a smile behind her hand when she saw him swallow and heard him clear his throat. Then, movement distracted the crowd and those immediately in front of them parted, stepping to one side or another. Scarlet gently lowered herself into a deep curtsy, pressing fingers into Matteo's arm, hoping to alert him. He must have seen Prince George too, because Matteo soon joined her in his most respectful bow. Scarlet left his arm to rush to her friend, grabbing the prince's hands in hers and raising on tiptoes so she could kiss his cheeks.

"Your Highness. It is good to see you this evening! Thank you for having us."

Prince George responded, "When my Scarlet wants a ball, a ball she gets, wot? Am I not correct?"

The lords and ladies nearby nodded in agreement and chuckled in appreciation.

Scarlet allowed her laugh to ring out around the room. "Oh, Prince George, you are too kind." She asked in quieter tones, "May I inquire after the health of your father?"

He shook his head and answered in a whisper, "He does not know me today." Then louder, he said, "Thank you, my dear, my father is quite well."

Nodding, she eyed him with sympathy. Then she turned to Matteo. "Might I introduce my new friend from France, Your Highness? He is very desirous to make your acquaintance."

The prince turned to Matteo and looked into his face for a moment, measuring. "Yes, I would enjoy meeting him as well."

After the introductions, Matteo bowed deeply. "I am so pleased to make your acquaintance, Your Highness. I have some ideas about France—how we can help. I thought that perhaps we could sit and . . ."

"Yes, yes. Not now." Prince George gestured that Matteo should follow him. "Perhaps you have not noticed—we are at a ball!"

Matteo frowned as the prince walked away.

Scarlet's laughter rang out again. She spared Matteo a quick apologetic glance and then said, "Our new prince is in great need of your merrymaking, Prince George. He is so *serious* all the time." She pouted. "Perhaps we can find him a partner for our first dance?"

Prince George clapped his hands and whispered something to the summoned courtier. Then he waved his hand in the direction of the orchestra. Instruments began the first notes of the opening set.

The courtier brought back an exquisite woman, dressed in emerald green, diamonds rising up her neckline in a great glittering cascade and filling her headpiece.

Prince George said, "Your Highness, may I introduce Her Highness, Princess Elizabeth of Hungary. And this handsome gentleman, Princess Elizabeth, is our own newly claimed Prince *Legitime* of France."

Matteo bowed low and took her offered hand in his own, kissing it. "Would you do me the honor of dancing this first set?"

She nodded regally to him, and they turned to wait for Prince George and Scarlet to lead out. The crowd backed farther away, pairing off. The music became louder, and Prince George and Scarlet began dancing.

The prince had declared every set to be a waltz, a new dance just gaining attention in Europe, mostly in Germany. No one had yet attempted it in England, even among the braver, more daring members of the *ton*. But the prince had made mention of it in his invitation, and those who wished to impress him had learned it before the ball. Although scandalous, few new debutantes attended the prince's balls, and those married members of the *ton* showed a great desire to indulge the prince.

Scarlet had little to worry her as far as scandalous dances were concerned; as a widow, society's strictures held little relevance. Most thought her quite an eccentric. It would surprise no one that she was already proficient at dancing the waltz. In truth, she had learned it herself in France, from a German instructor six months past. Scarlet shook her head as she often did at the prince's shocking attempts to gain attention. As she had witnessed often enough, he appeared to seek out scandal whenever possible.

Everyone waited, watching their graceful rise and fall and turns for several measures before Matteo and Princess Elizabeth joined them. They were soon followed by the other couples, until the room filled with brightly colored women swirling around men with jackets in equally colorful hues.

Prince George pulled Scarlet closer to him. "As much as I enjoy your company, dear lady, I find I am equally missing our dear Rupert, may he rest in peace."

Familiar sadness lowered the corners of her mouth. "He was a dear man. I miss him too."

Prince George eyed her for a moment. "Yes, but there is a new distraction. One Matteo Durand? Staying on your estate?" He waggled his eyebrows at her.

She blushed. "I mean no disrespect to Rupert. Matteo is just—"

"Deliciously irresistible."

"Your Highness!"

Prince George clucked his tongue. "My dear, how shocked you seem. It is perfectly acceptable for you to find a new love. Dear Rupert will not be harmed by it, to be sure."

Scarlet felt her cheeks burn, and she looked up into his eyes to see sincerity and real concern written in them. "Thank you. I find I am unsure how to proceed, but as Rupert's dearest friend, you have alleviated some of my worry."

"Not at all, my dear. Now, shall we discuss my sleeves? Are they not the most elegant cut of all?"

Scarlet grinned. "Why, yes, I was noticing their drape. They seem to flow out in great layers from your wrists, just so. Mark my words, by this week next, all the men will be wearing them."

Once satisfied, she knew he would move on to consult her about his cravat and the cut of his jacket. When they had, at length, exhausted all fashion subjects, she concluded with what she hoped would lead to a productive moment. "I admit, I wished to return from Paris with new fabrics and ideas for gowns."

Shaking his head, the prince frowned. "Again you were visiting Paris, that horror. Whatever made you wish such a thing upon yourself?"

Eyes wide, innocent, Scarlet said, "In my new position as your personal emissary."

"Oh, that." His lips pursed. "My dear, I hadn't expected you to actually visit. I quake at the nightmares you may have witnessed."

"Oh, it was not as bad as all that. But the fashion was abysmal. No head pieces, nothing new on their feet. The ladies looked positively dreadful. And the men! Not a single crisp cravat amongst the lot of them."

"No!" Prince George closed his eyes.

"They have lost their presentation." Scarlet nodded gravely. "I do believe they fear for their lives, trying to hide what wealth might be had among them."

Prince George sighed. "That is the true tragedy of the whole mess. We can be grateful for the Pimpernel and his blessed interference."

Scarlet considered him. "And their pastries! Not a good bakery to be found on the streets of Paris. All have closed their doors."

"Tragic! Fortuitous we lured our maestro, Chef Louis, to come and cook at Carlton House, is it not? Try the pastries tonight. They are his own family recipe."

"Well, I can be grateful for that. To think, I must return to England in order to taste a true French pastry."

The music ended and the prince bowed low while Scarlet curtsied. Smiling with kindness, he said, "Lovely as always to spend time with you. Would you and that French prince of yours return tomorrow? I feel we had better discuss what can be done."

Exultant, she kept her response to a nod. "Yes, of course. We will come as soon as we have had our morning repast."

Matteo approached with Princess Elizabeth, and the four of them switched partners. Scarlet's feet tapped with hidden anticipation to be held in his arms.

Chapter Seven

"AND NOW, YOU SHALL EXPERIENCE dance with a true Frenchman. May you never feel the same about another partner." Matteo's eyebrow quirked upward as he bowed to her, a confident grin on his face.

Scarlet curtsied low and laughed. "My heart is aflutter with anticipation." And it was, quite at that moment, pounding in her breast.

Matteo pulled her into his arms, and she rested her hand on his broad shoulder, felt his bulk and his strength as he held her other hand out to their side. They were mere inches apart, and she looked up into his eyes, feeling wisps of his breath on her neck. A great feeling of hopeful expectation filled her, and the last shackles of her hesitancy began to fade. Before she could say a word, she floated across the floor, almost carried in his arms. They whirled and spun and glided. The room was empty but for the two of them and their movement.

"You are magnificent, Matteo!" she said, her breath coming faster.

He grinned down at her. "And I am enchanted. You fit so well here in my arms."

"Tell me this is real." She searched his face, ending in his great brown depths. "That you feel it too."

Matteo's eyes darkened. "I have never been more moved by a woman." He paused, his eyes showing his sincerity. "I have a bit of a wicked confession to make."

Scarlet felt enticed and wary at the same time. "Do you?"

"Yes. I cannot forget our first carriage ride. You see, I became immediately addicted to the feel of your lips, and I must repeat the experience." He leaned in close to her ear. "Again." He looked down into her eyes. "And again."

Scarlet swallowed. "You are too bold."

"I am French." His lip quirked up in a half smile. Then he added, "But a gentleman."

Scarlet bit her lip.

"Lady Cavendish, you move me to distraction. Let us keep your lips unbitten, shall we? And while we are discussing this fascinating topic, might I add unwet by your lovely tongue as well."

Scarlet laughed, feeling her face heat. She knew her reactions to him must be obvious to all.

He persisted. "Perhaps you remember our moments together at the west barricade?"

She opened her mouth in surprise. Did he expect her to discuss this right now? Then she felt her courage rise, and she narrowed her eyes slightly. Running her tongue along her lips for the briefest of moments, she said, "I'm not sure to what you refer? Are you speaking of the moment when Bibot nearly cast you from the carriage?"

Matteo frowned. "No, not that moment."

Eyebrow furrowed, she pursed her lips. "No? That was memorable, was it not? Hmm. Were you in fact speaking of the moment when the carriage picked up speed and went racing around those corners?"

Matteo's frown deepened. "Not that moment either."

Scarlet made a show of looking about the room in search of the answer. Then, biting her lip in consternation, she said, "I cannot imagine what could have made such an impression, Your Highness."

Matteo almost faltered in his steps, his eyes glued to her lips and the teeth that pressed them delicately.

Scarlet laughed, bringing smiles to the couples closest to them. Then she moved her body closer to him and whispered, "How could I forget? You lit a flame, Matteo, that burns still."

He misplaced his foot but recovered quickly, and Scarlet laughed again.

"You mock me, my lady?"

Catching her breath, Scarlet recovered. "No, no, I do not. I am in earnest." The music stopped, yet they remained together. Neither wanting to be the first to look away, she felt overcome by the magic of their attraction. Quite heady with the rush of emotion, she swallowed first and then sighed. "Come, let us get a bit of refreshment before the start of the next dance. I fear we may not see each other again until we are leaving for home."

"Oh, that will not do." His head turned in all directions until he found whatever he sought. "Come." He tugged gently on her hand and rushed in that direction as quickly as propriety would allow.

Giggling unrestrained, she followed him, her small feet hurrying under the many skirts that weighed her to the earth. "Where are we going?"

"To the gardens. I see another exit."

She knew others would talk, knew they were creating a scene, even if a small one, but she could not resist. "Yes, this way." She hurried even faster, turning down a hallway and through a door that led out the side of the home into a small statuary with a fountain.

"This is just what we need." He took her hands and spun her around.

Laughing, she asked, "Do we?"

Then he brought her close and began the steps of their waltz again, this time without an audience. "I was not finished yet."

Her eyes sought his, heart full of wonder and blossoming love for this adventurous French nobleman.

"Might I have this dance?"

Although their bodies already glided over stone paths in the moonlight, circling a tall fountain, she smiled her excitement and said, "Yes, I would be delighted."

He grinned in response and twirled them both in a circle before returning to the regular three-count waltz rhythm. In his arms, she knew they could fly, move mountains, travel the world, and conquer whatever dragons crossed them. She felt the joy and fun of the moment bubble up inside her until she tipped her head and laughed with abandon as they spun.

His face lit in appreciation, and he joined her with his own laughter. Then he pulled away and, while still holding fast to her hand, ran with her farther into the gardens.

After a few moments, they approached a maze and slowed in front of it.

"Dare we enter?" Matteo's eyebrow rose in challenge.

"We might never return, be lost to its depths forever."

"A delightful thought, if I am being candid."

Scarlet looked up at him through her lashes. "Agreed."

He reached for her hand, and they moved forward through the first of the tall hedges that marked the beginning.

They had not walked two steps before Baron and Baroness Pinckney approached.

"Lovely dancing, my dears. I must say, the French could teach us some wonderfully daring moves." Lady Pinckney looked meaningfully at Matteo, who appeared to misunderstand.

"We do have excellent instructors, Lady Pinckney."

She pouted and sidled closer to him, which caused him to lean more into Scarlet, who nearly lost her footing from the shift in his balance.

They caught each other's eyes and fought smiles.

Disappointment dimmed Scarlet's heart, but a glimmer of sense also returned. For once, she was grateful for a Pinckney interruption. "Ah, my lady! How lovely to see you, and we are of the same mind—a tour of the gardens."

"Yes, they are far lovelier in the daytime, though. Not entirely sure what we are thinking, out here at this time of night." Lady Pinckney gestured to the night sky.

Not rising to her bait, Scarlet said, "Well, as for us, we were just about to conquer this maze. But I thank you for your arrival, as I recognize minutes have passed and we are neglecting the most talked-about social event of the Season." She pressed into Matteo's forearm.

"Ah, yes, too true, my lady. Baron, Baroness, shall we make our way back to the ballroom?"

The baron's eyes twinkled as he said, "To be sure. I do believe we could catch a chill out here."

With that, the four of them made their way to the terrace and through a pair of back doors into the ballroom.

Several ladies approached Scarlet, with hopeful eyes turned in Matteo's direction. She made all the introductions, and Matteo bowed over each lady's offered hand. He asked the woman nearest him for the next set.

Before they could make their way to the floor, Suzanne and Andrew approached. She reached out a hand to stop him. "Comte Durand?"

Matteo turned in surprise. "Suzanne de Molier. How fortunate to meet one of my fellow French." He bowed over her hand.

She stiffened. "Some of us are truly French, while others are merely pawns of the Revolution. I wonder how you could break away from your dear Éléonore."

Scarlet frowned and opened her mouth to speak, but Matteo stopped her with a hand on her arm and said to Suzanne, "I find it quite easy to leave any room in which Éléonore resides. But it was heartbreaking to leave our beloved France, which is still caught in her snares."

Suzanne bowed her head in acknowledgment.

Matteo returned his smiles to his new partner and led her out onto the floor.

Andrew, who stood at Suzanne's side, whispered something into her ear. She held her hand up to her mouth in surprise, and her cheeks turned a shade of pink. "I did not realize." After a moment, her eyes narrowed slightly, and she watched Matteo closely.

Lady Pinckney eyed the entire exchange with great interest, her expression calculating. Scarlet interrupted her thoughts. "Does our Prince George not look smashing in those new sleeves? I love the manner in which they drape down his forearm."

Anyone within hearing distance turned to notice the drape of Prince George's sleeve. He responded to their attention, lifting his sleeves for all to take note, and winked at Scarlet.

As soon as that set was completed, her next partner whisked Scarlet away. And it continued throughout the night. She noticed that Matteo barely had a moment before another lady was presented to him and he obliged her with a dance. Once, their eyes met, and he wiggled his eyebrows. She wondered how he was faring, fending off and appeasing all the curious minds of the *ton*.

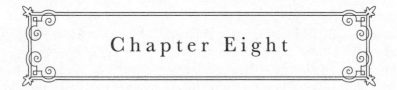

Chapter Eight

ENCHANTING. SCARLET SHOOK HER HEAD in awe. She and Matteo walked together through an archway, lit by candles flickering in the refreshing outdoor air, a tunnel of sorts, leading to a tented space beyond where all the tables were set for dinner. A thin, translucent fabric lined the walls, decorated with cascading artificial flowers.

In one of the smaller tents, Matteo and Scarlet sat near His Highness for dinner. He never included his wife, Princess Caroline of Brunswick, at any of these events, so Princess Elizabeth sat at his right with Scarlet at his left. Matteo sat on the opposite side of the table, farther down.

His Highness's laugh shifted Scarlet's attention back to him. "I shall have a river, my dear, flowing water, down the center of this table at my next party. Mark my words." He leaned to the side, almost too far, and a footman rushed to right him again. "Yes," he emphasized. "With fish swimming in it, flowing toward a fountain, right in the middle." He swung his arm to demonstrate the direction and nearly upturned Her Highness's cup.

Giggling, Princess Elizabeth responded, "Oh, do! I only hope I am here to see it." She laughed at everything Prince George said, which pleased Scarlet because she was able to glance about the room and study the people in it.

Matteo was flanked on either side by two of the lovelier new debutantes of the Season, twins. She hid her smile when he said, "Charming. Two perfectly pleasant women who look remarkably similar." He leaned toward one. "I enjoyed our dance, Cordelia." She giggled in her hands.

"That was I, Your Highness." The young lady at his other side, apparently Cordelia, smiled.

"You?" Matteo whipped around in mock surprise. "Then who is this lovely creature?"

"I am Amelia."

"Amelia and Cordelia. I must be the most fortunate man at this entire ball to be sitting between the two of you."

They each fluttered their eyelashes at him, and he glanced back and forth between them.

Scarlet said, "Their father is the Duke of Cumberland. Have you yet been introduced?"

Matteo nodded. "Yes, I have, and a fine man he is. He has invited me to come hunting with him on Thursday next and then to take tea with the family."

The girls nodded and each put a hand on his arm. He again swung his head between the two as they vied for his attention.

Scarlet hid her smile behind a sip of water.

The servants offered course after course. Matteo entertained them all with his many childhood exploits in France. Even the prince was wiping laughter tears from his eyes. Scarlet felt the warm relief of Matteo's acceptance into the English court and among the nobility.

The man to Scarlet's left, one Lord Panning, leaned toward her and placed his hand on her knee. "When will you allow a more intimate friendship? I have been more than patient."

Her eyes found Matteo, whose gaze sharpened on the two of them, as he looked from one to the other.

Scarlet smelled the bourbon on Lord Panning's breath, and his hand clutched her leg tighter, slowly moving toward her thigh. She stood, dislodging his unwanted advance. "Oh, my lovelies. Oh, my dears. What an incredible event this has been. Has it not?" The crowd murmured in assent, nodding. She ignored Matteo's questioning face.

Her abrupt rise commanded the attention of the table. "Prince George, we would like to thank you. Might I have a moment to address the group?"

He nodded, his eyes alight with amusement.

"You are a wonder, and tonight has been a grand masterpiece." The guests clapped their hands in appreciation while the prince nodded in Scarlet's direction. She turned to those sitting around her. "I must applaud you all on your adornments, your lovely dresses, the drapes of your sleeves. You have bejeweled Prince George's ballroom, though none as gloriously ornamented as Prince George himself." She nodded her head in his direction. "And now, perhaps, a bit of poetry?" She clapped her hands as the guests responded in agreement.

"What shall we call this one?" She tapped her chin in thought. "'An Ode to the Pimpernel'?"

An excited chorus of women's voices answered in obvious agreement. Scarlet placed a hand on her breast and stared off across the room. "Who is the Pimpernel? That rogue of a man. I long to tell."

Sighs and squeals sounded from down the table.

Scarlet continued. "Expert, cunning at disguise. Our eyes wonder at his size." She held her arms out to demonstrate a broad chest.

"And his nose—"

Lord Panning scoffed. "Nose, indeed."

"Well, yes, his nose." She held a finger up in the air. "*And* his clothes—"

"And what about his hair?" Cordelia called out, covering her mouth with one hand.

"Exactly. Does it have that wavy flair?" Scarlet paused, demonstrating where a wave would rest on the top of Lord Panning's balding and scaly head. "Perhaps . . . he is an old, coddled creature?"

The ladies at the table murmured in dissent.

"A tired and worn out preacher?"

Prince George's amused laughter brought smiles to even the men.

"Who is our paragon, The man we all depend upon, Saving many a life From that despicable knife?"

The Comtesse de Molier's hand went up to her throat, and she shared a look with her husband.

"Who has seen his face? He hides himself well, England's own elusive Pimpernel."

The prince clapped and shouted, "Bravo!" The whole of their table followed suit. Then he stood also, which signaled the rest of the guests do the same, before they all began making their way back to the ballroom.

Matteo circled the table and came to stand behind Scarlet, helping her pull back her chair farther. He turned to face Lord Panning. "I do not believe I have had the pleasure of an introduction."

Scarlet said, "Oh, yes, of course. Your Highness, Prince Matteo, this is Lord Panning."

Lord Panning bowed, and Matteo nodded his head with a slight bow in return. He said, "Lord Panning. I couldn't help but notice an obvious flash of revulsion cross the lovely Lady Cavendish's face while you were leaning in to talk to her just now."

Scarlet's mouth opened in startled amazement. "Matteo—"

He placed his hand upon her own where it rested on his arm, and waited with raised eyebrows, looking expectantly at Lord Panning. With no response forthcoming, Matteo continued. "As a dear friend of hers, I would hope never to see such a look of discomfort cross her features again. If you are ever so fortunate as to secure any ounce of her attention in the future, I expect to see only expressions of supreme well-being shining from her person."

Lord Panning's sallow face sputtered and stammered. Then, swallowing, he said, "I can't see how her sense of well-being is any responsibility of mine."

"Ah, good. Then we are in agreement. You may leave her to others of her acquaintance, who feel it an honor to see to her happiness." Matteo's eyes turned to steel, and he stared at Lord Panning until the man nodded curtly and walked away from them.

Scarlet turned her face up to Matteo's in amazement. "What are you doing?"

"I just thought it would be helpful for him to know you are not without friends or protection."

She looked down to hide the sudden knot of emotion that threatened to overpower her. When had she last felt the protection of another? She did not know how to express her gratitude for something that seemed such a simple gesture to Matteo. She squeezed his arm with her fingers and walked with him toward the ballroom, fighting to relax the lump in her throat.

Within moments of their entrance, both were surrounded by people vying for their attention. Scarlet smiled at Matteo as he left her side to dance with a young girl who beamed in triumph at securing him.

During a lull between dances, Simon walked past her and brushed the left side of his coat three times. *The library in fifteen minutes.* Her eyes swept the party. What could have happened to require a rendezvous? Meeting Andrew's gaze, he directed hers to Suzanne. Scarlet turned away as if she hadn't seen him, and her heart clenched. *News from France.*

She sensed Matteo's presence before she saw him. He came up behind her, and the air between them crackled. She knew that if she stepped back an inch, or maybe two, her body would be pressed to his. She lifted her foot, ready to close the distance, but he stepped forward first, and she felt his breath lightly tickle her neck. The smell of his French soap enveloped the air around her.

His voice low, close to her ear, murmured, "Might I have another dance with the lovely Scarlet Cavendish?"

Scarlet closed her eyes, allowing the moment to linger, and then she turned to face him. Teasing, she said, "What will all of your women think of me if I monopolize Your Highness for two of your coveted dances this evening?"

"I must get revenge for this *Your Highness* nonsense. Somehow, I will catch you unawares." He eyed her in mock irritation.

Lady Pinckney arrived in that moment. "Oh, Lady Cavendish. Your Highness. There is such a to-do. I don't know what to even think, but I overheard the most shocking news! Surely you will want to hear post haste. I rushed to your side, Your Highness, as soon as I heard." Her hand rested on her heaving breast as she sidled up, pressing against him.

He inched back from her and said, "What is it? Surely it doesn't involve me as you have implied."

"Oh, but it does. I am sorry to be the bearer of such news, but I have just heard it straight from the mouth of the Comtesse de Molier. She doesn't know I was listening, naturally. But she said that she has heard from her compatriots in France that Éléonore Duplay is coming here to England, could arrive this very night, as an emissary from France." She stepped back, a look of triumph in her features. "I knew you would want to be the first to know, as I hear she is a particular friend—"

"She's no friend of mine." Matteo's curt response caused several near them to turn their heads in curiosity.

"Well, I meant no harm. I understood you grew up together, that you've known her for years . . ." Lady Pinckney allowed her voice to trail off.

Matteo's face had turned to stone and his eyes were fierce as he stared her down.

Scarlet looked from one to the other and then gently placed a hand on Matteo's arm. "I cannot imagine why she would come all the way from France, if not to gaze upon our fashions, my dear. Last I saw her she was in a dreadful state. Oldest dress I ever saw on a woman of her renown—fit her so ill she nearly sagged. It is no wonder she has come to spruce herself up, so to speak. Must keep Robespierre happy, if you take my meaning? Even unmarried as they are . . ."

Lady Pinckney's cheeks turned pink, and she brought a hand up to her mouth. "Oh, I see. Well, we can have nothing much to say to her, that is sure. Fashions indeed."

Matteo bowed crisply and left to walk across the room. Scarlet watched him until she saw Prince George motion to join him in conversation.

Lady Pinckney said, "Awfully touchy, is he not?"

Scarlet turned to her. "Would you not be, if his situation were yours? Excuse me, will you?" Her steps quickened as she made her way to the library.

She paused at the doors, listening, before she stepped into the room. Giggling carried out into the hall. She peered in and grinned. The curtains bulged with the bodies of two people.

A woman's voice, slightly muffled, said, "Simon, are you sure we will not be discovered?"

After more giggling and a thump against the back wall, Scarlet called out, "Hello! Is someone in here?"

The occupants went silent and still.

"Yoo-hoo! Behind the curtain! I fear I have misplaced my fan. Do you see it there?"

A muffled female voice responded, "I don't see one here, no."

Scarlet pouted. "I was just right there earlier today. Are you certain you don't see it?" More movement followed but no response. Scarlet shook her head. "Would you mind if I take a look myself? It was a gift from a dear friend, you see." She moved toward the curtains, ready to pull them aside.

A voice squeaked, "No!"

Simon pulled the fabric aside. "Lady Cavendish. How pleasant to see you this evening. Might I introduce to you the lovely Penelope Finkle?"

Scarlet raised one eyebrow and her lips formed a delicate *O*.

A hand pulled aside more of the curtain, and a pair of eyes glanced at her and then found the floor. The lovely dress finally revealed itself, and a pair of knees must have curtsied beneath billowing skirts, which lowered in folds to the ground. "Pleased to meet you. Now, if you'll excuse me." She moved as swiftly as she could from the room.

"Really, Simon, you are too much. She may never look me in the eyes again, poor dear." She watched him for a moment. "And where is Franny?"

"Penelope will recover. She is a frequent visitor to the curtains in libraries, I am told, innocent-looking eyes or no. And Franny, of whom I thought you disapproved, is home with her mother this evening—seems to have caught a fever of some sort."

"After meeting Penelope, Franny is growing on me. Now Simon. Let us be quick about this." She gestured for him to follow her over to the fireplace, where they stood in the corner, respectably, in case they were discovered.

Simon began immediately. "Two families at risk—neighbors of the Durands'. Slated for execution in less than one week's time. Already in prison; children as well. We just received news through Suzanne tonight. An express came as the family was leaving for the ball, and Suzanne, not knowing what else to do, confided in Andrew."

"We must leave tonight, of course. You know what to do."

Simon nodded gravely. "I am uneasy. I sense a trap. More is going on here than is apparent at the surface. We must tread carefully."

Scarlet nodded. "With the utmost care."

Simon hesitated. "And secrecy. It would be best if Matteo remained unaware."

A rush of irritation disturbed her, and she knew her eyes flashed. "I will make sure of it. But, Simon, it is not out of distrust that I do so. I wish to spare his life. The moment he sets foot on French shores, they will put him on the scaffolding."

"You coddle him. He could be a valuable part of the team, with his inside knowledge and bravery, were he to be trusted."

"What are you saying?"

"I have my own reservations about him, you must know. His loyalties. Can we be sure he would not be swayed? He is suspect in my mind, with families close to his own estate being named traitors so soon after his departure."

"Surely an attempt by Éléonore to flush him out. Simon, you take too much upon yourself with this. I trust him, and I will entertain no more conversation on the subject. Meet at rendezvous point four at the break of dawn." She couldn't think about how her emotions undoubtedly clouded her opinion of Matteo, nor could she bear to consider him anything other than lovely and heroic.

Footsteps sounded in the hallway, and the door slowly cracked open. The curtains closed around Simon and Scarlet as voices entered the library.

The Comtesse de Molier said, "I cannot think why she would come here. Are we at risk? What if she ships us back to France?"

The comte replied, "Now, my dear. Surely she has no power here."

"She will find a way. Éléonore is such a force in France."

"But here, she is nothing. Perhaps her presence will be indulged by the prince, perhaps not. But her words and her threats mean nothing to us."

Scarlet looked into Simon's face, trying not to disturb the curtains. She suspected she understood the motivation for the unprecedented visit. And her heart felt uneasy at her own sudden imminent departure, leaving Matteo to Éléonore's clutches.

Chapter Nine

SCARLET AND MATTEO SAT QUIETLY in the carriage as they rumbled through the streets toward the Cavendish estate. He tried to review all the people he had met, memorizing faces and names, hoping to fit himself tightly into their society to garner support for his homeland, but his thoughts continued to jar to a stop as Éléonore's impending presence interrupted in his mind. Why was she coming here? He feared he knew the answer.

"The prince would like to see us tomorrow morning. This is such great news, as he expressly mentioned that he wants to discuss the problems in France."

Clearing his throat, Matteo said, "I am pleased to hear it. After spending so many hours with the man, I was beginning to wonder if he has a sensible thought in his head."

Scarlet smiled gently. "And my head? Were you worried about the thoughts in my head as well?" Her eyes widened, and he felt drawn to her open vulnerability.

He moved to her side of the carriage and took her hand in his. "I have nothing but pleasant feelings about the thoughts in your head, be they about fashion or social engagements or filled with nonsensical poetry. I find I want to intimately know *every* little thought."

Her eyes misted over. "You are too kind, Matteo. It is so refreshing to hear you say such things. More and more, you are my breath of fresh air and my sunny day."

He brought her hand up to his lips and left a lingering kiss. Then he peeled back her glove and took off his own. With his bare hand holding hers, he traced circles in her palm and ran his fingers up and down the length of her hand. Scarlet's eyes found his and could not break away. He caressed her skin, enjoying its softness, and then brought his lips to the inside of her wrist, watching her. She swallowed and bit her lip. He reached forward to run his thumb along her mouth, his eyes roaming her face, taking in each feature. Her beauty filled him. He knew he could look at her every day for the rest of their lives and never see enough. "You are so beautiful, Scarlet."

The carriage came to a stop, and the footman opened the door. As they exited, Scarlet smirked. "Your Highness."

Matteo turned to her. "What?"

"I said you may call me *Your Highness*, remember? No one gave you leave to use my Christian name, though you do."

Matteo growled and reached for her hand, pulling her closer. "I will not." Looking down into her face, sincerity replaced the teasing. "Though you deserve it. You are a remarkable woman." He closed the small space between them, hesitating a moment, his lips hovering a breath away from her mouth. Her eyes sparkled up at him, warm and inviting. And he paused, drinking in the thrill of expectation. Then he pressed his lips to hers. As soon as he felt their softness, he craved more. Her bravery, kindness, humor, intelligence all combined to make her lips even more delicious to him. He moved his mouth over hers, struck with a great urgency. Again and again, until the soft sound of Buckley clearing his throat interrupted. Scarlet's lips moved in a smile beneath his mouth, and he pulled away.

She turned her head and said, "Yes?"

Devoid of emotion, Buckley said, "Is there anything else you need for the evening before we retire?" Then his mouth lowered in disapproval.

Matteo smiled in chagrin. He stepped back from Scarlet but held her hand in his own.

Scarlet answered, "No, thank you, Buckley. Comte Durand was just leaving, and Annabeth will attend me in my rooms."

"Very good, my lady." He bowed crisply and returned to the house.

Matteo turned his gaze back to Scarlet's. "My apologies. I quite forgot myself." He searched her face, unsure what to do about the emotion that surged through him. "I have never felt this way. I am overcome. You have my heart, my soul. I cannot live another moment without you as my own." Clarity cleared the misty fog in his mind, and that single desire crystalized at the center of his thoughts: Scarlet, forever and every day his own. He lowered himself to one knee, holding her still-bare hand in his. "Lady Scarlet Cavendish, would you do me the great honor of becoming my wife?"

Scarlet's free hand went up to her mouth, and her eyes shone with new tears. "Oh, Matteo." She pulled him to his feet.

Hope flickered, and he tried to communicate the depth of his feelings with the strength of his gaze.

She said, "It is too soon. Ask me again another day. I cannot imagine refusing you anything. But for now, it is too soon."

He tried to keep most of the disappointment out of his eyes; nevertheless, he saw acknowledgment of it cross her features.

She reached for his face, gently cradling his cheek in her hand. "Do not misunderstand. You have become my everything. Every day I long for you, love you even, but I need more time."

Exultant victory surged through him. Bringing her hand to his lips, he said, "I am yours. And every day I will wonder if today is the day you will be mine. I can be patient. I will wait, with joy even, knowing I have your love." He bowed to her, squeezing her hand in his own, and then turned to walk down the path and around the house to the dowager cottage.

Chapter Ten

Paris, France

TWO WEEKS OF KNITTING. DAYS of heat under the scalding sun. Scarlet almost forgot she used to be clean and comfortable. The memory of Matteo's impetuous proposal remained a constant strength and comfort; she grinned inside thinking of it. But to all around her, she grunted in concentration. The grime caked in the lines of her hands dirtied the yarn as a brown fingernail moved over each stitch and she counted her knitting. An old hag-like woman with wild gray hair, she muttered numbers to herself. "Forty-five, forty-seven, forty-nine." Those numbers might mean nothing to anyone else, but to her, they spelled a name. She raised her hand into the air. "Jacques Pierre!" Then she returned to her counting.

Most of the crowd gave her no mind. She sat with a brooding circle of women who claimed their spot every day, front-row witnesses to the executions. Spies for the Revolution, their daily tasks consumed them: knitting code, making lists with their stitches, eyeing every person with looks of supreme suspicion—their breathing heavy, their concentration unmatched. Skin feverish and hearts racing, the women anticipated with great pleasure the next denouncement, first worked with their own fingers the coded numbers in each line of knitting. Visitors could almost smell the blood on them.

Just like this morning, every morning they arrived early, staking out their place of honor among all the guests of Paris to watch the beheadings. A heckling clutch of hags, screeching and fluttering and calling out as each victim took the stage.

"Jacques Pierre!" The woman shouted again.

The crone next to her breathed old onion into her face. "Eh? Jacques Pierre. Pretty sounding one, that."

Gray strands shook as she nodded proudly. "That he is. Too pretty." She cackled with laughter.

The ladies around her joined in a contagious upheaval of brooding energy.

The executioner, all in black, arrived on the platform of the guillotine, and the crowd screamed in a rallying cry. He raised his hands to the air and took his place at the back, near the knife. All eyes watched his hands as he grasped the rope and began to pull it downward; one thin coil formed at his feet. The blade inched toward the sky, a flash of light glinted off steel, momentarily blinding. The attention of the crowd rose upward, anticipating its summit. When it reached the top, they let out an exultant shout Paris felt in its very soul.

Several streets over, prisoners in moving carts heard the cheers. They toppled against each other, when a wheel dipped into a rut while creaking through the streets to *Place de Grève,* where *La Guillotine* awaited their necks. A young boy, crouched in his small corner of the cart, reached for his mother's hand. She held it in her own, reflexively, too terrified to offer more. Yet he, seeking only to comfort, squeezed with his dimpled fingers in reassurance. As their eyes met, her shoulders relaxed, and the lines on her face smoothed. And then she leaned to cup his face and kiss his head. "Peace, my child."

He nodded, eyes shining.

Nearby, Andrew heard the echoing shout as the members of the league waited in position. Lord Courtenay, tasked with the toughest aspect of the day's rescue, leaned forward on the balls of his feet, his face smudged and clothes tattered, smelling of whiskey. Not a drop had passed his lips, of course; he shook his arms and opened and closed his fingers.

The old hag began a slow chant, her intended distraction. No one would die today. "*Descendre. Descendre.*" Come down. Her low, monotone sound continued. "*Descendre. Descendre.*" Come down. Come down. She pounded her hands into her thighs as she repeated her incantation.

The women around her took it up immediately, feeling the hypnotic rhythm as they swayed to their own drums. "Down, down, down."

Soon the rest of the crowd joined and a feverish expectation rallied the people. Louder their call, "*Vas-y! Vas-y!*" Pounding on thighs led to stomping of feet and shouting of voices. "Go on. Bring it down, down, down."

The carts outside the prison walls continued to creep forward. A young girl with blonde curls sat silently inside the lead cart, eyes squeezed tight, hands over her ears. Her brother reached a hand across her shoulder and pulled her closer to him, tapping to get her attention. When she looked, he produced a wooden horse from his pocket and began to make it trot and dance in front of her. The chanting seemed to shake the very walls of Paris and shudder in hearts already pounding within barred carts. But the girl smiled and reached for the horse.

As the conveyance rolled nearer and the chanting grew ever louder, the old hag could hold her position no longer. She jumped from her ledge at the very front of the stage and leapt out upon it herself, shouting and pounding her thighs with her fists, surely bruising them. She swayed with the rhythm and reached for the sky, calling to the blade to lower.

Sensing her audience growing larger, she began to prance as an aristo might. She put on airs. She curtsied and flaunted and flipped her hair. She strolled along, with imagined umbrellas. All the while, the crowd chanted. If one strained an ear, as the old woman did, the closer sound of carts nearing the square could be heard, but the crowd took no heed, intent as they were upon her antics. She made her way to the block itself. She swayed, she danced, she pulled at air under the blade, willing it to descend. Then, as the carts rounded the corner, almost visible, she placed her own head on the block. The crowd's calls rose in pitch. She writhed, she wiggled, she begged the blade above her to drop.

Hearing the wheels enter the square, she jerked her head up. Relief filled her, but she stared at one entrance, eyes and mouth open. "They've gone! They've gone!" She pointed her long and slender finger at the empty carts pulled by donkeys, without even a driver. "Ghost carts, they are! Ghosts!" Her shriek echoed against the walls around them. Eerily in the now-silent square, cart after cart rolled in, led by the habitual pace and path of the donkeys, but empty of any visible human soul.

When the first cart pulled to a stop in front of the platform, the crowd let loose. Guards shouted, tearing down the street from whence the carts had come. People hurried, searching up side alleys and back again.

Many ran away, spooked by the evil magic that invited ghosts at the scaffolding.

The old woman jumped on top of one of the caged carts, shouting, "After them! We must go in pursuit!" With her sharp slap of the reins, the donkeys moved forward in a slow trot. She stood atop, shouting and urging them onward. Out of the square they moved, too slow but quick enough. People clung to the bars, stealing a ride until they tired of the donkey's slow gate. Down the streets of Paris, away from the square, away from the throng, the cart continued, other carts following.

A sister cart journeyed in the opposite direction, Lord Courtenay at the reins. Until almost in unison, continuing far enough that they'd lost all stragglers, the donkeys stopped in two separate alleys. Their passengers dropped to the ground, arms shaking from the exertion of clinging to the axle underneath. The young boy pulled his mother to her feet, a victorious smile filling his face as he rushed to thank Lord Courtenay. Former prisoners, not quite free, rushed and huddled under the benches and seats of two waiting carriages.

Drivers urged the horses onward. Two entire families now moved in cramped, hidden safety away from the busiest crowds of Paris, out toward the barricades and the surrounding countryside.

Inside the carriage, Scarlet moved through her change of costume quickly as she shed evidence of the old woman. She hoped to never wear it again; any other disguise would be preferable to this one she had grown to loathe. While she worked, she slowed her breathing and tried to shed the evil feeling that always surrounded the guillotine. Too many weeks sitting at its feet wore at her. With a shudder, she applied a veil and black outer layers. New gloves covered her dirt-filled fingernails. She pulled the gray strands of her wig back into a knot at the base of her neck. Bits of her filthy costume, rolled tightly, fit in the valise at her feet. She sat atop hidden passengers—mother, father, and son concealed under the carriage benches. She drummed her fingers as they pulled closer to the exit at the east barricade. She worried for those trying to get past Bibot.

"Papers!" the man shouted.

Scarlet handed over her papers in silence, a breeze catching the lower edge of her veil, causing it to dance at her shoulders, but it did not rise to reveal her face.

The man looked them over. "Éléonore Duplay! I did not know. Forgive me. But of course you must go through, and at haste!" He waved frantically for the gate to be opened, and then he bowed low as Scarlet nodded her head in his direction. The carriage passed through the gate and made its way out across the countryside.

A rider approached the barricade, calling out, his voice reaching their carriage. "We have an urgent message from *Place de Grève*! All able citizens are needed. Two families of aristos have escaped in the very act of delivery to *La Guillotine*. You must go in pursuit, man! All of you!" The man waved his hand in a sweeping motion, and large numbers of them turned and rushed toward the center of Paris.

The rider's shouts brought Scarlet's heart into her throat. But Simon, her coachman, continued forward as if nothing were amiss. As soon as they were out of sight, the hatch from above opened, and he winked at her.

Scarlet removed her veil and placed a hand on her heart, willing herself to calm. "Welcome, to all our passengers. Please stay hidden and silent until we have come safely to our rendezvous point."

***

Once at their location in the woods, they built a fire and passed around tea. Scarlet began to pace in nervous agitation.

Simon joined her.

She said, "Still we have heard nothing?"

He shook his head. "The last we knew, they all safely hid in the carriage just as our group did and headed toward the west barricade."

"Curse that Bibot! Our check-in point would have contacted us by now. Something is wrong. They are in danger."

Simon gestured for one of the men to come forward. "Shall we send someone?"

Scarlet shook her head. "I must go myself."

He shook his head and opened his mouth to protest, when a man came running forward, clutching his side.

"It is I, Courtenay."

"Come," Simon said. He and Scarlet ran to him, bearing his weight between them as Courtenay's legs buckled.

"Quickly, bring some bandages," Scarlet called out.

Courtenay gestured with one hand. "They have Andrew."

She faltered, grabbing for Simon's arm with her free hand.

"Stopped at the barricade. Bibot discovered the lot of us. We tried to fight them off, but it was no use, not with the crowd. I broke free to get word to you immediately, but Bibot himself nicked me with his sword." He loosened the pressure at his side, and blood dripped into his palm.

They lowered him gently to the ground, and one of the league applied the bandages. Courtenay continued. "They took the lot of them back to *la Place*. About to be beheaded, all of them, post haste." He paused, coughing. "We could not have known. I misjudged you, my lady. You are . . . remarkable." He clutched his side and gritted his teeth from the pain.

She studied him; he was still in good color. He would recover—a blessed mercy.

Scarlet's own knees went weak. She grabbed for her scarf and began to wrap it around her face. Her wig still in place, the bun came loose, and matted gray hair fell down around her shoulders.

Simon grabbed her forearm. "What are you doing?"

"I must go back. I cannot simply allow them to die."

"I am coming."

Scarlet nodded and ran for the nearest horse, and then they took off at a gallop through the woods. She pushed aside a heavy feeling of dread. The family must live. And Andrew must return to England's safe shores. She urged her horse onward again, hoping to beat time, but a part of her knew she was already too late.

They arrived in the square during the slow, sleepy hours of the late afternoon. Shops were closed, and the remaining guillotine audience lolled about in the hot drunkenness of the over-indulged, resting out the high-sun hours.

Simon approached a group of children. "Tell me what has happened today. We heard we missed a real show."

The children stared suspiciously up at Simon and began to back away from them both.

One boy glanced at Scarlet and then sharpened his gaze.

She breathed in quickly and held his stare.

He said something to the group and they ran off together, but he stepped forward until she could see the deep brown of his eyes.

"It is you," he said.

Scarlet nodded. "We need your help. What has happened?"

"They were caught. Brought back here and beheaded shortly after." The boy looked down, avoiding her eyes.

"How many?" Scarlet dreaded the answer.

"Five, a family, three children." He reached into his pocket. "I saved this, just in case." He held out a small wooden horse.

Scarlet's eyes welled with tears and she reached for the horse, clutching it in her hands. "Thank you." Her voice caught in her throat. "All Frenchmen?"

He nodded. "The family. They say some broke free, but one Englishman is under guard nearby."

Simon and Scarlet shared a look. Her heart constricted, and a great weight of dread filled her.

Pushing it aside, she studied the boy, measuring him.

Simon asked, "What is your name, my friend?"

He stood up proudly and squared his shoulders. "Abelino."

Scarlet smiled. "Well, Abelino. I believe it is high time you joined our league. What say you?"

He nodded, his mouth set in a straight line. He pushed his shoulders back and stood taller, on the tips of his toes. "I would be honored."

Simon placed his hand on the lad's shoulder. "Can you tell us where they have taken the Englishman?"

He nodded. "Come this way."

They had to run to keep up with him, sticking to the shadows as he scampered through narrow alleys, dodging piles of garbage.

He led them to an older home with bars on the upstairs windows. "Bernard LeFevre dragged the Englishman up the stairs."

They ducked into a dark corner as the sentinel walked past, eyeing their very spot.

Scarlet asked quietly, "Any idea how many are up there?"

Abelino shook his head.

"Thank you, my friend. You have done well."

He blushed and looked up proudly at her. "I'm small, but I am always around. If you ever need me, ask near Île Saint-Louis." He bowed to them and ran off into the dark.

Scarlet watched him go and then indicated for Simon to follow her back a couple streets away from the guarded prison. "We have to move tonight. I don't trust that LeFevre will allow Andrew to live much longer than tomorrow."

"Consider that he could be laying a trap."

Scarlet nodded. "I have considered. We have no choice but to free him anyway."

"We must outfox the fox, eh? Shall I run to our checkpoint and alert the men?"

"Yes, send as many as we can spare with the Mercier family to England. Have them return the ship to France post haste. All others should come here immediately to the inn around the corner, the one with the tavern next door, and we will have a plan."

Simon raised his eyebrows. "Which is?"

"I don't know as of yet. I'll watch the house to try and determine at least how many patrol the place." She heard her voice speaking, but even as she said the words, she felt an odd sense of detachment, as if the energy had drained from her, sucked in by a heavy despair.

As soon as Simon left her in the shadows, her darkest thoughts rushed at her in a desperate invasion of all hope. She sank to the ground. The loss of the entire DuPont family clenched at her heart and forced breath from her lungs. Wrapping her arms around her own body, she gulped and swallowed cries into silence. Her chest shuddered with the effort and shook with each new wave of desperate sorrow. She had failed them. They could have left through another gate, waited until the dark of night, anything but face Bibot.

She imagined the eyes of a child, large and hopeful, and she cradled the small toy horse.

Unbidden, thoughts of her parents, shackled by the Spanish, haunted her. She tried to blink them away. Their memory always came forward in moments of despair or failure. Her mother's eyes, desperately drinking in Scarlet's face, her head turned toward her only daughter for as long as the captors allowed. If Scarlet had come home earlier, she could have warned them. She should have run to them as her brother had done.

She should have saved them all: her parents, her brother, the DuPont family, the children. Despair squeezed her chest tighter. She succumbed for one minute more, gave sorrow its full reign, and then she commanded herself to calm. For Andrew. She would not fail him too.

She measured her breathing, unclenched her fists, and tasked her brain to focus. Her shudders slowed and her sobbing ceased. Never would she feel carefree, but at least some sense of reason had returned. Wiping tears from her eyes, she made her way through the darkness back to a hiding place that allowed her to watch the prison residence.

In the twenty minutes she waited, only one guard walked past. She knew more must wait inside, but perhaps Bernard underestimated the league's ability to find Andrew. With any luck, they could whisk him away in the dark of night. As she considered the possibility, the beginnings of a plan formed. And with that new hope as fuel, she ran off through the streets. If she moved quickly, she just might get their costumes in time.

Returning to the inn with a cart in tow full of fabric and bottles of wine, she rushed inside to summon the men. "Gentlemen. Let us make haste, empty my cart, and take everything up to our room, shall we?"

As quickly as they could, they changed clothing in their room and reassembled again on the street. Each person dressed in black, with a red-, white-, and blue-striped band tied to their upper arm, the tricolor cockade stitched in the center. Many of them carried bottles of the cheap wine.

All were prepared for whatever may come. They knew the league did not leave its own. They would remain in France doing all they could until Andrew was once again among their number.

As they neared the home, their voices became louder and more rowdy; they punched each other and swayed back and forth. By the time they had approached the door of the house, flickering light illuminated the front window. A man came to the door and cracked it open. His voice demanded, "Who goes there? What do you want?"

Scarlet held her breath, watching from the shadows.

The largest of their number, Morgan, grumbled, "Here with reinforcements. Now open the door."

The man inside hesitated and then said, "What reinforcements? I was not informed."

Morgan said, "Well now, whose problem is that? We're all here and with wine to share. Are you going to let us in, or should we march all the way back to Robespierre himself only to be told to come back to you again?"

A few of the other men took to grumbling. "Come on now! Let us in."

The door opened wider. "You can stay right where you are, but I'll take the wine, first thing." He waved to the men behind him and they stepped out into the night, assuming wine bottles from the closest men.

Morgan said in a half whisper, "There's talk of the Pimpernel attempting a rescue. The man inside is his particular friend."

The guard's eyes opened wide.

"I would think you'd be grateful for extra numbers guarding your prisoner tonight." Morgan looked up and down the street into the dark.

The guard also looked out into the street, scanned his eyes quickly over the men, and then shrugged and held the door open wider. "You have more wine, you say?"

Morgan said, "That's the spirit! Wine we have, gentlemen. It's going to be a fine night after all."

The men laughed and pounded each other on the back as they entered.

Scarlet breathed a sigh as she watched each of her league members. If all went well, the rescue would be swift and quiet. She crept away, work yet to be finished. The gentlemen would soon be guests in the Paris home of Lady Scarlet Cavendish, emissary to France, at the soiree planned for the next evening.

Chapter Eleven

MATTEO OPENED HIS EYES TO the sounds of his valet preparing clothes in the next room. Memories of his evening with Scarlet filled his mind and welcomed the day. His face broke into the largest, most ridiculous smile he felt sure anyone ever saw on a man lying alone in his bed. Edwards would think him addled if he were to peek his head inside and witness it. But it could not be helped. Discovering that you were in love with a person as glorious as Scarlet deserved a few early-morning smiles. He planned to smile every morning in just such a manner, particularly those mornings that involved her beside him.

Energized at the thought, he jumped out of bed and called, "Edwards. Good morning, Edwards!"

His valet leaned his head through the doorway to his adjoining dressing room. Eyebrows raised, he said, "Good morning, my lord. Shall I ring for breakfast? Or your morning tea?"

"No, thank you, but I feel in great need of an early ride. Could you prepare my riding attire? And then I will change quickly for a bit of breakfast with Lady Cavendish."

Clearing his throat, Edwards held out a slip of paper. "She had this note delivered early this morning."

Matteo tried to stop his smile from reappearing but was completely unsuccessful. His goodhearted valet averted his eyes and pretended not to notice. Matteo took the paper from Edwards's hand and sat at his writing desk.

My Dear Matteo,

I am saddened to be writing a farewell after the perfect evening we had, but it must be so. My dear aunt is ailing, I am afraid, and calls me to the north to attend her. I daren't refuse, as she is near the last remaining relative I have on this earth. Please continue to feel at home on the estate. I have instructed the servants to attend to you as they would me. I will be thinking of you in each moment and long for the day when I can return. I have sent on my regrets to the prince, but I am sure he expects you and will enjoy your company this morning.

With all my love,

Scarlet

Allowing his hand to drop to his side, he leaned back in his chair, staring out the window.

She left?

He rubbed his face, unsure what to think. He had been certain until this moment that time was his only obstacle to pass before she became his, body and soul. But now . . . She had never mentioned an aunt to him at all, ailing or otherwise.

In all fairness, they hadn't discussed their families at any great length. He supposed it was because his was all but gone from the earth, and he assumed she would not want to talk about her deceased husband.

But as he sat, letter in hand, a splinter of doubt lodged itself, and he opened his mind to the idea that something could be amiss. He questioned the one thing he had been sure of—her affection. *With all my love,* she'd signed the letter. But had he spoken too soon? Declared his love, proposed, and then scared her away? And perhaps she still held strong feelings for Rupert. Of course she always would, he assumed. Or worse, what if she was free with her attentions to many? He thought over her behavior at the prince's ball.

The most maddening realization, that he couldn't see her, look into her face to judge for himself, drove him to restlessness. Her sudden disappearance represented only another test of his patience to endure before he saw her again and could ask her himself. With that, he called for Edwards. "Let's get me on a horse, man. I will be out for several hours at least."

Edwards nodded. "Very good, sir."

After a good long ride, Matteo walked back to the dowager house, wiping sweat from his brow. At a distance, dust from carriage wheels rose above the bushes that lined the lane. He groaned. With any luck, they were come to visit Scarlet and upon discovering her absence, would leave straight away.

But the carriage did not stop in front of the main house. It continued on instead down the drive toward his own. He picked up his pace and arrived around the side gardens just as the carriage door opened. His feet stopped midstride, though, when he saw Éléonore's hand and leg exit. He considered turning and running toward the back of the house, but her voice stopped him.

"Oh, Matteo. I am so glad I caught you."

The irony of her word choice not lost on him, he stepped forward and bowed crisply to her. "What are you doing here, Éléonore?"

"Always my greeting from you. Tsk tsk, Matteo. One would think you've forgotten your manners."

"I could say the same of you, showing up continually where you are not wanted."

"Oh, come now, must we be so antagonistic? Can we not simply sit and drink tea as old friends do?"

He considered her for a moment, feeling no small amount of curiosity about why she was here in England, so he decided to play her game. "I apologize for my state, but if you don't mind a bit of horse on a person, we may sit together outside on the terrace." He gestured for her to walk with him around to the back of the house.

After a moment she said, "You have done well for yourself here in England."

Matteo clenched his teeth. "It is hardly my home or my land or my own estate, but I am comfortable, yes."

"France is still home to all its loyal citizens. You could be numbered among us if you wish."

"I am loyal to France forever. Some of its citizens are a bit troubling, I must admit. Chasing a fellow around, tying him up, and attempting to rid him of important appendages like his head. Those things are a bit difficult to swallow, but France—France is a delight and my homeland forever."

Éléonore frowned. "You have changed, become a danger to the Revolution."

"You sent me to the guillotine, Éléonore, tied my hands. If not for my rescuers, I would be dead, even now as we speak. And you say I have changed. Because I do not like your bloodthirsty methods? It is you who has changed."

"There was a time when you were just as disgruntled with our wealthy neighbors as I have been."

"I was young and hot-blooded. Criticizing neighbors because they wouldn't share their tarts or allow us to pluck apples from their trees is entirely different from sending entire families with their children to the guillotine simply because they inherited title or affluence."

"We were children, yes, but denounce them we did. Think of it as gathering evidence, my dear, from the mouths of babes."

Matteo felt his blood run cold. "You would not use the innocent ramblings of a youth, *my ramblings*, to bring dear friends to their deaths!"

Éléonore turned to him with a smug smile. "I have all the letters we wrote, in my keepsake box. We accused every neighbor of something, I am sure. Remember when we saw the Jardins whip the poor urchin outside the gates? And why? Because he wouldn't stop begging, and Lady Jardin did not approve of his dress."

His throat dried. They approached the table set up at the back of the cottage. Praise the servants and their intuitive genius.

She sat daintily on the chair offered and began to pour out the tea for them both. "So, you see, you are helping me after all."

Clenching his fists, he used a considerable amount of energy restraining himself. "I forbid you to use my name or my letters to implicate people."

Leaning back in her chair, she raised a hand in question. "Forbid, darling? What position are you in to forbid me anything?"

A footman arrived. "The post has come with correspondence you have been seeking."

He reached for it. "Thank you, James." He tried to hide his great relief as he quickly moved the letter from the tray to his inside pocket.

Éléonore watched his hands with narrowed eyes.

He leaned forward. "Perhaps I may reason with you. I do not denounce these good people any longer. I have grown up to adulthood and have seen them do many kind things for the less fortunate outside their gates. The Jardin family, for example, opened up a school for the poor. They provide food baskets to their tenants and the needier families in the area." Then he accentuated each word with a tap at the table. "They are good people, Éléonore."

She shook her head. "No doubt you have been deceived over time. I would much rather believe the words of an innocent, truthful youth than someone as jaded and selfishly motivated as you."

Leaning back abruptly in his chair, he ran a hand through his hair.

She sipped her tea, watching him over the top of the cup. "I could be convinced to hold off on my denouncements, however—perhaps even burn the pile of letters."

His eyes narrowed in distrust. "What is it you want from me?"

She placed her teacup back on the table and dabbed her lips with her napkin. "Hand me the identity of the Pimpernel, and all the letters are yours. I promise not to denounce a single one." She sat back with a satisfied air.

"The Pimpernel? No one knows who he is! I've been trying for weeks to find him, with no leads, not one!" He snorted. "And if I did know the man, I would never deliver him to you, not if I had to die in his place."

She leaned forward. "So, you have been trying to find him!"

Matteo frowned at her. "Of course. I hoped to aid him in his rescues."

She scowled. "Well, now you will aid me in finding him. Or I begin denouncing families from our childhood, one by one." She paused, biting into a pastry. "Think, Matteo. It is a fair trade. You save the lives of six families in exchange for the name of one man. Until you find him, you work for me."

He considered her for a moment. "I have tried myself already, as I have said."

Éléonore smiled with satisfaction. "Your first task is to attend the Pinckneys' dinner party on Tuesday. Lord Simon Devereaux will be there, and we know he has ties to the Pimpernel. Trail him, watch him, intercept all notes he might leave lying about."

"I have agreed to nothing."

"Then the first of your families will die when my post reaches France."

Matteo stood, his tall body looming over her small one, breathing rapidly. He resisted the urge to toss her aside and instead considered his options. "I will attend, but I am certain I will discover nothing."

Éléonore stood. "Come, darling. You cannot enjoy this estrangement from your home. Return to us. The cleansing that you find so distasteful will not last forever, and then you will witness France's rise to greatness."

"Leave my home."

She approached him and ran her hands up his chest. He stiffened and reached to pull them away. Before he could stop her, a hand slid into his jacket pocket and took the letter. Reading the direction on the front, she said, "Oh, it's from dear Potier. How I miss that codger. He has been quite difficult to track down, until now." She again studied the direction on the front of the letter.

Matteo snatched it from her fingers. "He was like an uncle to you, like family."

"Sometimes our families can be so disappointing. You now have one more reason to help me."

His throat tightened. "Have you no more heart at all? What is it that beats in your chest?"

"Bring me to the Pinckneys' party as your guest."

"You are not welcome there."

"I will be, if I come with you."

Matteo's jaw clenched and flexed. What choice did he have? Until he found a better solution, he would humor her requests. "Very well. Come here on Tuesday, and we shall drive over together."

He called for a footman. "Please escort Miss Duplay to her carriage. She is leaving."

As soon as she rounded the corner of the house, Matteo ran in through the back door. He took the steps three at a time, calling for extra paper and ink to be sent to his room immediately. He ripped open Potier's letter. What would have been a comforting missive now filled him with dread. They had at last found a safe house and location. Potier had written in kindness to put Matteo's mind at ease. That consideration could have sealed his death.

Matteo rushed to the table and began writing furiously, feverishly across the page. The first note he wrote to Potier, telling him that he must change location immediately. He tried to be as vague as possible. But he was sure Potier would understand. He then proceeded to write notes to every family he had ever complained about to Éléonore when they were young. Curse his misguided youth! He wrote as quickly as his hand would allow. Soon he had a stack of seven letters. He called for Parsons, his butler.

"Please, man. Call for an express rider immediately. These letters must reach the shores of France as quickly as possible."

Parsons took them in his hands and hurried away. Matteo breathed deeply. As he exhaled, he prayed the letters would arrive in time and all recipients would be safe. For two more breaths he sat, commanding his heart to calm. Then he called for Edwards and began his preparations to visit Prince George. So much of France's future lay in His Highness's hands and in Matteo's ability to sway him.

Chapter Twelve

THE PRINCE WAITED IN AN area of Carlton House the staff called the rose satin drawing room. When the footman announced him, Matteo stopped just inside the door so he could take in the room in appreciation. The walls were a deep rose color, with draperies and satin curtains hanging in great folds of fabric along the ceiling and in every entryway. A chandelier hung in the center of the room, the glass a light-blue color with gold candle sconces. The floor was a matching blue. Great portraits and other works of art covered the walls. The ceiling, engraved with gold filigree, depicted paintings within carved and framed rectangles. Matteo bowed to the prince. "A pleasant room, Your Highness. Thank you for the great honor to call on you."

Prince George nodded.

"The murals on the ceiling, do they depict hunting excursions?"

"I believe so. The ceiling has been above me so long I hardly look at it anymore; it is so dashed difficult to continue looking up all the time. Gives me a pain right here in my neck." He winked at Matteo and gestured that he sit on a low settee across from His Highness. "I am glad you could come, Prince Matteo, even though Scarlet is unable."

Matteo grimaced. "You call me *Prince*. I feel it is a title I do not deserve, Your Highness."

The prince waved his hand. "Do any of us truly deserve our titles? Not when we get them, surely. But hopefully there are some of us who grow into them and do in fact one day deserve them."

Matteo nodded in appreciation. "Just so. Beautifully said. I may one day quote you."

He shook his head. "Ho ho! There will be none of that, sir, no. Mustn't disrupt my delightfully *scandalous* image." He reached forward and picked up a pastry to place in his mouth. "We have the most wonderful French chef. Please, help yourself to some of his delicacies."

Matteo raised his eyebrows in appreciation. "Now this, I could never refuse." He sampled two or three. "You have discovered my weakness. I thank you for a taste of home." He closed his eyes as he chewed his last bite.

His Highness rested his hands in his lap. "Now, let us talk with purpose. France is in great need of assistance."

Matteo wiped his hands on his napkin, cleared his throat, and said, "Yes. Nobles are in need of evacuation immediately. All of their lives are at risk. They live at the whim of a few minds. If the wind changes direction, the tide of goodwill follows and they are sent before *La Guillotine*."

"Yes, yes. I know all that. We are already doing as much as we are able. The Pimpernel has done a great service—"

"Does he work under your direction?" Matteo's eyes widened in surprise.

"He does, but I give him all manner of leeway." The prince leaned forward in his seat. "You know, I have never even seen the man. He refuses to disclose his identity even to me."

Matteo raised his eyebrows. "But surely someone must know who he is. How do you contact him?"

His Highness shrugged. "We have our methods."

His personal needs weighing him down greatly, Matteo debated in his mind what to communicate to His Highness. Watching the prince for a moment, he said, "France has one desperate need, more important than all others at the moment."

He nodded. "The *dauphin*."

Matteo opened his mouth and then closed it. "You astonish me."

"Nothing so astonishing, I assure you." He humphed. "We do keep ourselves abreast of the happenings to our nearest neighbor. The *dauphin* is in dire straits, the poor lad. If rumors are to be believed, torture and abuse are his daily bread. The stability of your country, and quite possibly ours, rests in his safekeeping."

Matteo sat up straighter in his chair. "I am so pleased at the depth of your awareness. Something must be done. Rumors are indeed grave. His treatment is beyond cruel, starvation and illness his constant companions. Incarcerated in the Temple prison along with Marie Antoinette and her daughter, though the lad is purportedly in a separate, dark room all by himself."

Frowning, Prince George said, "We are investigating what can be done. But we must tread carefully. We cannot do anything that would be seen as an act of war by the governing body in France. And you can be assured that kidnapping Louis-Charles would be an act of war."

"Will you consult with your advisors?"

"No. Not at all. We must not let them know a thing. I will keep it from my father as well. No, this must be handled with great discretion by military in my service, by the Pimpernel, and by some very loyal friends in Hungary."

Matteo's face relaxed, and his mouth turned up into a small smile. "I thank you. France will be greatly in your debt. Preserving the royal house of King Louis could save my country."

Lifting a cup of tea to his mouth, the prince took a sip. "I also need to discuss with you a sensible manner in which to approach the new governing body of France."

"They are imbeciles."

"So they appear to be, but I must discover ways to negotiate, to deal diplomatically with them."

"I can help with that. I know them well. Unfortunately, in the beginning, I worked closely with some to bring about a hope for new freedom in my homeland." Matteo could not lift his eyes from the floor so great was his shame.

Continued silence brought his eyes up to search Prince George's. The man did not seem pleased. "You were misguided. People need the crown, a strong monarch to guide them, to give them purpose. To keep them in hand."

Confused, Matteo felt unsure, though his fellow citizens of France had certainly dashed all hope and celebration he had felt in gifting power to the people.

Prince George interrupted his thoughts. "There is more you can do *here*, Matteo."

Matteo frowned. "Scarlet tells me that more and more often. I find I have a difficulty believing or accepting the idea."

After his meeting with Éléonore, he felt more of a danger to France than anything. His mind twisted and turned over whether to share her threats with the prince.

Chuckling, the prince rested his cup on the table. "Scarlet can be a persuasive woman. You may as well give in and believe her. She will not rest until you do."

Matteo chuckled in return. He did not say more, but he did not think there would ever be something he could do here in England as important as saving lives from *La Guillotine* in France.

Adjusting his sleeve, Prince George said, "I have a specific task in mind. It may not be pleasant, but I have no one else to ask."

Matteo leaned forward. "What is it? I will do my best."

The prince's mouth lifted in a crooked smile. "Don't say that until you hear what it is." He paused, examining his fingers. "I need you to keep an eye on Éléonore Duplay."

Groaning, Matteo asked, "Isn't there anything else you might need?" He could see the wisdom in it. No one would understand Éléonore and her motivations better than him. But His Highness did not realize the blackmail Matteo was suffering; he couldn't possibly understand the power she had over him, or could have, if he let her.

The prince eyed him with sympathy. "I understand she tried to send you to prison. You were once childhood friends, were you not?"

"We were." He sighed. "And she uses that to her advantage whenever she can." He paused. As awful a prospect as time with Éléonore promised to be, he was grateful for the excuse to escort her to the Pinckneys' dinner party. "I can see I am the best person for this job, however dreaded it may be."

Leaning forward, Prince George patted him on the knee. "Thank you, Matteo. I cannot shun her. For diplomacy's sake, she must be included in some important state events, parties, balls, and the like. But I am not comfortable with her here, and I want to keep her away from everyone as much as possible."

"I understand. It will be especially easy with Scarlet gone. I will want to escort someone." He could not keep a tinge of bitterness from his tone.

The prince winked. "In love with the woman, are you?" He laughed good-naturedly. "As is half the *ton* and nearly all of my court. I daresay I would be too, if I were free to fall in love." He chuckled again. "She will return soon enough. She is always flitting about in one place or another, but she always comes back."

This new information joined a jumbled puzzle of pieces Matteo was trying to sort but had so far been unsuccessful.

When the prince stood, Matteo joined him. "Thank you for meeting with me this morning. I hope we can do this again. I find I am in much need of a loyal Frenchman's thoughts on any number of things. Please be available for me to summon here even on the smallest bit of notice."

Bowing, Matteo said, "I would be honored. France will be greatly in your debt, and as I cannot trust the current government to even recognize our great need, I will thank you in our behalf."

"I do this for my own country's safety." The prince turned to face a large map laid out across his table. "Whoever reigns in France after the current terror is over will have great power. I hope to ensure our friendship."

"A wise aim." Matteo moved to leave.

Prince George said, "One more thing. I will be having a French nationals ball, and I hope you will come. Keep Éléonore as sequestered off as is possible. Our French citizens are understandably petrified of the woman. And watch her. My sources tell me nothing is below her notice."

Chapter Thirteen

Paris, France

SURROUNDED BY FRENCH SOLDIERS, HER own men, dignitaries, and a few local gentry who dared socialize in public, Scarlet hoped to flaunt a convincing enough façade that she would dispel all suspicion.

Returning to her conversation, she placed a hand on her chest. "Oh, but you are deliciously funny, monsieur. I'm sure your little Marguerite will thank me a million times for this conversation. May I wish you every happiness, albeit premature? Surely she will accept your offer? How could she refuse such a man?" She patted the arm of this new acquaintance, one of the French soldiers for the Committee of Public Safety. "Please, try the pastries. I had them brought over specially from England. We employ a French chef there, you see."

The irony was completely lost on her new friend, Monsieur Crevier. He grinned and promised to try them.

The strain of the evening began to tighten her stomach. More likely the strain of the entire stay in France weighed on her. Knitting at the base of the guillotine had proved to be her most trying deception yet. Day after day in such company, pretending to revel in the bloodlust, had drained almost all the light she had inside. Losing a family and almost losing Andrew had shaken her. She doubted herself and craved home.

And now, French soldiers and dignitaries mixed with her league and other French and English nobles in an evening soiree she hosted in her Paris home, just twenty-four hours after their successful escape from LeFevre. This sort of frivolity required a different kind of strength, one she hoped she could maintain.

A bold move, she knew she risked much, even though most in the room carried some form of diplomatic immunity. And she had found time and again, if she stood strong and in the open without flinching, it did more for her deception than cowering in the dark. People rarely suspected the obvious.

Interestingly, the Baron de Batts, a Hungarian by birth, also mingled amongst her guests. The tension in the room felt thick at times. The baron loathed any member of the Committee of Public Safety and did nothing to hide his hatred. As a Hungarian citizen and friend of the English, he maintained the strongest immunity and therefore felt free to make his antagonistic sentiments clear to all.

Scarlet took a deep calming breath. If they could just get through this night, all would be well. Their cover would be complete, and they could travel to England in the morning. She almost began to calm but jolted back into high awareness when Bernard LeFevre himself entered through the front door. His eyes scanned the room, narrowing when he found Andrew.

Andrew noticed him immediately but let his eyes slip past the man as if he did not know him.

Impressive control of emotions.

Soon Monsieur LeFevre took purposeful strides in her direction. She pushed all thought away and found her inner blank and ridiculous state, which she grabbed with both hands. With any luck he would be convinced of her utter idiocy and inability to do anything at all to harm the Revolution.

"Why, Bernard! How good of you to come! We have so many of your dear soldiers here and members of your committee." She reached her hand out to him.

He bowed over it. "You have a diverse group here. Many of my men, as you mentioned, and many of yours as well." He raised an eyebrow, watching her closely.

Fishing.

She blushed and placed a hand over her mouth. "Oh, you flatter me, monsieur. I wouldn't say *many*, no. Perhaps one or two have succumbed to my charms, poor dears. They never do recover, you know. Totally lost to me; even when they marry, a piece of their hearts remains loyal." She shook her head sadly.

She bit back a smile as she noticed him grit his teeth. "You misunderstand. Your rescue efforts last evening. Your same men are here."

She tilted her head in complete confusion, and then she brightened her face in open discovery. "Oh, yes! You mean the pastries. You would have heard, being French, about our near-disaster with the pastries. Oh my, yes. Nearly destroyed. Our chef, poor dear, keeps us well supplied here in France whenever it is we come. But they were just a bit on the stale side, so we employed a local chef, but let me tell you—although French, he simply could not bake a single thing, so then we had to employ a group of runners to gather every good pastry in Paris, from all different bakeries, and difficult to find they were—"

"Surely you jest. Please do not continue in this mockery."

"Oh, believe me, I wish I were in error, but France hasn't a single good pastry chef. We can attest to that, as we searched up and down the streets. I heard it once said that you would elevate your chefs. Well, perhaps you have, and now, my dear Bernard—now, there is no one to bake your food."

He ran a hand up and down his face and used one finger to loosen his cravat.

"Or perhaps they are lolling about their days in your horrid *Place de Grève*, wasting away good talent." She shrugged delicately. "Well, whatever the reason, the tragedy has been averted, and we have pastries for our party." She smiled up at him with a vacant expression of pure relief.

"And the Pimpernel? You know nothing of him?"

"Why, monsieur, of course I have heard of the Pimpernel, the greatest hero in all of France! Who hasn't? Isn't he just so entertaining? Sneaking all sorts of people right out from under your very fingers. Why, just the other day, did he not ride out of Bibot's west barricade himself, with none the wiser?"

Turning red in the face, Monsieur LeFevre said, "Is he here, madame? I wish to speak with him."

"Here? Here, in my home? I hardly think so. As well-liked as I am, I am sure the Pimpernel has better things to do than to entertain me." She leaned toward him and in a mock-whisper said, "It's more likely he's over at your prison right now, what with you and your soldiers so happily situated. What a perfect opportunity."

His squinty eyes opened wider, and he turned from her briskly, calling for two of his men to follow out the door. Once outside, he shouted for his carriage.

Slowly, she let out a large breath of air.

Another French soldier who had been standing several feet behind them stepped forward. "You mock him, but you should not. His thirst consumes him. Never satisfied, he has doggedly decided that all the guillotine deaths are insufficient. He will keep trapping the unworthy, seeking out those who would stand in his way until every drop of aristocratic blood, every dissenter, every dirty spec in our homeland is annihilated." The man stepped nearer.

She could smell his sweat and weak attempt to use soap.

"And what's more, he is fixated, completely distracted by the filth of two people. I have heard him say that France will only truly be cleansed when the blood of these two men has been spilt."

Scarlet stilled her features and stared blankly at the soldier.

A thirsty gleam appeared in his eye as he said, "And would you like to know whose?"

Scarlet shook her head and was about to decline, when he interrupted, "The blood of the Pimpernel and Matteo Durand."

Clutching a drink in her hand, she willed her hands not to tremor. "Oh, soldier. All this talk of blood and pastries has quite worn me out. I do believe I need a refill of our fine lemonade. What say you? Would you care for another as well?"

The soldier stared at her with stony eyes and shook his head. "No."

She turned from him and made her way to the lemonade and Andrew. There, she turned her body to face the room and announced, "Ah, my dear guests. We are so glad you have come. It is these conversations that need to keep happening. I daresay, we have so much to share, so many fashion secrets to divulge. Why, the very manner in which you weave your lovely fabrics . . ." She laughed. "But I digress, and I fear I shall lose the attention of every man in the room. I thank you, my dears, for coming. We set sail for England in the morn, but upon our return, we shall have another party, *oui*?"

Those nearest clapped politely and nodded their heads in agreement.

She raised her lemonade. "Wonderful! It is decided then. We will spread the word when next we arrive, and we hope that you all will join us." She turned from them to place her cup on the table. In an undertone she said, "I am glad you are well."

Andrew nodded. "Not nearly as glad as I am. Brilliant escape, if I do say so myself."

Scarlet grinned. "Of course you would say so. You were involved in it, were you not?"

Andrew smiled. "Naturally. Though it is a pity."

Scarlet tilted her head in question. "Oh?"

"Why, yes. Only one of my fine captors was able to make it to the party." Andrew looked down at her with lidded eyes and then winked.

Scarlet laughed, some of her tension leaving. "Perhaps they were a bit tied up?"

Andrew laid a finger aside his nose. "Just so, my lady. I am sure you have the right of it. Although, Simon must have been carrying an obscene amount of rope on his person, somewhere or other."

"Remarkable man, that Simon. It's uncanny what a good costume can do for a person." She looked around the room and sighed. "When will this night be over?"

Andrew glanced down at her, sympathy showing in his eyes. "You are a wonder, my lady. One of our more trying escapades, and here you are, as bright and brilliant as ever."

"Costumes come in all shapes and sizes, you know." She smiled at the Baron de Batts, who'd caught her eye across the room.

Andrew raised one eyebrow, still his most preferred expression. "And I think, if I dare suggest such a thing, that you are a bit more anxious to get home than usual. Some pleasurable distraction there? Hmm?" His eyes teased. She knew he tried to lift her spirits.

She couldn't stop the blush that spread across her cheeks. Then she stopped trying and succumbed. She sighed. "Home has more draw than ever. You are correct." She could think of nothing more strengthening than the arms of a certain Frenchman. Her eyes stung, and she tried to shift her thoughts.

Andrew placed his hand at the small of her back and leaned closer to her ear. "We will be there in no time." Then he straightened and announced a bit too loudly to those closest to him, "I daresay, I am feeling fatigued. Perhaps it is time to end the evening early, begin again tomorrow?" He looked a bit abashed, apologizing with his expression. The women giggled and then nodded in compassion toward him. As he made his way across the room, people began their own plans for departure. Scarlet smiled in relief. They would be on their way to the ship before daybreak.

***

The carriage pulled up in front of her home as the sun climbed above the horizon. One of Scarlet's most taxing missions, followed by the longest night, had finally closed with the glorious rising of the sun. She felt the weight that had been sitting on her chest fall off around her, and she allowed the peace of her land and the birds and the smell of fresh dew wash over and cradle her wounds.

Memories flooded her with warmth. Her first sight of the place, with Rupert at her side; the smell of freshly stirred dirt and the first signs of new growth; dear friends and balls and parties—all of it combined to create one happy sensation and the essence of her home. She swayed in her spot, the housekeeper calling, "Are you well, my lady?" She came forward, offering to assist Scarlet into the house.

Scarlet smiled. "Oh, my dear Mrs. Bussworth. I am afraid I'm a bit fatigued but happy—just reliving some memories is all."

Mrs. Bussworth's eyes crinkled at the edges. "So many good ones to choose from, my lady."

"And many more to come." Matteo rounded the house, his face showing a healthy glow of exertion. "You have returned." He approached slowly, a bit cautiously, to her side.

Mrs. Bussworth curtsied and turned back to the house with a smile.

Scarlet reached for Matteo, and he immediately supported her, pulling her into his embrace. She clung to him, melted into his front, and tried to block out the pain of the past week, but she could not. All her emotion, kept carefully in check, came flooding to the surface, and she found herself crying with abandon. She had failed; a dear French family lay dead. All the pent-up frustration and pressure surfaced, and she wet his lapel. So sudden was her outburst that she didn't have time for embarrassment.

He held her, cocooning her and resting his chin on her head. As her sobs subsided and her body stilled, he ran his hand along her back, tracing circles with his fingers. He said, "Would I could shield you from all sorrow, that you would never have a moment like this again." His grip on her tightened.

She pulled away so she might look into his face, her eyes widening as a single tear travelled down his cheek. "Matteo, what is it?" She reached up and caught it with her finger.

His expression held warmth. "Your pain. I couldn't help but feel a bit of it myself."

Her heart filled. What manner of man was this? No questions. He seemed to know what she needed. And tears. Tears for her sorrows. She considered him, searching his face through new joyful tears of her own. "This is the first moment of true happiness I have felt in many days." She rested her hand against his cheek.

A great feeling of unity passed between them. The distance closed. He searched her face as if to drink her in and then tilted his head and pressed his lips to hers. She leaned into him for comfort, for the warmth she knew she would find; but the minute their lips touched, a hot fire ignited, and she struggled to hold back with the proper decorum, to gently kiss only once, twice, a third time because she couldn't resist.

He tried to pull back then, but she reached for him, stepping up on the tips of her toes to keep him close. He responded immediately, meeting her lips anew with his own, lifting her around the waist and pulling her closer to him.

Neither knew how long they stood thus, but at length, she felt a change between them, a tired sort of sigh, and she knew they must stop. Still holding her, feet off the ground, Matteo leaned his head back to look into her eyes. The love she saw in return to her own filled her with wonder. His eyes full of joy, he rested his forehead against hers and smiled.

She smiled in return, giggling a little, the change from utter misery to bliss so complete she surprised herself. Matteo spun her around, and she felt her heart would explode. Never had she felt more joy in the mere presence of another. A great completion of herself began piecing itself together. What she lacked, he provided. When she could go no further, he filled her with strength and love and joy. This moment, this feeling, *this*, she wanted for the rest of her days. "Oh, Matteo."

He gently placed her on her feet but kept one of her hands in his own. Then he bent one knee in the dirt in front of her house as he'd done before, with the morning birds as witness. Scarlet, unaware of anyone but Matteo, watched him kneel before her.

"You said you needed time, and I pray these past weeks have been sufficient. Scarlet, you are my completion, my whole. You have become the very reason I breathe. Make us both happy and please, agree to be my wife." His eyes were full of love, of hope.

Scarlet knew she was tired, vulnerable, needy; but she also knew she no longer felt any hesitance. She wanted only Matteo, every day, Matteo. And so she said, "Oh, yes, Matteo. Make me the happiest of women and marry me straightaway, as soon as we are able."

He picked her up again and swung her around and around in front of the house. They laughed, and he set her down. Then, grabbing her hand, he ran with her around to the back of the house, through the beds and hedges and along the paths until they reached her rose garden. "Here," he said. And he sat her down on a bench under an arch of roses.

Between breaths, she asked, "What is this?"

He shrugged. "I had planned to propose here, in this spot. See, they have bloomed while you were gone. And I pictured you right there." He picked a rose from a nearby bush and handed it to her. "With this." He sat beside her and again took her hand in his.

She leaned her head against his shoulder and yawned, the past twenty-four hours catching up with her at last. "Right here," she echoed.

Within moments, Scarlet fell asleep. Matteo smiled, enjoying her soft breathing until he was sure she would not awaken with movement. Then he lifted her gently in his arms, carrying her up the back walk and into the house. Once inside, he gestured with his head to the nearest servant to help him. The maid led him to Scarlet's room, where Annabeth waited. He gently laid her on the bed and crept out, closing the door softly behind him.

Chapter Fourteen

SCARLET STOOD IN A GRAND foyer outside the sanctuary doors that entered into the great hall. She breathed large deep breaths of happy satisfaction. Her brother-in-law had offered to give her away before he and his wife had left on an urgent trip to Wales, but Scarlet declined and instead stood alone. She preferred it this way—at least, she had when she had planned the wedding. She smiled, thinking of the planning—a beautiful, frenzied excitement, as she'd organized all the details. She and Mrs. Bussworth had pulled off a masterpiece, she was sure of it, and in only three weeks' time.

She took in the details of her dress and laughed out loud, and then she laughed louder at herself, standing in the foyer of the sanctuary, finding amusement in her wedding dress. She hoped Matteo would be able to hide his amusement. She wore yellow—bright canary yellow—with a bold headdress of teal and peacock feathers. It rose to great heights on her head and then cascaded down her back in folds of feathers and ribbon and fabric. The dress bumped out behind her in the largest rump of the Season. And the fabric trailed below it, gathering in ruffles as it flowed to the floor and on down two feet after her. At her sleeves, she had stitched together ribbon and fabric in great mounds, the layers hanging all about her arms, down to her fingertips. She was a walking display, one big distraction. Which is exactly what she hoped.

She and Simon had discussed at great length how close they had come to losing their personas and their disguises. Andrew and Simon both were linked in one way or another to the Pimpernel, and more and more people tied her to them in friendship. The soiree in her home and much of what she did at the parties amongst the *ton* were to help dispel any suspicion that she would be a significant risk to the committee in France. As long as they discounted and underestimated her capacity, she and her league would be safe. She had used the evening soiree in Paris as another measure to prove the vacancy of her brain and the ridiculous focus on fashion eccentricities. They hoped LeFevre would think nothing of grand consequence could come forth from a mind such as hers.

The wedding was meant to distract even further, to confuse and to pull attention away from Scarlet Cavendish the spy, to Scarlet Cavendish the fashion expert and eccentric young widow now happily married to a French prince. She hoped it would work. So much depended on the Pimpernel's identity remaining secret.

She scoffed at the idea that any would suspect her. People *would* guess she somehow possessed an intimate knowledge of the league. She hoped to portray in an even stronger degree that her involvement was that of a frivolous eccentric, toying with her famous and elusive friends.

Her safety in France also depended on the new title from the prince. As long as she never gave them reason to believe she acted as an enemy to France but only as England's emissary, she would be shielded, to a certain degree, from the power of the Committee of Public Safety.

She moved to the window, still waiting for the music to cue her entrance into the great hall. Outside, birds sang a lovely chorus. It was all the music she needed.

Of a sudden, so much in her life had come together in blissful perfection; she almost failed to believe it could be happening. Her thoughts turned to Matteo, waiting at this moment near the altar at the head of the hall.

Then her music began, and the doors swung wide open. Every head turned in her direction, and every pair of eyes gazed upon her. She paused for a moment to take them all in, making eye contact with many. Simon winked at her, and Andrew's smile stretched his cheeks. Then she turned to find Matteo, and everyone else in the room disappeared. His face shone with a brilliance she felt was almost unearthly. As she began her journey down the center of the church, a strong sense of community enveloped her, and the welcoming love from the man at the front almost consumed her. She was sure to be overcome from the whole of it. But her feet kept moving and her heart kept beating, and soon she reached for dear Matteo's outstretched hand and heard her marriage vows.

Could her heart stretch to include a full life and love for another man? She had wondered, worried, but here she saw it could. The human heart could contain much more love than she'd thought possible. She wondered and thrilled at the thought of further increase with children. She was filled with such an out-of-body expansion and space that she asked the universe if there was no limit to the heart's capacity to love. Perhaps it could grow to accommodate forever without end if she would but remain open to love.

She heard the words, "Yea, that thou shalt see thy children's children . . ." and she knew the ceremony was almost at an end. Matteo quirked an eyebrow, his glance taking in her headdress. She smiled and bit back a giggle.

"In the name of the Father, and of the Son, and of the Holy Ghost. Amen."

"Hello, my wife." He was not Matteo the escaping French prince, Matteo the desperate lover, Matteo the hopeful affianced, but Matteo her husband. And the feeling could not compare to any other. Belonging and longing filled her. She would never again be alone in the world. And at that moment, she knew she would never experience enough of Matteo. She would always long for more.

"Hello, husband."

He grinned at her and winked. Then together, they turned to face the church congregation. He took her hand in his and held it up as they faced the pews. The people all rose in a great cheer of congratulations.

They hurried together down the aisle, hand in hand. When they crossed through the doors, children threw rice and cheered. All the people from the town and many from the staff attended outside the church, celebrating and shouting and wishing love and happiness on them both. Amidst all the cheers and the love, they found their way to her waiting carriage, where they were whisked off down the lane.

Matteo turned to her and pulled her against him. "At last. My dear Scarlet, at last."

She giggled and wrapped her arms up around his neck as he pulled her onto his lap and looked down into her eyes. "You are the most beautiful woman I have ever seen. You are at once stunning and clever and kind. Three times beautiful: your face, your mind, and your heart." He eyed her headdress. "Even with this lovely large spectacle on your head." He tried to stop his laugh, but it choked out through his closed mouth.

Scarlet laughed again. She felt she could not stop. Everything was too wonderful for words, and the happiness bubbled up inside of her. "Could we be any happier, Matteo? Truly?"

Matteo shook his head. "There has never been a happier couple than you and I. But we will be happier still." He held her hand in his and kissed her knuckles. Looking into her eyes, he said, "It is my vow to make you happier still, that the years ahead will always promise joy on the horizon. You will always know that your next smile, your next laugh, is just around the corner."

Scarlet's eyes shone with unshed tears. Trying to swallow her emotion enough to speak, she said, "May it ever be so. May we find joy amidst the storms that are sure to come." She reached her hand up to his face, so close to her own, and held his cheek tenderly. Then she tilted her head ever so slightly to the side and pressed her lips to his.

Matteo cradled her so that she fit comfortably against his arm, his lips still moving over hers. He murmured against her mouth, "We have but a moment. Then I must share you again. Remember, my dear, I am yours to command. You have won me over heart, mind, and soul."

Scarlet looked up into Matteo's eyes and saw the truth of what he was trying to say. "I believe you, Matteo. And I accept all you offer, joyfully. I must be the most blessed woman in all of England. Married to a prince this very day—"

"'A prince,' she says. Must you!" With a great growl, he tickled her wherever he thought might make her squirm, until she screamed for him to stop.

"Oh, Matteo, please, I cannot stand it."

"Call me a commoner."

"I will not, Your Highness."

"What?" Then he tickled her more and more insistently. "Call me a commoner." He stared down into her eyes, and they stopped, each lost in the other.

She watched his breath coming quicker and felt her own pulse race faster. "I cannot, for you will never be common to me. Even had you been born so, I would still not call you common. You are a prince in your heart, born noble in goodness. Your care for your country, your love for your fellowman—these speak more of your royal standing than any title. So my prince you will always be . . . Your Highness." As she teased the last title, she squirmed from his grasp and moved to sit on the opposite side of the carriage. "Now, if you promise to behave, you may come sit beside me. But I must work some kind of magic with my hair before we stop. It has become all disheveled."

He moved to sit beside her. "I like you disheveled."

"Be that as it may, we cannot exit to meet the staff in this state."

Matteo smiled curiously at her. "We already know the staff."

"Yes, but we must present you as lord of the estate. The current marquess and marchioness are moving permanently to the ancestral Cavendish estate in Whitmore with the hope that you and I can manage things here on our own." She smiled, grateful. "It is their wedding gift to us. Now, the staff will want to greet you accordingly. It is an important tradition and an honor I would not deprive them of."

"Then greet the staff we must." Matteo nodded. "And after—"

She interrupted, holding up her hand. "And then we prepare for the wedding ball."

Matteo grimaced. "And why, again, is it we must have a wedding ball?"

Scarlet paused, her expression serious. "For France."

Matteo leaned back and laughed. "Right you are. For France." He reached for her hand again. "At times I wonder who is the French national and who is the English. Grateful I am for a wife who loves the people of France as I do."

Scarlet smiled, and inside she nearly screamed with desire to shout her identity to him. She *should* tell him. She *would* tell him all about her role as the Pimpernel. Just as soon as she was sure he would be safe in France. She knew if he discovered where she travelled and what she was doing, nothing could stop him from following after. And she doubted her ability to keep him safe. The faces of the DuPont family flashed in her mind. Those dear children who would no longer know joy, would never experience the love she felt.

"What is it?" He ran his hand along her forehead and down her hairline, tucking a tendril behind her ear. "Your eyes went dark. A great worry passed right before me across your brilliant greens. Tell me."

His expression was so earnest, his smile so hopeful, what was she to say to him? "I worry for you, Matteo. I can't keep you safe."

He chuckled and watched her face. "And why would you need to be keeping me safe?" He lifted her legs and laid them across his lap. "You are a formidable foe, I give you that, but my dear Scarlet, it is I who has promised to his dying breath to love and cherish and protect you."

She shrugged, grateful to not have to say more. "It is a worry all the same."

Matteo rested his hands on her knees. "I shall do my best to not need rescuing, my lady."

Scarlet eyed him with partially concealed skepticism but noticed their familiar surroundings. "I am sure Henry has taken the longest possible route from the church to our home, but we are now coming down the lane. Come, let me introduce you to your kingdom."

As the carriage rolled to a stop, a footman opened the door and the entire staff, from the upstairs maids to the outside gardeners to the stable hands, lined the entryway to their home. She looked proudly on them all then she turned to Matteo. "Welcome home, my lord."

Matteo helped her exit the carriage. Her hand secure on his arm, they turned to walk up the path lined with their staff. She watched their expressions. Many had been here serving Rupert long before she'd come to the estate. Her shoulders relaxed as great loyalty and kindness reflected in their faces. They straightened as she and Matteo approached and seemed pleased when Matteo addressed them. From the looks of things, the transition to Matteo would be emotionally easy for them all. Rupert had chosen his staff well. And because they were always treated well, they were loyal and excellent in their service.

After an interminable tour of the house and many accolades from Matteo on everything from the dust-free mantle to the meticulous kitchen, they finally arrived at their adjoining chambers. Annabeth, her maid, and Edwards awaited them. Their apparel for the ball would be nothing short of awe-inspiring and would require several hours of work.

Matteo's eyebrows rose. "Grateful we are for your help. Perhaps we might have a moment first?"

As soon as Annabeth removed Scarlet's headdress, they left as discreetly as possible, eyes on the floor, a small crooked smile playing around Annabeth's lips.

When the door closed, the quiet of Scarlet's bedchamber relaxing them, Matteo exhaled. His hand found the knots in Scarlet's neck and began applying a soft pressure until she moaned. He brought her to a chair at her dressing table and continued the kneading at her neck with one hand while the other found each pin in her hair, letting down sections at a time until it cascaded in thick waves down past her shoulder to the middle of her back. He ran his hands through it to its ends. She closed her eyes and tipped her head back as relaxation rolled over her in great waves. His hands began a gentle massage of her head.

With a great sigh, she said, "I would have married you just for this skill." She leaned her head into his hands.

"Your every pleasure is my greatest aim, tonight and every night." He moved his hands to her neck again and lightly ran his fingertips over her skin. Pulling her hair back, his lips found the spot just below her ear.

All too soon, Matteo ended his ministrations, Annabeth and Edwards joined them, and their preparations began.

Scarlet bit her cheek to stop a smile when she heard Matteo say, "What outfit is this? Where are my usual clothes, man?"

Chapter Fifteen

"I THINK YOU LOOK HANDSOME."

"Well, that is something, but coming from a woman in your current attire, I hesitate to lay much weight to your approval." His eyebrow quirked as his gaze searched her from toe to headdress. A chuckle escaped. "What can you mean by dressing us in such a manner?"

His incredulity gave her pause to question. She had pushed the ridiculous to its upper limits, hoping their decoy would further dispel any possible suspicion of her involvement in serious rescue attempts from France. And by involving Matteo, perhaps convince a few suspicious minds of his new allegiance to wealth, pleasure, and fashion. "I have a reputation to uphold, my dear."

"Am I to now share in your love of fashion extremes?" He gestured to the embroidery on his sleeves.

Her finest seamstress had designed a pattern on his jacket. It started up at his neckline and travelled down his front on each side of the buttons. From afar, it looked like a beautiful swirly pattern of bright colors. Jade and orange weaved through rounded, flowing lines of purple. But if one looked closely, the shape of a dragon being hunted by a knight revealed itself. The image of the knight began at his neckline on the back of the jacket and swirled amongst a grove of trees.

"For France, darling. If we appear thus, we set ourselves as the supreme leaders in fashion. And besides the prince himself, everyone will turn to us." All true, naturally, but an equally important great disguise and sleight of hand were at play as well.

"And you feel that men of substance, men I would care to influence, will have any respect for me at all? I am wearing *purple breeches*. Could I not simply wear my usual tan or black?"

Scarlet shook her head. "Matteo, trust me. You look wonderful and will be the envy of the *ton*, and most especially, Prince George. He will turn to you for your brilliant fashion advice, mark my words." When Matteo began to protest, she continued. "And that will carry over into other, more important subjects." She placed a hand on his arm. "I know you do not feel like yourself. But look at it as a costume of sorts. That is the only way I can stomach it." She waved a hand over her own clothing with a flourish.

She'd forgone any side bums and instead built up an immense rump at the back of the dress as she had for the wedding ceremony, but this rump was so large she didn't know how she would ever sit down. The fabric of her dress fell in layered folds down to the ground. Her sleeves draped from her shoulders in ever-wider lace. When it reached her hands, it sat precisely at her wrist on the tops of her hands but fell in great abundance on the underside of her wrists, down to her knees.

Matteo grinned and kissed her hand. "I quite like the dress, actually. This jade color matches my jacket and lightens your eyes. I am a bit mesmerized by them, flashing back at me the way they are. And I am astounded—yes, that is the word—utterly astounded by your hair and adornments."

He couldn't stop himself. She could see he tried, but a laugh escaped before he turned and cleared his throat.

The headdress towered above her head. Annabeth had built it up as high as it would go. Then she'd divided Scarlet's hair into even sections, inserting fabric to help it hold its shape. At the very top, sections of her hair rounded and billowed out into a large bow, standing higher than Matteo. His eyes travelled upward in order to see the very top of it.

"You may laugh. Of course my presentation is ridiculous but not so dreadful when you remember that someone actually imagined it up. I'm quite proud of it; genius, I daresay."

"Too true. Only a genius could think up something of this nature. I will never argue with your great mind. Now, shall we venture below? Greet our guests so that we may all the sooner bid them adieu?"

She stepped closer to him. "Thank you, my husband, for all of this. I too find I am anxious for everyone to leave. But never fear. We have the rest of our lives to linger and love and enjoy each other." She leaned closer to him and whispered, "Would that we could run up these stairs and begin right now." She recognized the returning fire in his gaze. Breathing in slowly, she turned and placed a hand on his arm.

Everyone they'd invited had come. The ballroom, gardens, library, and drawing rooms all overflowed with happy conversation and music. Scarlet enjoyed two dances with her love and then rarely saw him again during the next two hours.

Seeking a moment, even a touch of his hand, she made her way through the house with a hope to encounter him. She moved slowly, stopping by anyone she passed. All gushed over her adornments, wondered if Annabeth could show their own ladies maids how to accomplish such a hairstyle. At length, she determined to give up her search and return to the ballroom, surely the most likely place to reencounter Matteo.

Simon approached her, an urgency in his face he rarely displayed. Her own gaze sharpened, and she felt a familiar speeding of her heart. He tapped his elbow once before commenting on the weather and the lovely wedding and the flowers. He wished to talk to her immediately. Her eyes held a question, but she tittered in a nonsensical way. "Oh, Lord Devereaux, why of course you must see the roses. They have bloomed and smell divine. Pick your favorites for Franny. Was she able to make it this evening?"

She placed her hand on his elbow, and he walked as quickly as their charade would allow.

Simon glanced all around them, pointedly avoiding the small clusters of people also sharing the gardens. "Here we are. Do tell me about how you came to find all these different varieties, my lady."

She led them farther in through an arbor and toward the shed at the back of her garden. Blessedly alone, she opened the door and ushered him inside. "What is it?" Dread filled her. "What news?"

"I received this letter today from our contact at the Bastille. That family we lost, the DuPonts . . ."

Scarlet's heart sank. The wedding preparations and festivities had helped ease her heart about her failure in France. "What about them, Simon?"

"We have the letters of denouncement."

She studied him with interest. They had been trying to discover how to stave off the denouncements, or at least to hear about them as early as possible. It seemed their spies had discovered a treasure of knowledge.

"Prepare yourself, Scarlet."

Simon's eyes held such sadness, her heart pained within her. "Tell me. What could be so awful?"

Instead of speaking, he handed her the letter itself. It read,

The DuPonts denied food to the poor thrice in my eyesight. They refused to share of their great abundance and, at one point, while going at unacceptable speeds in their carriage, barreled down an elderly man in the middle of the road. He was thrown to the side into the mud, breaking several bones, and they, unaware, because they didn't even slow to take a look. The man would have died had he not friends nearby who happened upon him.

Scarlet shook her head. "If the aristocrats of France had only been more giving, perhaps some of this awful terror could have been avoided."

Simon's eyes held an uncharacteristic amount of sympathy, and he gestured with them for her to look again at the letter. "It is signed."

"Oh, yes." She brought the paper up closer to her face. "Matteo Durand." Her throat felt tight. "It cannot be." Her hands trembling, she lowered the paper.

Simon continued to watch her with intensity.

She continued. "Have we checked the handwriting? How could it be him?"

"Of course. I have checked and checked again. He denounced them the week before he arrived here in England. Those I have asked say he has an old childhood grudge against the DuPonts for whipping him. Apparently he was caught taking apples from their tree as a child and beaten soundly for it."

"I do not believe it. He would never."

Simon held out his hands. "I did not want to believe it either—"

"Of course you wanted to believe it. You have not trusted him, ever. Before we even left to rescue him, you accused him."

"That I did, but I have since come to know him, or so I thought."

"You do know him. This can be explained. I am sure of it."

"You are too close to the situation."

"What are you saying? That my instincts can no longer be trusted?"

"I am saying that you should maintain secrecy until we know for sure. I see nothing here that even hints at his innocence. He is responsible for people's deaths, Scarlet. What do we really know about him except that he dances the waltz with perfection and knows how to win over the ladies?"

Her mind flew in all directions. The very strength of the ground beneath her began to give way. "I will prove it to you. He is as innocent as you or I." She turned from Simon.

"Just be careful. All our lives are in your hands. Your own life, even Abelino's. Do not bare yourself to Matteo."

She ran from him, his words filling her mind as she hurried back through the rose garden. Thorns tore at her gown as she rushed by, cutting through narrow, underused walkways. Almost unaware of everything around her, she began to run faster. Where was Matteo? She had to find him, to look into his face. A mound of pink fabric stepped into the middle of the path, blocking Scarlet's escape. She nearly ran it down.

"Upon my word! Lady Cavendish. What is the matter?"

Scarlet stopped, annoyance filling whatever room remained in her heart for emotion. "Lady Pinckney, if you will excuse me. I must find Matteo."

She smiled a coy, secretive smile. "Then you are in luck. For we have just left him this instant, over by the gazebo in front of the pond."

She looked too pleased with herself, but Scarlet had no room to care. She turned from her and walked toward the pavilion. What would she say to Matteo? How could she discover his innocence? She wanted to blurt the whole of it out in front of him, to lay out the accusations against him and hear his response. He would deny it. She would see the truth of it in his face, and then they would figure out how his signature came to be at the bottom of that letter. She turned another corner, following a path of hedges and arbors with vines, when the sound of a voice froze her feet where they stood.

"Thank you, Matteo," Éléonore purred. "And Robespierre sends his thanks for your continued loyalty to France."

Her laugh rang out and grated Scarlet's raw emotion. What did the woman mean, continued loyalty? Dread filled her and weighed her to the earth. Her feet felt too heavy to move.

"I must return to the ballroom."

Matteo's voice sounded pinched, tired. Did he dread returning to her?

Éléonore chuckled. "Does your love know about us? Does she know you seek me in the dead of night?"

Scarlet stepped closer to hear what she most dreaded, and Éléonore's next words tore at her last threads of hope.

"Does she know that I still cause your heart to pound? It pounds now, Matteo. I feel it against my own." Her voice sounded breathless, almost airy with desire.

Scarlet could bear it no longer. She ran down the hedgerows in a straight line back to the house. Entering through a hidden servants' passageway, she made her way as quickly as possible back to her rooms. She must spend a moment gathering her thoughts.

One thing was certain: Simon was absurdly and dreadfully correct. She could not bare herself to Matteo. For now, she would need to continue her charade until it almost consumed her. She must play the fool at home as well as in public. That thought brought such a wave of exhaustion, she reached a hand out against the wall to steady herself until she reached her room and fell onto the nearest stool. Too painful to address, her feelings tightened into the depths of her core; she pushed them deeper. Then she breathed, building the courage to return to her guests. Knowing she would be surrounded by people, she braced herself for the overpowering loneliness.

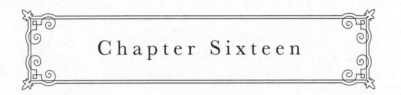

Chapter Sixteen

MATTEO SEARCHED THE HEDGES WHERE they stood and hissed, "Stop it, Éléonore. Someone might hear you. Leave Scarlet out of this."

"I am only having a bit of fun. No one is here to witness." Éléonore ran a hand up his arm. "I must admit I enjoy this side of you. So vulnerable."

Matteo flinched away. "I have nothing more to say to you. I have done my best. Escorted you everywhere you asked—the Pinckneys' dinner party even—listening at every turn. Tell your committee to back away from Potier."

"All in good time. I have another task for you. The French nationals ball. I am certain our illustrious Pimpernel will be in attendance. If you can bring me his name, all will be forgiven, letters destroyed, Potier saved."

"As you wish." Matteo gritted his teeth in frustration. Éléonore had forced an encounter with him on the very day of his wedding, tormenting him for her own pleasure. All he wanted was to end this conversation as quickly as possible and find Scarlet.

He had heard news of several of his old neighbors, thanking him for the warning. But he had not heard from all, and he knew that Potier and his family remained in the gravest danger. *Curse his wretched youth*. He'd lamented his youth more often than ever these past two months.

He sought the balm of Scarlet. She had become his light, his everything, and he needed her in this moment more than ever. His pace quickened as he moved toward the ballroom. Her smile, the touch of her hand, would be sufficient. He could not burden her with his plight tonight, but he would confide in her tomorrow. Perhaps between the two of them and the prince himself, they might discover a solution, or at least a way to get word to the Pimpernel.

A flash of yellow captured his attention, and Suzanne de Molier stepped forward from the hedges on his right.

He startled. "Lady de Molier."

"You traitor!" She swung at him with her palm, missing his cheek by a hair as he dodged away.

"What is the matter with you?" Matteo took two steps back, eyeing her.

"The DuPonts."

Matteo stared at her in confusion. "What about them?"

"All dead because of you. Don't play stupid with me. You may have fooled the others, but I know your true character. I saw the denouncement myself."

Matteo's hands went cold. "What are you talking about? Have the DuPonts—?"

"As you well know, met with their fate at *La Guillotine* three weeks past, at your own hand. Denounced them, you did. And what for? Because of a childhood beating?" She stood before him, breathing hard, looking as if she would give anything to swing at him again. "I loathe you."

Matteo staggered back two more steps. Éléonore had done it. She had gone ahead and used his name. He choked out his question, "And the children?"

"All of them. Including their young grandchild." Suzanne watched his face. "Could you really not know?"

His words, his *evidence*, had killed an entire family. Matteo shook his head; staggering, he lost his balance and fell into a hedge. The heavy branches caught his fall, scratching his face and poking into the backstitching of his new jacket. In a daze, he righted himself, pulling off sticks and leaves, tearing the fabric in the process and loosening the threads. Turning, he began walking toward the house. "I must find Scarlet." He stumbled twice but managed to stay upright.

A servant stopped him at the door. "My lord, you look unwell. Might I pour you a bit of brandy?"

He did not remember answering, but he followed the servant to a pantry near the kitchen and drank whatever the man gave him. He leaned his back against the wall and closed his eyes. How would he ever leave this new inferno? When would he finally escape Éléonore's claws? She did whatever she chose whether he obeyed her wishes or not. But if he didn't, Potier was sure to be next in line.

If not for Scarlet, he would leave England immediately, head to France, and rescue Potier himself. He could sneak into the homes of all those who had not returned his correspondence and warn them all. He should go, Scarlet or no. What choice did he have? Waiting in England, dressed like a fop, dancing attendance on the prince had not saved the DuPont family. He might be doing some bit of good here, yes, but urgent needs awaited him across the Channel. Needs that were so immediate, they could not wait for the pleasure of the English court or the attention of the Pimpernel, were he ever to respond to Matteo's pleas to show himself.

Scarlet. Thoughts of her filled his soul like the cool breeze of a summer day. A bit of relief loosened the tightness in his chest, and he desired to hold her as he never had before. Hers was the comfort he sought and desperately needed. His feet found their strength, and he began again to make his way to the ballroom.

The sight upon entering jarred him. He wasn't sure what specifically about it startled him. Scarlet swirled through the room in the arms of the prince. They laughed and bantered in a ridiculous manner as they always had. The prince held her closely as he always did, and he looked to her with a deference and respect that Matteo appreciated. But Scarlet appeared different, her eyes more vulnerable, her expression needy. He had not seen that raw need in her face, not since the night she'd returned to him from her aunt's, sobbing in his arms. What had placed such a look on her face, and why had she turned to the prince for comfort?

Matteo waited until the music ended and then approached them from behind. The prince saw him first and whispered something to her that made her body stiffen. *Odd.* Reaching them, he placed a hand at the small of her back, above the huge rump. He bowed to the prince. "Your Highness."

He could hardly contain his urgency to pull his wife into his arms. "Scarlet. Might I have a moment?" She paused and then turned to him with a blank look of confusion. "Is it our dance already? Oh no. We danced our two at the beginning. Surely you remember . . ."

He played along. "Yes, my dear, we did. I was hoping we might drink a lemonade and have a bit of walk through the gardens as well? Might we?" He held out his arm, gesturing that they could walk in the direction of the food and then out onto the adjoining terrace. He tried to show with his eyes how much his request meant to him.

She searched his face, but her eyes never lost their vacant stare. With a sigh, she said, "If we must, Matteo. But let us be quick about it. If we are out on the terrace, no one can see our costumes or the lovely manner in which we complement each other. I did not have our seamstress spend such a large amount of time on your stitches for nothing, you know."

A tendril of doubt began to grow in the back of Matteo's mind. Could she really care so much about the clothes they wore? He shook that thought away and led her out. In an undertone, he murmured, "I need you, Scarlet. I cannot wait to hold you. Yours is the only balm that will help me now."

She laughed overly loud. "Oh, Matteo. Our wedding night will be here soon enough. Surely you can be patient for a few more hours with our guests."

The ladies nearest them gasped in shock, putting hands to their mouths. An older matron ushered her daughter away. A few men smirked at Matteo, some smiling in sympathy.

Matteo burned with mortification. "Scarlet, that is not what I meant at all."

"Oh, of course not, my dear. Come now, I find I am a bit parched. Let us get our lemonade and be quick about this moment on the terrace, shall we?"

Matteo stopped, turning her to face him. "Are you well?"

She looked away for a moment and then found his eyes, her own flashing. "I am well." Then she swallowed, and a bit of hurt passed through her eyes. "Quite well. It is all for France, you know." For a second, he saw a look of regret cross her face, and then she closed off completely.

Stunned, Matteo moved forward mechanically, handing her a lemonade and then escorting her outside. The night air felt cool on his face, and he turned his head to feel it.

"You've scratched your jacket."

Remembering his fall into the hedge, he said, "Yes. I had a bit of a mishap outside. It can be mended, surely."

"How did you come to be rolling about in the hedges?"

He turned to her. Before she could school her features, he saw suspicion and even jealousy on her face.

He reached for her, pulling her into his embrace. "Scarlet, I have had terrible news. I stumbled outside upon the hearing of it. I long to tell you."

She stiffened in his arms and stepped back. "News? Oh, dear. I had hoped to keep it from you."

Had she heard about the DuPonts already? Could she know of his involvement? Deep shame filled him with an irrational desire to hide. His own stupidity, pride, self-righteous blame, had brought an entire family to their deaths.

"Perhaps someone mentioned that purple is not the color of the Season after all. Instead of being the first to wear the color, you are on the cusp of being the last. I miscalculated, darling, and I'm sorry. We will do better next time."

What game was she playing? He looked around. No one could possibly overhear. "We are alone—"

"Too true. Let us return to the ballroom. We have been out of eyesight long enough. Shall we dance a third time? Shock everyone just a little bit? They will expect it of us, so much in love as we appear to be."

"Appear . . . ?"

Lady Pinckney arrived at their side. "Oh, Lady Durand, Comtesse. I'm so happy I found you. Have you heard? Oh, I'm sure you haven't. It is fresh from France. I heard only this very moment, but the DuPont family—all of them, even the grandchild—have been executed. Oh, that awful France. When will it stop?"

Pain filled Matteo's head, and lights flashed in front of his eyes.

Scarlet's body went still, her face a stone. She turned to him with unyielding eyes of steel.

Emotion so great it paralyzed him rose up inside. He had to finish the evening, be generous to his guests, but he didn't know how. "Excuse me." He bowed curtly to them both and entered through a side door, seeking the men and the cards and the brandy.

"Tsk tsk, Matteo. Trouble with your new love?" Éléonore slinked in front of him.

He grabbed her wrists before she could touch any part of him. "Leave my home. Now."

"No need to get angry, *mon ami*."

"We had an agreement, and the DuPonts are already dead. Get out, and never return."

Her eyes narrowed into slits and she hissed while speaking. "You don't want that, darling. Because others would suffer. This is what I do. You must know. I am cleansing France, and I will continue to do so with your name unless you do exactly as I say whenever I say it." She changed her tone to a more placating one. "Potier walks every morning down the lane and across the field to a pond to fish, just like he did when we were little. Such a dear man, really."

"Get out, Éléonore. You have done enough evil for one night."

"As you wish." She nodded her head. "But I will be in touch."

Matteo didn't know how he made it through the rest of the evening. He couldn't remember what he said to the prince over cards. He didn't even know if he heard the conversations going on around him. But the night did pass, and finally the guests departed. Scarlet stood in silence next to him at their front door as they bid goodnight to the last of them. Her hand rested on his arm, but he felt no warmth from her. When the door closed and they had thanked Buckley, she turned without a word and headed up the stairs.

"Scarlet, wait."

She faced him. "Matteo, the guests are gone. There is no more need to pretend. Let us only sleep." Her eyes showed a touch of compassion in an otherwise vacant expression. "Are you not tired? Surely you long for your bed."

Numb, becoming hopeless, he was too tired to convince her that forever, his idea of bed would always include her. Too tired to reach for her when all he needed was to feel her embrace. Too tired to even speak when all he wanted was to pour out his troubles in a heap at her feet. Instead, he watched her go, and the despair in his mind robbed him of any further energy. She turned at the top of the stairs and entered her room. The door shut with a final snap behind her.

Had she locked the door between them? He didn't dare try it, because he couldn't bear to know. Instead, he endured Edwards and his preparations for Matteo's wedding night. Finally, when the man left him, Matteo crawled into his bed and sank beneath the sheets alone. Tomorrow. Tomorrow would be better. Scarlet must feel tired, overwhelmed. Things would be better tomorrow.

He tried to block out the faces from his childhood, the DuPont family visiting in his uncle's home. The young girl riding around on his back as he pretended to be a new pony. The father shaking his hand as he went off to school, acting as his father would have. Even that ridiculous and much-needed beating when his youth had led to recklessness. Tears flowed, and his body shuddered with the sobs he had repressed all evening.

***

Hours later, Scarlet crept into his room and watched him while he slept. His body convulsed now and then with the sobs of a young child during sleep. Tears welled in her eyes. Had she caused this pain? Could she not crawl into bed beside him and wrap her arms around his quivering frame? Oh, how she loved this man still. Even knowing he had betrayed her, even knowing he had sent an innocent family to their deaths over a childhood grudge, she loved him. And blast that wretched love. She would be miserable all her days because of it. With a soft sigh of despair, she turned from the room, climbed into her own bed, and curled into a ball knowing she had to endure only another hour of her sleepless night before the sun would once again appear, and she would be on her ship to Calais.

Chapter Seventeen

Paris, France

THE EFFORT TO BLOCK ALL thought of Matteo from her mind exhausted her far less as soon as she donned her new costume and began life as Renée Moreau the Seamstress.

Claire Lacombe, noted founder of the Society of Revolutionary Republican Women, fingered Scarlet's fine lace. "Amazing. So intricate. A name is written right there, clear as day, but you can't see the pattern unless you know exactly what to look for." She reached her hand out to grasp Scarlet's in her own. "Come to our meeting this afternoon. Pauline Léon needs to meet you and see your talents."

An odd sort of gratitude reminded her of her mother's patience in insisting Scarlet become proficient at needlepoint and tatting lace. The irony of its current use almost brought a smile to her face. "I do hope it will help. I thought of the idea watching those knitting women by the guillotine." She created a look of shy humility. "Thank you, Mademoiselle Lacombe. To think I will be assisting you, a famous actress, in this great Revolution." She squeezed Claire's hand in her own.

"Please, call me Claire. We are to be sisters in arms, after all." Claire held tight to her hand in return. "You've come at the perfect time. We are running out of ways to communicate our denouncements. The infernal Pimpernel seems to get wind of half of them." Claire shook her head in disgust. "We must prove to Robespierre that women have a place in the new society. We are a force that cannot be denied. The more we denounce, the more we prove to him our loyalty." A feverish excitement flashed through her eyes, and her skin flushed.

Scarlet inwardly cringed in disgust. Was everyone in France in a crazed, bloodthirsty frenzy? She swallowed a hint of apprehension that tried to build a lump in her throat. "Where shall I meet you?"

***

Smell. The first sense to completely overload as she stepped into the square. Rotten female sweat and filthy body neglect overpowered the small breeze that tried to clean the air. Knotted hair and torn clothing found every available stone as they all sat facing a platform at the head of the contained space.

Claire grabbed hands of jeering women as she passed, gesturing in greeting to the crowd who welcomed her. Scarlet's face showed wonder as she waved shyly to a few women. Inside, she wanted to vomit in disgust. *These* were the women running this society? Most sat indecently, skirts falling up above their knees. They called to one another and picked at their stained teeth. More than one bit blackened fingernails while cackling some story to the woman at her side.

Scarlet pulled at her blonde braids. The wig was all but glued to her head, and she felt confident it would stay. Several dirt-smudged faces eyed her with disdain. If she had come alone, she was certain these women would not have borne her presence for long. Her costume was neat and comely, her stitches were precise, and her steps were careful. She was the Seamstress.

Of all the factions warring to rule France, Claire Lacombe, Pauline Léon, and the Society of Revolutionary Republican Women placed their hopes and allegiance with the Jacobins: those aligned with Robespierre and Saint-Just on the Committee of Public Safety. However, most shop owners remained unsympathetic to the Jacobin Republic. And they did not agree with these women's goals or aims. Scarlet supposed their very presentation disgusted the more well-to-do shop owners, and Claire's women resented their snobbery. A strong antagonism had developed between the groups.

The new identity as Seamstress helped Scarlet communicate with both, because she could mingle with the merchants as a merchant herself and also trail after Claire, and no one would question or suspect that she belonged with neither group.

They didn't know it yet, but the shop owners' lives were at risk. The tide of goodwill would shift, and they would be denounced. One of her more important rescues, everything needed to play out just right. Scarlet could allow herself no missteps.

Eyes alight with expectation and just a bit of hero-worship, she picked up her pace as they neared the front of the platform where she assumed they would meet Pauline Léon, the cofounder of their group.

Scarlet almost stopped walking when a woman on the stand turned to face them. Where Claire was light, she was dark. Where Claire gave off energy, she sucked it in. Her eyes looked like holes, pits into an abyss that held her soul. Scarlet stopped a shiver and pretended to be unaffected.

Claire seemed not to notice Pauline's lack of enthusiasm. She approached her, indicating Scarlet. "And here she is. Just wait until I show you her work, Pauline." Claire pulled Scarlet closer to her side. "This is my new friend, Renée, come to us from Marguerite. They call her the Seamstress."

Scarlet stepped forward, unsure how to greet this woman. Surely not a curtsy. Pauline nodded to her and sniffed. "Let's see this tatting."

Claire said in a hushed voice, "Not here. No one must suspect."

The two shared a look, some kind of inner struggle sparking between them, and Scarlet let her eyes wander up near the rooftops. She sharpened her gaze as she noticed movement up there and followed a crouched figure who ducked behind the chimney. She hid a smile. *Abelino.*

Pauline's voice made her jump. She shouted out over the assembled group, "Please welcome our newest member, Renée."

Smiling shyly, Scarlet turned to face the women as they slapped their thighs.

"Now let us begin," Pauline continued.

Claire motioned for Scarlet to follow her, and they moved away from the platform and over to the right where they crouched down on their own bit of stone. Claire's face filled with rapture, eyes shining, watching Pauline's every expression. "She is magnificent."

Scarlet tried to echo some sort of similar sentiment but could not. She giggled instead and said, "She scares me a little bit."

Claire's hoarse laugh made Scarlet jump. "She has that effect on everyone. Don't let it bother you too much."

"We must have a constitution." Pauline began talking in more urgent tones.

The crowd cheered.

Did they know what a constitution was? She chided herself that she had underestimated them.

Pauline emphasized each word. "And that constitution must include the rights of women. We will not be forgotten, waylaid, or ignored. We are the rebellion!" She threw her hands into the air. "Where would Robespierre be without us?"

The ladies slapped their thighs in mad agreement. Scarlet wished for a handkerchief to block out the worst of the smell that had intensified with all of their movement.

One of the women called out, "The bakers are hoarding food! Soon, there won't be enough for us all."

A toothless woman to their left shouted, "And the price is higher today than yesterday. It's going to cost more than my rent just to buy a loaf of bread, make no mistake."

Pauline raised both her hands, and the crowd quieted. "We have written some requests for the merchants among us. Tomorrow we will post them in all the stores." She pulled out a paper, unfolded it, and began reading. "Number one, a pound of bread can cost no more than sixteen *sous*." The crowd stood in shouting support. "Number two, the constitution must be written and our rights as women protected." More shouts and dancing amongst themselves expressed their great delight. Pauline's voice rose to be heard. "Number three, no one will hoard or otherwise store food. All will be purchased and the excess shared by all." She held her hands up to forestall further crowd response. "And this, my sisters in arms, this I saved for last. Robespierre has heard us. He has listened to our arguments, and a law was made demanding that every citizen must wear the tricolor cockade." The women jumped in their places, gesturing wildly about.

Claire leaned closer to Scarlet. "A good victory, that."

Scarlet nodded. "I can tell. It's all so exciting! I must sew a cockade into my clothing at once."

The soldiers wore an armband with the red, white, and blue cockade, and she remembered her own men fooling LaFevre only weeks ago.

Then all at once, the crowd stood and the women pushed themselves forward toward the alley leading back to the main street where most of the shops were located. "Tell them now, Pauline! Let them put on their cockades while we watch."

Scarlet and Claire jumped to their feet. Pauline hurried past them, shouting, "To the baker first. Our food will not be polluted with filthy traitors."

"Prove your loyalty! Show it on your arm," a woman screeched near Scarlet's ear.

Pushed along with the frenzied crowd, packed in amongst arms and ratty hair and filthy bodies as they entered the alleyway, Scarlet schooled her features and even shouted out with the rest of them, "Prove your loyalty."

Claire turned to her and winked, people jostling by them. "Isn't it wonderful?"

As they approached the shops, a group of owners, already gathered, pressed closer together. As loud as the Republic of Women were, Scarlet guessed that all the nearby streets had become aware that something was afoot. The merchants' faces, unwelcoming, held up hands, asking the crowd to stop. The man in front said, "There is nothing for you here. Go back to your homes."

The women laughed, and one called out to him, "Not until you prove your loyalty."

Another shouted, "Give him an armband, Pauline."

She stepped forward through her women and came to a stop directly in front of the man. They faced each other, about two feet apart. Then she pulled out her paper once again and read out, in a strong, clear voice all their new demands and the cockade law. The longer she read, the more disgruntled noises Scarlet heard from the people gathered behind this man. She assumed them all to be shopkeepers, workers, and owners.

When Pauline read the last bit about how every citizen must now wear an armband, the merchants were visibly upset, and one woman shouted, "I will not wear such a thing, lest I be branded a prostitute, in cohorts with the likes of you."

A hiss followed her remark, and several of the women near Scarlet clenched their fists.

Another merchant called, "No one wears those but the Jacobins."

Shaking a fist in the air, another man, a blacksmith, said, "Go home! Make your own bread then. Wear your own bands."

The tone of the interaction darkened, shopkeepers demanding that Claire and Pauline lead the women away.

One merchant woman stepped around the baker in front of them and walked right up to Claire. She placed a finger on her chest and pressed into her, hoping, no doubt, to push her backward, but Claire was much stronger than she looked. The merchant leaned into Claire's face and sneered. "*Filthy.*"

Scarlet raised a hand up to her opened mouth.

The women around Claire hissed and growled in a low guttural noise. Claire grabbed the merchant woman's hair at the back of her head and yanked it to the side. Others grabbed her arms. Pauline's women all circled Claire as she forced her captive to the ground, jerking her head around by the hair. Claire called out to her group, "Are we dirty women?"

They shouted, "No!"

Claire called out to the shopkeepers, "We are no dirtier than you are. You merchants, with your inflated prices and fancy clothing, have made us who we are. If we don't have new dresses or fancy bath oil, it is because our last *sous* go to buying bread to feed our families." She leaned forward and hissed into the woman's face. "How dare you keep food from our families!" Claire bent the lady's head back so that her neck was exposed. "A lovely neck, no?"

"Guillotine! Send her to *La Guillotine*!" Pauline's crowd was held back from tearing into her only by their curiosity.

Scarlet looked away from the captive woman, who trembled and cried out whenever Claire pulled on her hair. Pauline tied a cockade armband around the woman's face as a gag.

Then Claire used the fistful of the poor woman's hair to yank her to her feet again. She forced her to walk forward through the revolutionaries. The merchants stepped closer, their faces menacing but also fearful. Claire let go of the woman and shoved her back toward the first man. "I'd better see red, white, and blue on you tomorrow."

Ripping the gag from her mouth, the woman snarled, "Never," looking much braver now that she was once again surrounded by her friends. "I'll never join with the likes of you."

More people poured out of the shops around them, wearing angry expressions, shouting. One sneered, "You'll starve before we let you control our prices."

"We'll feed our bread to the pigs!"

The Republican Women of the Revolution pushed past Scarlet, rushing toward the merchants. As if a great switch snapped in two, they controlled themselves no longer. Nails were out and teeth bared, as they cut at, yanked, or pulled anyone close to them. Pauline ran nails down a woman's arm, gleefully celebrating the blood that dripped. The merchants responded. In no way running from the violence, they reveled in the opportunity to inflict pain on their gruesome contenders.

Scarlet crept backward until she felt a wall behind her. She must leave the square as quickly as possible without anyone the wiser. She shook her head in disgust. The street had become a mass of human limbs grappling at each other, pulling at hair, kicking, flailing, biting to get at an opponent. Whistles sounded down the opposite alleyway. Could there still be an active police force here? Soldiers? She used the accompanying confusion to hide her escape.

As she ran down an alley, the tinkling sounds of glass breaking followed her. She wondered anew, as she did every time she entered France, how the situation could get any worse.

Chapter Eighteen

SCARLET IMMERSED MORE COMPLETELY INTO her new role as Renée. She finished tatting two more lace borders for gowns, both with fictional denouncements. The guards would never find these families, because they did not exist. The real families, whose names she had been given only days before, were safely on their way to England. If anyone investigated, they would discover that a break in the guards' secrecy had occurred after the Seamstress delivered her stitches. Simon helped Renée cover her tracks.

Claire's lovely blonde locks bounced in the Seamstress's shop window. She bubbled more energy than usual, and Scarlet felt a bit of dread, bracing herself for whatever news would leave the woman's lips.

"You are the most blessed of all revolutionaries, my dear! And blessed I am to be the one to bring you to light."

Renée giggled. "Oh, Claire. You always have some grand thing to say. I am but a seamstress." She gestured around her quiet room, piles of fabric and thread filling the corners.

"Ah, but your humility is part of your charm. You are a gift. And none other than Robespierre himself has become aware of you."

Scarlet's heart sank. "Oh, dear, oh no. What if I fail?" She did not have to disguise her emotion, though she gave it a different cause.

Claire placed a hand on her arm. "You will not fail. But he does want to meet you. He has a particular question and wonders if your skill will come to use for the Revolution."

When Renée did not respond, Claire said, "Did you hear? You, Renée the Seamstress, will go down in history as an aid to the Revolution. And a woman at that. Your success is our success."

Scarlet straightened her shoulders and brightened her eyes. "You are right. I will hide my insecurity. This is our moment to rise." She smiled the best she could.

"That's better, and more's the luck, because I'm the one who gets to go with you. Me, meeting Robespierre."

Greater dread filled Scarlet. "Will we meet Éléonore Duplay, do you think? She's such an inspiration."

Claire shook her head in disappointment. "I wondered that very thing. But no, she is still in England, so not this time."

Scarlet's relief was difficult to hide. "Wonderful. I mean, I *am* disappointed to miss Mademoiselle Duplay, of course, but to see Robespierre himself."

Claire wrapped her arms around Scarlet. "Now you are catching on. This is much bigger than you or I." She stepped back proudly and said, "Go wash your face. His carriage will be here any moment."

"What? He is coming now? I have so much work to finish."

"Don't worry about that at all. Everyone will understand. Oh! And you are to bring some of it, to show him what you can do."

Scarlet controlled the shaking of her hands. Had she ever met Robespierre? No. But what if LaFevre was in attendance? "I'm sure they have thought of this, but how do we ensure my methods aren't seen by some of his advisors? It won't help at all if people start to become aware of our secrets."

Claire eyed her and nodded. "Right you are. I will mention it when we arrive. The more secrecy about this whole visit, the better. In fact, I would feel more comfortable if others were not aware of your identity at all."

Scarlet nodded. "Just so. I am pleased that so many call me the Seamstress." She grabbed some of her better examples and placed them in a satchel. Then, following Claire out the door and locking it behind them, she exited just as the sounds of carriage wheels echoed down their street. Heart pounding, she reached for Claire's hand and tried to bring happiness to her face to hide her fear.

She let out a great breath and relaxed her shoulders when the carriage door opened to an empty bench inside.

As they moved through Paris, Claire's energy turned to an absolute giddy fever the closer they came to the Bastille.

"Why are we going to the prison?" Scarlet clutched her satchel closer to her body. She wished she had maintained a closer form of contact with her league. They knew her general whereabouts, but her next check-in time was still days away.

"He keeps his offices at the Bastille now. He says it inspires his mind to greatness."

Scarlet nodded and reached inside to find her spectacles. Placing them on her face, she nearly went blind with their strength. She knew her eyes appeared large and distorted under the lenses.

"Oh, *ma Renée*. I did not know you needed those."

Scarlet blushed. "I do. But I don't usually wear them. Not very flattering. I just don't want to miss anything."

"Such a dear one, you. And so dedicated." She squeezed Scarlet's hand in sympathy.

Scarlet nodded and returned the pressure on Claire's hand. She calmed her breathing and tried to act as though she were meeting a long-admired hero. The loathing she felt for him and all he did to France hid itself behind countless other thoughts Scarlet shoved in that direction. She pulled her bonnet closer over her face, and her eyes found the floor. Blonde braids draped over her shoulders. Hopefully very little of Scarlet Cavendish remained recognizable to a casual viewer.

They pulled up to the towering stone walls, and guards waved them past. Arriving in the committee's carriage offered at least a free pass *into* the prison. Guards opened their carriage door and escorted them, Claire bouncing with glee, across a stone courtyard and through a door at the opposite end. They travelled through a maze of passages and poorly lit hallways. Scarlet kept meticulous track in her mind. At length, they arrived at a closed door with three guards standing outside. Four raps were answered by a muffled voice inside. And then, despite all her dread, Scarlet stood before the vilest man of the century. Her eyes could not leave his face.

He seemed calm, almost reasonable. "Come here, my dear. I long to meet the mastermind of so ingenious an idea." He held out his hand to her.

She willed her feet to move and placed her hand in his, grateful for the gloves. She won victories over herself when she did not jerk away at his kiss, and she forced a curtsy in return to his bow.

"Did you enjoy the carriage? I don't use them myself—such a spectacle of excess—but I see them as a useful method to transport people here." He gestured for them all to be seated. "Please, show me this work of yours. I am fascinated with your abilities." He smiled with encouragement and patted the seat beside himself.

She opened her satchel, but before she could speak, Claire began. "All in the tatting. You must first see the lace."

Scarlet cleared her throat. "Yes, we are able to tat names in the lace, in symbols, code. And therefore send any message or denouncement without anyone else becoming the wiser. We can add it to our gowns at the hem, our sleeves, or our . . . neckline." She cleared her throat and blushed.

Robespierre took the lace from her hands and studied it. "I cannot even find the message, and I am looking for it. Where is it? Will you show me?"

He searched Scarlet's eyes, and she blinked. Did she see actual kindness in his own?

She looked away and stammered, "Well, it is right here, you see." She pointed out the letters and shapes in white hidden in an elaborate pattern in the lace.

He brought the lace up close to his face and studied it, following where her finger pointed. "Ah, yes! I see it! Ingenious." He turned to her again. "You have a gift. This will save us, save the Revolution."

"The ladies at the guillotine gave me the idea, with their knitting." Scarlet looked down again at her lap.

Robespierre lifted her chin with his finger. "You seem a virtuous sort of person."

She looked away again and shrugged.

"You understand what we aim to do here. Virtue is exactly what we are after. This terror . . . will *bring* virtue. It is the only way. If we do not enforce our laws with violence, all the *sansculottes* will. You saw what they did at the Bastille. Violence without law must be stopped. We bring terror as a means for peace." He seemed so earnest, searching for her approval.

In her silence, she realized he waited for an actual response from her. What could she say to that? Even in her charade, she could not manage an agreement.

Claire jumped in. "Oh, monsieur. Citizen Robespierre. You are the savior of us all, the one who will bring about our liberation. As women, we long for the day when we too will receive equal justice."

He nodded politely and then returned his focus to Scarlet. "Renée, is it?"

She brought her eyes back up to his face and nodded, thankful that the thick lenses distorted her view.

"What do you think?"

She swallowed. "I long for the day when France can be free. I long for justice, for peace. For a great love to exist amongst its people. That is the virtue I am seeking for in France."

Robespierre searched her face in silence for a moment more. "You have spoken the inner feelings of my heart. Do you trust that I long for these same things?"

Scarlet started to nod her head but was saved from the most difficult lie of her life when a great pounding shook the door.

"Enter." Robespierre stood immediately and went to the door of his small office.

Scarlet took in the rest of the room. They sat in a humble space with a small desk and five rough-looking wood chairs. To their right, a door to another room remained closed. She wondered if Robespierre actually slept here as well. Who would want to sleep at the prison? She shuddered.

Claire leaned toward her, motioning with her head to the door. "What's that all about, I wonder?"

A man spoke in low tones to Robespierre, who stiffened and gestured decisively with his hands. Then he turned and said, "Well, we have one of its founders right here. Perhaps she can shed some light on the matter." His hand pointed right at Claire.

Claire stood and came toward them. "How can I be of assistance? You have but to ask." She blinked her lashes and widened her eyes hopefully.

Robespierre indicated that the man should enter the room. Scarlet shrunk farther into her seat and pulled the bonnet lower over her face, making sure her glasses were pressed up to her eyes. LaFevre took the seat Robespierre indicated.

"Please tell our good guests what you just told me." A coldness replaced the earlier supportive tone, and Scarlet began to worry for Claire's safety.

LaFevre began. "The merchant shops along Rue de Rivoli have all been destroyed, their supplies raided, their windows broken, their wares pilfered." He turned his eyes to Claire in question.

She stood taller. "We went to the shop owners. We demanded that they follow the law. They were not wearing the colors. They refused to regulate the price of bread. They hate Jacobins. Denounced us for being poor. When they flat-out refused our demands that they follow the law, fighting broke out. It was us as much as them clawing at each other, but you will be happy to hear that we beat them, humbled their arrogance, and brought them to the dust." She nodded with a smile.

"And their shops?" Robespierre asked.

Claire shrugged. "I had nothing to do with that. After our skirmish and the merchants had called for a truce and backed away, Pauline and I returned to our homes. Renée as well. But the ladies out in the street, they were angry and riled up. They feel they have a right to that bread, the same as everyone else. But with it priced so high, they can't eat it. So I wouldn't be surprised if their hunger pushed them to do things a person normally wouldn't."

Robespierre nodded. "You say they denounced the Jacobins."

Claire nodded. "They did—accused us of being prostitutes and Jacobins as if one were akin to the other."

Robespierre and LaFevre shared a look, and then they stood.

Claire continued. "Our group is anxious for the constitution. We hope women's rights are remembered in the new government. That you acknowledge our great service to the Revolution when it's time."

Robespierre reached for her hand. "We reward loyalty where it is due. And we are grateful for your assistance in finding those who would breed unrest amongst us. We see it is not just the aristos whose political leanings must be purged."

Claire beamed with joy. She clasped her hands together in front of her with supreme happiness. And then she took her seat.

"But we have been interrupted. LaFevre, if you could leave us now, we must finish our business here."

The man glanced curiously at Scarlet, but when no one offered explanation or introduction, he turned and left the room.

"So now, my dear. I hear your talents are not limited to just these supremely hidden stitches."

Scarlet shook her head. She wanted this to be over as quickly as possible. "I have also devised a clever way to conceal a weapon, a knife for example, within the sleeve of one's jacket or within the folds of a skirt."

Robespierre's eyes sharpened. "Who else knows of this talent?"

Claire leaned closer to him. "No one. We have been careful that only the two of us, and now you, are made aware."

"Good. Tell no one else. This skill, though genius, could be harmful as well as helpful."

Scarlet nodded.

"Might I ask, could I be the first to receive of your gift? Would you create such a clever little pocket in my own jacket before anyone else's?"

Scarlet cleared her throat. "Of course. If you would have your jacket delivered to my room, I will make it my first priority."

"Oh, no need for the wait. Please, take this one." He removed his coat and held it out for her to take.

She reached for it and felt his loathsome body heat on it, imagining his body odor still identifying it. She folded it carefully, away from her body, and then draped it over one arm. "Very well. I will have it ready tomorrow."

"So soon?"

"Yes, I plan to start work on it this very night so it is ready."

Robespierre reached for her hand and held it in his own two. "You take such care. It is a rare and valuable quality. I thank you."

Scarlet nodded, her throat making a weak attempt to swallow. She needed to leave this man's presence. Her ability to maintain character was currently tested to its fullest.

Thankfully, he released her hand and turned to Claire. "We must plan, you and I. The shop owners who abhor us must be identified and denounced. We cannot have so strong an aversion to our party. France's security relies upon it."

She sat higher in her chair and began panting in anticipation. "Yes, of course. We can take care of that."

He nodded. "Lure them in. Gather them together in one place, a public location. Their very attendance should seem traitorous. And then we will take care of the rest. They must be a public example. In one week's time, I will send my soldiers, but I will wait for news from you of the hour and location." His eyes had gone cold, all kindness departed.

Scarlet longed for her shawl, but her mind had begun to spin, and as quickly as Robespierre planned, she counterplotted. Now, her most important rescue must be scheduled in days instead of weeks.

Chapter Nineteen

Too EARLY TO BOTHER EDWARDS, Matteo donned breeches and a coat. A good long ride would do much to clear his mind before Scarlet awoke.

He allowed thoughts of his disastrous wedding night to plague him slowly, an easy trickle instead of the deadening crash that threatened to flow. His wedding day felt as terrible to think upon as it was wonderful. Not ready to face the DuPonts' deaths again, he went over all his interactions with Scarlet, the strength of his mount beneath him a comfort.

Making his way to a wide-open field, he urged his stallion into a hard run, giving the eager animal full rein. Most of his conversations with her had been delightfully full of joy. She seemed excited and looking forward to their long life together. Only at the end, when he himself felt as devastated as he had ever been, had she changed so drastically.

Was his impression of her a mirror of his own sordid feelings, his disgust with himself, his horror at the evil in Éléonore? Could he have imagined or made her reactions seem worse than they actually were? These new thoughts gave him a place to start and the beginnings of hope.

Foaming about the bit, the horse had worked up a good lather, and Matteo gradually slowed him down to a walk. They followed the edge of a stream, Matteo hardly noticing his surroundings as his mind spun.

Suspicions crept in, thoughts of how little he knew Scarlet. She played so many parts, acted differently depending on who they were standing near. How could he be sure which part she was playing when? And where, in all these layers, did the real Scarlet hide? Why did she hide? Perhaps the books or the servants or some family history would help him better understand the woman he married just twenty-four hours ago.

His thoughts flowed naturally to the DuPonts. If they had died three weeks ago, then Éléonore had already denounced them before she had even arrived in England. Perhaps their deaths were her first angry reaction to his escape from

France. He clenched one fist. Would he never be free of that woman and her claws?

He reached the stables and left the reins with a waiting stable hand.

Again, a battle began inside him. He should be in France. He must personally ensure that any and all of his acquaintances escaped. And his first priority would be Potier. But how could he leave Scarlet? Particularly now, when misunderstandings threatened, he felt a duty to heal the problems and to build a happy relationship with his new wife. But surely that could all wait. People's lives were in danger. As soon as he could be sure no one else would die because of him, he would spend the rest of his days winning back Scarlet's heart—if he had indeed lost it, which he hoped he had not.

Stepping back into his bedchamber, he nearly ran into Edwards, who had entered at that moment from the dressing area.

"How may I be of assistance, my lord?"

"Edwards. Impeccable timing. I need to be up and dressed and about my day. Could you inform me also where I might find Lady Cav—Durand?" On any other day, he would have stopped for a moment to relish that name on his lips.

Edwards paused just long enough for Matteo to glance up at him. "She left you a note, Your Highness."

"Please, Edwards. No need to address me as Your Highness."

"She expressly required it of me but not at every encounter. It seems I am to surprise you with its use."

Matteo grinned. Perhaps her sense of humor had returned. He held his hand out, taking the note Edwards offered.

A sense of foreboding began in his chest. She had sealed it and everything. He had never understood her seal, a small flower. Knowing how much she adored the floral parts of her grounds, he had only assumed it to be a flower of some historical or familial meaning. Breaking it, he opened the page.

Edwards turned from him and reentered the dressing room.

Dear Mattteo,

You will likely not be surprised that I have chosen this morning to go on some visits that are long overdue. It might be well if we have a week or two to grow accustomed to our new relationship. You can familiarize yourself with the running of the estate. And I can pay attention to my much-neglected aunt and other friends who have been awaiting my arrival these many months. I hope you are well. Do not overly distress yourself. Until next we meet,

Scarlet

He crumpled the note in his fist. What could she mean by this? The niggling worry he had felt since awakening began to deepen into a much greater anxiety. She would run to avoid him, escape to her aunt. How could she think he would not be surprised? It was the day after their wedding. The day after they should have consummated their relationship. The day they should still be abed, commanding servants to leave them be. "Edwards!"

"Yes, Your Highness."

"Edwards, if you call me that again, you will be immediately dismissed from my service."

"Yes, my lord."

"Thank you. I must be dressed. I will visit his true Highness, Prince George, this morning."

"Is he expecting you?"

"Well, no, not at all. In fact, I am sure I am one of the last he would expect to show up at his home today."

"Then, might I suggest you send a card first, to see if the prince is amenable to visitors?"

Matteo felt grateful for this saving bit of advice. "Yes, very good. Will you ask someone to take care of that for me?" He splashed water on his face at the basin.

After he was dressed and Prince George had sent back a card welcoming him for a visit, he set out in the carriage to Carlton House.

Today, the prince received him in a room outside his bedchamber.

"Come in, come in, Comte Durand." The room was still dark, and the prince sat on a low settee, holding a cloth on his head. "I have a pounding headache and find the light disturbing. I hope you don't mind the dark?"

"Not at all. I regret that I have a similar sensation in my own head."

"Do you?" The prince raised an eyebrow. He waved a hand to the closest servant. "Please bring a cool cloth for Prince Matteo."

Matteo shook his head but chose to let the matter of his new title drop. "Your Highness, I am sorry you are unwell. I wonder, do you feel up to a conversation of a grave nature?"

Prince George waved his hand at a chair near him. "Certainly. You talk. I'll listen. If much more is required, I don't know that I am capable yet. It is dashedly early in the morning the day after your very late and exciting wedding ball. I fear I drank too much."

Matteo placed an offered cloth on his own head, enjoying the cool sensation for a moment. "I am happy you enjoyed yourself. But I come because here it is, the day after my wedding, as you say, and Scarlet has left, visiting her aunt again."

Prince George nodded then winced. "Left already, has she? You will both need to talk through some things. I am not sure what has come amuck between you, but it's nothing a few conversations and full evenings in bed cannot solve."

Matteo would think of that later. "The worst I am about to tell you. I come to you, placing my life and the lives of many French families in your hands."

The prince pinched his eyes closed and placed a hand on his forehead. "Oh, come. It cannot be as bad as you make it sound. You are a dramatic one, now I remember, trying to talk politics with me at a ball." He leaned his head back farther on the settee.

"I am being blackmailed."

The prince opened one eye. "Mademoiselle Duplay?"

Matteo nodded. "As youth, we pretended to denounce our neighbors if they did selfish and cruel things. We kept a notebook."

He groaned. "And she is using the information now?"

"Yes, already one family has suffered because of my foolishness."

"The DuPonts."

"Yes. They were like family to me. Stood in often when my own parents were gone, even punished me for swiping some apples." Matteo stopped, a lump in his throat.

"Sorry I am to hear it. Has anything been done to warn the others, the unfortunate French neighbors in your notebook?"

"I have written them all, and several are already out of France and away from her clutches. But I believe many remain. I don't know. I haven't heard from them. There is also one friend and his family who is in the gravest danger. Éléonore claims her soldiers watch his house, and it is he she holds over me most of all. My butler and dear friend, Potier."

The prince nodded slowly, careful not to agitate his head. "Have you given this list to the Pimpernel?"

Matteo couldn't stop the expression of annoyance that crossed his lips. "I have not, though I have tried every way I know to reach him."

"Does Scarlet know your concerns? At times, she is the best manner in which to reach that man."

Matteo blinked in surprise. "I did not know she was so well connected. She does not know. She left before I could confide in her."

"Leave a list of the names with me. I will work on my end, but you must also strive to reach the Pimpernel through your own means and continue your correspondence to France. Reach out to anyone you trust."

"I will. There is one more thing."

The prince turned to face him, tilting his head and opening one eye to see him. "This sounds dire."

"If I return to France—"

"Terrible idea. You would be killed immediately or imprisoned and give more work for everyone else to do to save you."

Matteo held up his hands. "I am aware. But *if* I return to France to warn these families, to rescue Potier, will you care for Scarlet? Will you watch out for her all your days and lend the Crown's protection to her?"

Prince George waved his hand in slight irritation. "She has had our protection long before you arrived. Rupert was a dear friend to me and my father. Her financial needs and that of protection will be met. She *is* quite wealthy, you know. But we can do nothing about healing her heart."

Exasperation filled him. "I don't know if she would suffer from my loss at this point. She left without even an expression of sorrow."

"She loves you. You can be sure of that. Might not be sure of anything else where she is concerned, but of her love, never doubt."

Matteo did not answer. Part of him knew the prince spoke truth. But he wasn't sure her love for him could save them. It obviously had not kept her in town for very long.

"Thank you, Your Highness." He pulled a letter out of his jacket pocket. "Here are the remaining people still in danger as well as my man, Potier, and his family. Please, do all you can for them."

"I will. You can be sure of that. Now, go home and get some rest. We've, all of us, had a long night."

Matteo stood, handing his cold cloth to the waiting servant, and bowed before he left the room. An uneasy knot began to grow in his stomach. He had not done enough. People were still in danger, and he knew the prince's efforts would not suffice.

As he rode in the carriage, his mind began planning his return to France. He had no other choice. He must cross the sea and personally see to it that more did not die at his hand. Rushing into the house, he handed Buckley his hat and gloves and almost began a list of instructions to help him get packed and ready when the man held out a note.

"Oh, thank you, Buckley." Ripping it open, he groaned when he saw the signature. Éléonore. She had written to remind him of their upcoming plans to attend the French nationals ball. He reached out for something to steady himself.

Buckley's concerned voice interrupted. "Are you unwell, my lord?"

He gratefully grasped the man's forearm. "I am well. A bit disturbed by this news, that is all. I will be traveling in three days' time. Could you see to it that all will be in readiness for me?"

"Very good, my lord. Might I ask, where you are going?"

"To France."

Buckley said nothing, but his disapproving stare struck Matteo right in the chest.

What could he do but nod and walk up the stairs? He had no other choice but to disappoint some. He could not allow another innocent person to fall victim to his mistakes.

But first, he had to attend the now odious French nationals ball and search out the Pimpernel. He felt less and less attached to the elusive hero. Weeks had gone by, and still no word from him. If he were worthy of Matteo's respect, surely he would have reached out by now.

Chapter Twenty

The Seamstress finished the remaining stitches for Robespierre's jacket, and she slipped a knife inside the sleeve to test her work. No one would be the wiser. She hoped her other alterations would also remain hidden. His jacket now contained weapons against him as well as places to conceal those for his own use. Grateful she was to the apothecary for the special deadly package, delivered late into the night. She had treated the powder with caution, wrapped in paper so it never came into contact with her skin, and carefully sewed the scroll into the back yoke of Robespierre's jacket. If only she could find a way for the awful man to receive his clothing that did not involve her presence.

Claire walked in through the door on the street. "Renée! Oh, Renée, there you are."

"Hello, Claire. Perfect timing, for I have just finished his jacket."

Claire's face turned worshipful. "Have you dared to put it on?"

She ran a finger down the sleeve, her face hungry. She began to caress the fabric until Scarlet said, "Oh, stop. Put it on, for all our sakes."

Claire smiled. "His power excites me. All of Paris bows at his feet, you know." She slipped her arms into the jacket and hugged herself.

A loud rapping startled them both. "We are here to see the Seamstress."

Before Scarlet could walk the four steps to the door, soldiers opened it and entered the room. Claire immediately removed the jacket, tossing it over the back of a chair.

The men eyed her and said, "Citizen Robespierre sent us for his jacket."

Scarlet reached for it and held it up by the collar. "Here you are. Just as he requested. Please handle it with care."

The men nodded, obviously more than curious about the whole situation, but they said nothing, and the first man did carefully fold the garment over one arm. "He also sent this as correspondence." He held out a folded slip of paper. "We are to wait for your response."

Scarlet reached for it, opening it carefully. Claire came to stand beside her. The note said, *Write the date and time of the event in your special manner.* He wanted it in code.

Scarlet nodded. "Just a moment." She dipped a quill in ink and scratched out tomorrow's date and the other information as requested. She waved the paper, the air drying it, and handed it back to the soldiers.

They watched her with raised eyebrows but knew better than to interfere. Turning, they opened the door and exited out onto the street.

Claire bounced on her toes and squealed. "Corresponding with Maximilien Robespierre. Oh! Do you suppose he would ever replace Miss Duplay with someone younger, more blonde? Or maybe he needs more than one mistress."

Fortunately, the Seamstress did have a reputation for virtue and an upstanding character. She did not have to listen to Claire's raptures any longer. "Really, I hardly find that appropriate to discuss. Please."

Claire laughed and hugged her while floating out the door. Before she closed it behind her, she said, "The invitations are out and the responses back. Every one of the merchants we invited to hear Olympe speak plans to be there tomorrow *with* their families." She whispered, "Imagine how many we will send to the guillotine for this. More than anyone else has ever denounced, I would imagine." Her mouth split into a wide grin, and then she closed the door behind her.

Scarlet closed her eyes. This assignment wore on her more every day. That Claire rejoiced in the deaths of so many, that she would cause these deaths through trickery, that she had invited innocents to hear Olympe de Gouges, a known traitor, as though the Jacobin women supported her, only to cart the shopkeepers off to their deaths—Scarlet shuddered.

She walked to the window, searching the street. When she felt sure no one would interrupt, she rushed to the bucket of ashes by the fireplace where she had hidden the lists of the denounced. The act of pulling them out during daylight hours caused her face to flush and her breathing to quicken. One slip at a time, she placed the pages onto the flame, watching each name, each denouncement, wither and curl and blacken, disappearing forever.

Several hours later, as the Seamstress made her way down darkened streets, her mood darkened further at the great deception. Posters lined the walls, and everywhere, people could be heard discussing Olympe de Gouges, noted playwright and author. They looked forward in happy anticipation for her to arrive on the morrow to address them.

Also lining the streets with the posters were feet, dozens of boots— soldiers, dressed in black, hiding in the darkness, ready to rip the shop owners from their doorways. Scarlet glimpsed them in the shadows. So, Robespierre did not want to wait until the square filled with people. He hoped to grab his victims in the act of leaving their homes to circumvent word getting out to others and any attempts at escape. With this intent, all through the night, boots waited outside homes.

While Scarlet and her men worked.

***

Morning dawned bright and early, and only small numbers began to gather. Soldiers watched the streets with a smirk of satisfaction. Some of the working classes from neighboring boroughs trickled in. Olympe stood on a platform, glancing at her time piece every now and then, her face serene but aware. Shops lined the square, her platform at the head, in the shadow of the church. Its bell tolled ten times.

Approaching her on the right, the Seamstress welcomed her and stepped closer to speak earnestly and in quiet. "Most are not coming today. They have heard their necks are at risk in such a gathering. I concur. Please reconsider. Come with us. Your own neck might need safekeeping as well." She held her breath, hoping Olympe would change her mind.

As the sun rose in the sky and merchants did not leave their shops, soldiers became impatient and began pounding doors and breaking through locks. Empty stores were ransacked. Beds, cold from lack of use that night remained, mocking the soldiers who kicked them aside. Up and down the street, every single shopkeeper or worker had disappeared.

Wary, the Seamstress watched it all, hoping to convince Olympe of her foolishness. Time grew short as soldiers' tempers flared.

Voices carried from the front of the bakery. "Do you think they used magic?" one particularly burly guard asked. "We've been watching their shops all night."

Another rushed out of the shop. "No, not magic. Look here." A small red flower in the center of a paper caused them both to grimace in fear. Anyone fooled by that little red flower had to answer to Robespierre himself.

The members of the Society of Revolutionary Republican Women watched as Olympe shook her head and then embraced the Seamstress. Their speaker straightened her back and then stepped up to the platform to begin. A few women jeered and shouted to her.

"Today, I came here to illuminate three different forms of government. But I don't think I will have time to give my whole speech, so I will say just the following: We are at a crossroads in France. Now that the monarchy has been toppled, we may choose who are to be our rulers. I feel it is time to warn you. At this very moment, those in power are preparing new shackles for you, new ways to stifle your freedoms. We no longer have our king, that is true—may he rest in peace—but losing a king did not make us free. New leaders threaten worse than any monarch ever did, and at the head of the evil and the lawless in Paris is Robespierre himself. He represents all that is wrong in France. From him, we should run for our very lives."

A group of five soldiers approached from the back of the square, spreading out, prepared to surround her.

She watched them come for a moment and then said, "Robespierre! Have you the courage to imitate me? I suggest we take a bath in the Seine, but in order to wash away all the stains you have acquired . . . we will attach cannonballs of sixteen or twenty-four to our feet; then, together, we will rush headlong into the flow."[3]

As she finished her last words, the soldiers bound and gagged her, leading her away from the crowds.

Scarlet slipped into the shadows.

The women cursed and called and shouted at Olympe as she left. All those who would have supported her, not present.

***

Scarlet frowned. "Andrew, why would she not come? I told Olympe we could get her out. I explained clearly that her life was at risk."

Andrew reached for her hand. "You said her last words denounced Robespierre, warned the citizens about him?"

She nodded. "Yes—bold words, but she could have lived and spoken many more words from England."

"Maybe her work was not to be accomplished in England. Her plays, her essays and papers, all taught the people, showed them a better France. Even though she has gone, she is not silenced. Her words remain, and she died declaring her truths."

Scarlet wiped a tear from her cheek. "What do I do with people who won't be saved?"

---

3 On November 5, 1792, Maximilien Robespierre gave a speech defending his political position. Olympe de Gouges penned, *Response to Maximilien Robespierre's Justification, Addressed to Jérôme Pétion*. These words are an excerpt of her arguments (*Réponse à la Justification de Maximilien Robespierre*, accessed Nov. 20, 2017, www.olympedegouges.eu/response_max.php, Nov. 2017).

Andrew pulled her into an embrace. "Ah, but Scarlet. It is not your work to save every soul—just some, just those you can. And this time, we have saved many, a cargo-hold full of merchants."

She allowed a small smile and stepped away. "And what a rescue!"

"One of my favorites to date, I will admit. Shopkeepers shutting doors as if to sleep for the night, Robespierre's men expecting that they sleep in anxious anticipation to hear dear Olympe."

Scarlet grinned. "The merchants said they didn't even stop as they entered their homes—just kept walking."

Andrew swept his arm. "In the front door, out the back."

"And off to our boat. With all those men watching their front." Scarlet frowned. "I do believe the soldiers eventually watched the back doors as well, but we left before they got around to it."

"So often it is just the same. The Pimpernel whisks people away from under the very nose of the committee. Rescuing some, in fact a good many, is better than none, is it not?"

She leaned into him once more, listening but not believing. Again, she saw the faces of her parents as their carriage drove away, heard the crying voice of her brother as he kicked shins, the Inquisition leaders frowning their disapproval. "It all seems so hopeless at times."

"And you have saved a baker. Protected the wonderful French pastries from extinction."

Scarlet smiled and moved toward the deck rail, wrapping a blanket farther around herself. The wind on deck started to pick up.

"What a relief it will be, to be home." Andrew stopped himself from saying more.

Scarlet murmured, "If only home provided the comfort it should." She longed and dreaded to see Matteo. How could she continue to survive this emotional nightmare?

"We will arrive in just enough time to attend the French nationals ball." Andrew stared out over the strait. "Suzanne will be there." He grinned.

She turned to him. "Is this an announcement of sorts? Have you something to tell me?"

He blushed. "Not yet. But perhaps. Perhaps soon."

"She is a dear. I approve, Andrew. Perhaps you will have better luck with the French than I have done."

Chapter Twenty-One

MATTEO LED ÉLÉONORE OUT ONTO the floor. "People are scowling at me. You have ruined my reputation."

"Ignore them. This is for Potier. Now, tell me what you know."

"I arrived only an hour ago. I know nothing. Simon is here, but Andrew is not. Perhaps the Pimpernel himself is not even here."

Éléonore stepped away as they moved through the steps of the dance. When she returned, she said, "Tonight is the night to be bold. Do whatever it takes. Find the Pimpernel, or Potier will answer for your crimes."

Matteo finished the dance in silence, smiling politely to the others, but refusing to acknowledge Éléonore.

When the music stopped, she said, "If you have news, offer me a lemonade, and we will go discuss it in the library."

Matteo turned from her and nearly collided with Scarlet.

A bit shaken, he searched her face, hoping. "Welcome home, my dear." He moved toward her, ready to pull her to his chest and breathe in the wonderful scent of her hair, but she held out her hand for him to take.

"Hello, Matteo."

Trepidation furrowed his eyebrows. "Would you dance with me?" he asked, bowing.

She nodded. "Of course. I would not miss a dance with my handsome French prince." She giggled to the ladies at her side.

The music for the waltz began. Matteo pulled her into his arms, cherishing her nearness. "I have missed you. So much I long to tell you. Perhaps tonight—"

"Oh, I hardly think we will have time tonight. I have arrived just hours before, rushing to change so that I could be here. I might long for my bed before too long."

Matteo's mouth moved in his most charming smile. "Then you and I will be of the same accord. I too long for it, and you."

Scarlet's cheeks burned red. "Matteo, really."

His heart soared. She was still affected by him, blushing in his arms. Hope filled him, and he swung her around in their waltz with greater energy and finesse.

She sighed. "You are such a good dancer."

"But why this sigh? I am yours. You may dance with me any time you like. It is something to celebrate, no?"

Scarlet looked down and then asked, "You say you are mine. And yet, I arrive to find you entertaining Éléonore Duplay. Was she not once the holder of your heart?"

His mouth opened before he knew what to say. Surely she did not suspect his disloyalty. All the guilt for his duplicitous search for the Pimpernel, however insincere, came back to him full force, and it must have shown on his face.

Creating more space between them, she looked away. "I see." She tried to leave his arms and turn from him.

"No, Scarlet. You do not understand. I feel nothing but disgust for that woman. Question the prince. I dance with her here on assignment from him. But she is a torturous, evil woman and is stripping away my peace every day more."

For a moment, Scarlet's eyes held hope. Then her face went blank again, and she stared at something across the room with a vacant expression.

Their song ended, and Lady Pinckney approached. "You have promised me dance after dance, and not one has yet been realized."

As the music began again, Matteo felt he had no choice. "We are in luck this evening, for I have a free set this very moment, if you would oblige me?"

She giggled and reached for his hand. He winked apologetically to Scarlet, but her gaze had wandered in disinterest. His heart sank a little more.

***

Simon shook his head in disbelief. "The man is a traitor. Too much evidence rests against him."

Prince George sipped his wine. "Your protective instincts do you justice and serve her well, except in this instance. He is not a traitor. I would place my life in that man's hands."

"But I have it on impeccable authority that he is actively seeking the Pimpernel. He told me so himself."

The prince put his hand on Simon's shoulder. "He is worried for his friends. Miss Duplay might denounce them. He hopes to give the Pimpernel their names, seeking their protection."

"A likely ruse. I heard Miss Duplay ask for information. He is answering to her, Your Highness; I know it."

"Simon, Simon. Have you considered that she might be forcing his hand?"

He shook his head. "How could she? What could she possibly hold over his head? And did you know it was his signature that signed that denouncement for the DuPonts? He is as deeply entrenched in this whole mess as she is."

"You must learn to trust, Simon. He needs your help now more than ever before. Whatever his reasons for seeking out this information, he will not betray the Pimpernel, mark my words."

Simon grunted in disagreement but said no more, bowed to the prince, and excused himself. His eyes found Scarlet as they always did. The woman appeared miserable. She laughed and teased as usual, but the spark of her life had gone. He could smash that weaselly Frenchman for being the cause of her misery. Simon wanted to call him out for it—pistols at dawn.

The prince says Matteo will not betray the Pimpernel, but what will he do when he has the Pimpernel in his very grasp?

He began a purposeful stride in Matteo's direction.

Seeing him approach, Matteo's face filled with a relieved smile.

Strange.

"Hello, Your Eminence. Might I have a word?" Simon's eyebrow rose in a teasing fashion.

Mouth turned up in half a grin, Matteo said, "Of course. I was hoping for one myself."

They moved toward a corner in the room where few people would hear them.

Simon began, "I know you have been hoping to talk to the Pimpernel—"

Matteo interrupted. "When I sent you that message, I did in fact hope to talk with him, to offer my services for France, but now, my reasons are far more urgent, of the direst emergencies. Please, it is imperative that I get word to him immediately. Many families' lives are at stake."

He seemed completely sincere and, in fact, frantic to help these others. As was, he fell perfectly into Simon's plan. "I will set up a meeting for you. You will not be able to see him, but you may tell him whatever you'd like."

Matteo breathed out a huge sigh of relief. "Oh, thank you, Simon." He leaned forward and embraced him, kissing both his cheeks.

Simon stiffened in surprise, pounding his back two times and then stepping away. "We will summon him here tonight. Come to the formal drawing room at one o'clock A.M."

The new light in Matteo's face gave Simon pause to question his own doubt in the man. Shrugging inwardly, he hoped to find out once and for all if Matteo could be trusted.

***

Lady Pinckney's slippers nudged his boots again. Their second set now, and Matteo's patience waned. Every time they came together in the dance, she managed to brush him or bump him or in some way come into contact with his person.

Giggling, she said, "Oh! Excuse me, Your Highness! You French are such excellent dancers; I must seem a bumbling fool to you!" She stepped in closer than was necessary, her décolleté brushing his chest. "Perhaps if you could teach me . . ."

"You are in luck, Baroness! For I have recently learned of a new French dance master who has come to stay in London. He is hoping to build a patronage here and would appreciate your support, I am quite sure."

When they came back together in the dance, she pouted. "That's all very lovely, but I was hoping that *you* would teach me. You have such excellent footwork. And your hands . . ."

Matteo coughed. "I have been much more occupied of late with the dealings in France and do not have a moment to spare. But I am sure Gerard would be a much better instructor than I."

The dance could not end soon enough. He longed to return to Scarlet. Perhaps they would now have time to work through whatever coldness had come between them. His eyes searched the room for her, and his teeth clamped shut when he saw her dancing with Lord Panning, whose hands fell lower down her waist than they should and pulled her closer to his chest than they ought. She leaned away from him and searched the crowd, obviously discomfited.

Lady Pinckney asked, "What is it?" She turned her head to see what had attracted his gaze. "Hmm. You must go to her."

Matteo did not wait but stormed through the couples, across the room. In a particularly intricate weaving pattern in the dance, he slipped in at her side, wrapped one arm around her waist, held her other arm across his body, and led her away as if he was her partner. He felt Scarlet's body relaxed into his own.

She breathed out a sigh and said, "Thank you."

Checking a clock on the mantle, he had fifteen minutes until his meeting with the Pimpernel, a precious fifteen minutes. He continued guiding her out the side doors and onto a terrace. Blessedly alone, he whirled her in a circle before bringing her up close to him in an embrace.

She giggled and then leaned into him. "Impeccable timing, as always. You are the only one to successfully keep him at bay."

His chin resting on the top of Scarlet's head, he said, "I will take care of this. He won't bother you again after tonight."

She leaned back to search his face. "That sounds ominous. What do you have in mind?"

"I'll start with embarrassment, blackmail, and end with threat of his complete emasculation."

"Matteo!" She tried to appear shocked, but he saw the humor in her eyes.

"I can think of no better deterrent. Some humans don't deserve to be men, but rest easy. He requires nothing so drastic."

Although Scarlet still eyed him with curiosity, she asked for no more details. Sadness crossed her face, and Matteo knew the blank look of indifference was coming before he saw it there.

A disturbing, screechy laugh interrupted them as the very man, Lord Panning, led Éléonore out onto the terrace with them. She swayed and teetered on her feet, falling onto the weak arm of her escort. When her eyes found them, she called out overly loud, "Oh, Matteo, darling! I need you, love. There's a tightness right here." She reached her arm around to her back, her finger trying to point to some unseen discomfort. Matteo almost laughed at the ridiculous request until he saw Scarlet's mouth open and felt her absence as she stepped back from him.

"Absurd, Miss Duplay. I would no sooner help you with such a request as I would kiss a snake."

Éléonore's eyes narrowed into slits.

He was undeterred. "You have obviously over-imbibed. Shall I get you some assistance to your carriage?"

"Matteo, the pure dove. *Pardonez moi* while I chortle at the absurdity." She leaned closer to Scarlet, and Matteo stepped between them, shielding his wife. Éléonore purred, "You must know he has tasted other lips, tasted *these* lips." She swiveled her hips and then turned, nearly dragging a stumbling Lord Panning with her. They exited down the stairs at the other end of the terrace toward another ballroom entrance.

Scarlet's silence unnerved him.

"Please, my dear, I abhor that woman. I believe she has my misery as her main purpose. You must know she means nothing to me." He tried to reach for Scarlet's hand, but she pulled it away.

"I know nothing about your relationship with Miss Duplay."

"I have no relationship." How could she not understand? Why would any moral man of sense be attracted to such a person? Did his wife have such little faith in him? If only they had more time together. He must prove himself anew, wipe all uncertainty from her heart forever.

Scarlet held up her hand. "Whatever your history, you are much closer than I imagined."

"But you don't understand at all. Please, allow me to explain."

A chime rang from inside the house, calling people to whist if they so desired.

Matteo's hand flew to his pocket watch; he had but three minutes to arrive in the drawing room. He turned with concern to his pale and exhausted wife.

Scarlet's body deflated before his eyes. With a great sigh, she said, "I am tired. Perhaps we may discuss things this evening. But for now, I will return home. It is nearly one in the morning."

He tried to show his heartfelt urgency with his eyes. "I would very much like to explain further this evening. Now, where would you like to rest? Shall I bring you some lemonade?"

She rested her hand on his arm. "Near the prince, if you would, and lemonade would be lovely, thank you." Her face remained drawn and pale.

He led her as gently and quickly as possible to a chair near the prince, who welcomed her with exclamations and raptures. Matteo promised to return and bowed his departure.

As he strode away, he asked the nearest footman to provide the lemonade. And then his thoughts turned to the Pimpernel and the grave danger to many families in France. Rushing to the drawing room, he hoped he was not too late. Just as he was about to enter, a grating sound reached his ears as it had far too often this evening.

Chortling, Éléonore said, "Matteo, are you following me? Hungry for another *rendezvous, oui?*"

Furious, he pulled her into an alcove just outside of the room where the Pimpernel likely awaited hm. "You must desist with the lies, Éléonore. Leave Scarlet and my marriage out of this. You know there is nothing between you and me. What we had as children was just that, *childish*, and now it is no more."

Still swaying from drink, she spat, "So you have said. Believe me, sir, I know where I stand with you." Her tone changed, and she ran a finger up his arm. "I'm just having a bit of fun. If she isn't secure enough in your love, what fault of that is mine?"

He shrugged her off. "Stop."

Time was passing, and he felt his frustration rise as he worried he would miss the Pimpernel altogether.

Voices in the hall interrupted his thoughts. "The Pimpernel. One A.M."

Éléonore stiffened beside him and burst out of the alcove, eyes madly searching up and down the hallway and then turning to the drawing room. "Where is he?"

Grasping for any idea, his mind racing, he said, "I was on my way to meet the Pimpernel now before you interrupted me. If you would just let me do my job and leave my personal life out of this, we could get a lot further along."

Her eyes glared at him with suspicion. "I am coming with you."

He shrugged, and with that shrug, gave up his precious rendezvous. He would have to save the families himself. "Follow me. We are meeting in the hallway by the kitchen. He will be there in a cupboard behind the door. We are not to see him, only to hear."

Éléonore rubbed her hands together in greedy anticipation. "I will not be so polite. In moments, we will know his identity. Robespierre will be pleased." Her eyes shone with a crazed energy as her hurried feet slinked down the hallway.

Matteo followed but looked over his shoulder. The toe of a shiny hessian revealed itself at the base of the drapes. He stared as long as he dared, watching his last hope of assistance in France disappear when he and Éléonore turned down a different hallway.

***

Simon had poked his foot forward under the drapes, hoping that Matteo would see it as he led Éléonore away. The little he could offer as hope seemed paltry in comparison with all Matteo carried on his shoulders in the form of worries and betrayal.

Confusion warred with Simon's conviction and understanding of Matteo's character. He had heard their conversation, purposefully dangled the one A.M. meeting near their alcove for Éléonore to hear, a test. He wanted to be sure of how Matteo would respond if given an easy opportunity to lead Éléonore straight to the Pimpernel.

But Matteo had led her away, given up a much sought-after meeting, and planned to spend a lengthy amount of time in a back hallway by the kitchen, putting another wedge of distrust in the precarious footing of his marriage.

What manner of man was he? Could he be all that the prince had claimed? Worthy of Scarlet's love? Simon stepped out from behind the curtains. It was time he found out. Checking his pocket watch, he decided that the Pimpernel had just acquired a secret meeting in a hallway outside the kitchen this very night.

Voices carried easily to him as he approached.

"I am finished, Éléonore. I have done my part. Is it my fault he did not meet his appointment?"

"You are finished when I say you are. Are you really so anxious to give up dear Potier? It will take me but a moment to send an express. Riders would carry it to the coast. It would enter a boat and fall into the hands of Robespierre himself in but one week's time. Even you could not travel fast enough to save him."

"Then so be it. You will get no further help from me. Go back to your snake."

"Then the letters of denouncement go in tonight. Each, with your signature. How long will you last in these English courts with blood on your hands? The more you denounce, the more distrust you will gain."

"I care not for their approval or yours. You have become the vilest of people, intent that my misery would equal yours. But in that, you will fail. Even if you take away all that is good in my life, even if you take my very life, I will never be as miserable or small or dark as you. You have sold yourself to become, what? You think you are his partner? His companion? You have believed a lie. You will never be anything so important to him. Certainly not his wife. You are his mouse, Éléonore, the mouse he plays with until he becomes hungry."

She reached her hand up to slap him, but he grabbed her wrist, wrenching her arm away. "Go, Éléonore. Go back to your snake."

She whirled in an instant and steamed down the hallway.

Simon whispered from his new location behind a doorway in the hall. "What an awful woman."

Matteo spun. "Who's there? Come out and reveal yourself at once."

"I cannot, but you have sought me this night. I thank you for leading the viper away. I followed because from what I understand, we have much to discuss."

"Yes, but allow me to verify your identity. Where was our initial meeting?"

"In the drawing room. I believe you may have seen my boot waiting for you?"

"Yes, and what time?"

"At one A.M. precisely, though you were a bit late."

Matteo chuckled into the darkness. "I thought I had lost my chance to talk with you."

"Never. The Pimpernel is always available to those in need. We aid as many as we are able. If we have been slow in responding, it is because the urgency of our missions has increased and we were detained more often in France."

Matteo's voice held a touch of something. "And I gave cause for suspicion. I do apologize. It seems my misguided youth has come to create disaster for us all."

"We have little time. What have you to tell me?"

"Éléonore is threatening my dear friend and butler and his family. She claims they are under watch every day."

"Potier, yes?"

"You know of him? Then you are getting him out?"

"All in good time. Who else is she threatening?"

"Is not Potier enough of a priority? She will immediately imprison him, before all the others." Desperation made his voice a little higher than his usual deep bass.

"And who are the others?"

A sigh filled the darkness with sound. "As a youth, I wrote journals, pretend denouncements, with Éléonore. We wrote them together, recording all the cruel and unkind things we witnessed our neighbors doing. She has these journals. I have with me a list of those mentioned in our writing. Three are already to safety. They have left the country. But the others—I have no way of knowing how they fare, except that they are, every day, in more danger."

"Leave the list on the ground near your feet. After you leave, I will take it with me to Paris. We leave at the first tide."

"Take me with you. I long for nothing more than to save my fellow French."

"You must stay. You are too great a target. They would arrest you immediately."

"I care not for my life. I have a personal responsibility. They might not be in danger but for me."

"Your neighbors would have fallen under suspicion soon enough. Potier would likely have been spared. But you must trust me. We will care for them and deliver them all safely to the shores of England."

"But Potier is of the utmost urgency. Éléonore will detain him in but one week's time. We have no room for delay or diversion."

Simon smiled in the darkness. So like himself Matteo sounded. He began to regret the many hours he had spent suspecting the man. "You must stay here. You are invaluable to the prince, and your absence would be difficult to explain. Your presence in France would put any mission at great risk. Trust us. You must trust us. You have my word that Potier will be safe."

***

Matteo made up his mind in that moment, but he did not at first respond. He would leave for France as soon as physically possible, after a talk with Scarlet this evening. But he said only, "Thank you. The list of names is here at my feet." Then he walked down the hall without so much as a glance behind him.

Weaving his way through the many couples lengthening out the night together, he knew Scarlet would be ready to leave. If he could find her quickly, they would be out and home within the half hour. By inquiring of the nearest footman, he discovered Scarlet had already left in her own carriage. Matteo remembered that they had arrived separately. As unsettling as it felt to have his wife leave without a word to him, he felt a small amount of relief that he too could leave as soon as his own equipage was ready.

Inside the front door of his home, Buckley took Matteo's hat and coat, directing him upstairs when he asked about Scarlet. Taking two steps at a time, he hurried to her bedchamber, knocking with great urgency. "Scarlet, darling. May I come in?"

He waited and heard no movement inside. Could she be in her bed already? Maid come and gone? Impossible. He walked down the hall and entered his own room. Their connecting door loomed before him. How many times had he eyed that barrier between them, wondering at his reception? A shut door, reminding him of all he had lost since his wedding day. He had no time for insecurities. They must speak tonight. Still nervous to try the knob, he stood in front of it for a heartbeat before reaching forward with his hand.

The knob turned. Great happiness filled him, knowing she had not locked him out. The door slowly crept open as his eyes searched the room. His heart beat faster, hope filling his mind. Convinced that conversation and time together could heal whatever had come between them, he pushed open the door faster and stepped into the room, softly calling, "Scarlet?"

Bed still made, desk clear, no evidence of her presence in the room. Confused, he stepped farther in, calling toward the back, into the dressing room. "Are you in there, Scarlet? Annabeth?"

Only silence responded. Tendrils of concern began to creep into his awareness. A piece of stationery grabbed his attention. Familiar handwriting flowed across the page.

Buckley,

Please be sure Comte Durand receives this letter in the morning. I will follow our usual methods and send word when I can.

S

Her usual methods?

He lifted the loose paper and reached for the envelope beneath. His name on the front, written in her curly script, brought his mind immediately back to the first day she had left him a note, when she had unexpectedly departed in the night to visit her aunt. He had never asked for more details of that trip because of his proposal and the happy weeks that followed, but his thoughts returned to her trembling frame in his arms just moments after her arrival.

A feeling of foreboding began to settle in his stomach. His hands tore through the seal and pulled out the paper inside. He scanned the letter. Short, to the point, but signed, *Yours*. A drop of warmth gave him hope that battled his confusion. She wrote of another trip to see her aunt. She feared that her dear relative did not have much longer to live. Apparently, she had a newly acquired case of lung fever, and the physician predicted her imminent demise.

Skepticism warred with empathy. No matter her reason for leaving then, she had left again now, and he was alone a second time in his marriage, a third time since meeting her. A heavy disappointment fell like lead into his gut, followed by a quiet resignation. He would have much preferred taking this journey to France with the memory of Scarlet in his arms to warm him. He searched the tabletop for a memento, something to carry with him. He pulled out a drawer under her mirror. A ring. He felt somewhat better carrying a part of her with him. He examined it and smiled. Flowers. If he remained safe and returned to this lovely estate, he would fill a room with flowers for her. With that small piece of hope, he returned to his own chambers.

Growing accustomed to the constant weight of unresolved distance in their relationship, he moved forward with his plans, pushing through the heavy unhappiness it created. Ringing for Edwards, he made preparations to leave at first light.

Chapter Twenty-two

SCARLET'S CARRIAGE SLOWED AS THEY approached *Place de Grève*. Cheers of the crowds jarred her anew, notwithstanding she had heard them often. She shivered at the sound. They drew closer, as she knew they must before heading down a different street and off to *La Conciergerie*, where she would pay a visit to her lovely friend, Marie Antoinette.

Imprisoned, separated from her son, Marie had become a political pawn, an attempt by the committee to negotiate peace with her relations, the Austrians. But Scarlet knew negotiations would not bring peace. Marie's brothers were no longer in power, and the ruling nephew had no care for his aunt at all, saw her as a distant relative and nothing more. The league must make every effort to set the queen and her daughter free, the *dauphin* soon after.

As they turned the corner and the guillotine came into view, Scarlet turned away. She had seen enough death from that blade. With every drop of the knife, she felt her failure all the more, saw the trembling families of those who died, saw her parents' faces more clearly, and wondered at the fate of her brother.

At times, she awoke from her dreams screaming his name, with the fresh fictional memory of his head dropping into a basket. She shivered again and willed the crowd to let them pass, to disperse with all haste so that her carriage could move again.

Her family had travelled to Spain, as they did every summer. As he had before, her father brought some of the banned books with him. The Inquisition, though increasingly distant from people's lives, had nevertheless banned multiple books, and her father provided those tomes for the neighbors to read. But Spain had become embroiled in a dispute over the Falkland Islands right around the time of their visit, and the Spanish were seeking ways to punish the British. Her parents, fresh pawns in this endeavor, provided too convenient an opportunity, and with her father's past service to the British Navy, a perfect example of Spanish dissatisfaction. The Falkland Islands dispute ended shortly after, and her parents' deaths seemed even more of a disastrous waste because of it.

An insistent voice distracted her, pulling Scarlet's eyes back to the carriage window. She searched the crowd for the source of the new sound.

Struggling against her captors, a woman was led across the platform, next in line to meet the guillotine. She shouted, forcing the men to slow her path. Scarlet admired her fire. She had a message to deliver before her death, and she was determined to see it received by whoever would listen. Scarlet brushed tears from her eyes, admiration at the woman's courage dimming the evil around them. This woman's bravery merited a sensible person to listen to her last words, whatever they may be. And Scarlet felt sure she was one of very few sensible people in attendance in that square. She strained her ears and focused on the woman's face.

As Scarlet drew closer to the stage, the woman's words became more clear. "Death is not the answer. When I die, you will still be hungry, poor, sick, and unhappy. Killing everyone who disagrees with you will not help France. Violence and blood will not win this war." She fell quiet and walked meekly for a few steps. Then she raised her hands to the heavens, steps away from her own death and shouted, "Oh, liberty, what crimes are committed in thy name!"[4]

Scarlet turned away as the knife dropped, suddenly ill, sick to her stomach. Liberty, an elusive dream, the idea of which moved men to passion, to revolution. Was there a group of humans truly ready to be free? If this mad violence was the manner in which men responded when seizing liberty for themselves, then humankind did not deserve freedom.

Several thoughts niggled at her, contradicting one another. Thomas Jefferson had come to France, had courted French assistance. His words carried over to America and to England's shores. *According to him,* thought Scarlet, *inalienable rights are ours from birth, kept from us only by tyrants who would rule.* True freedom gave rise to a glorious human spirit, a spirit that invents and discovers and climbs heights not heretofore attempted.

She sat back against her carriage bench. Certain that glorious human spirit just lost her head, Scarlet wondered anew, *What went wrong in France?* Chewing her lip, she closed her eyes. She would never understand senseless violence. Two

---

4 Madame Roland was among those executed by guillotine during the French Revolution. Before her execution, she is reported to have said, "O Liberté, comme on t'a jouée." (Austin Dobson, *Four Frenchwomen* [London: Chatto & Windus, Piccadilly, 1890, archive.org], 59). The quote used here is another attributed to Madame Roland (Mathilde Blind, *Famous Women: Madame Roland* [Boston: Little, Brown, and Company, 1898], 310, archive.org).

moving forces of human nature battled for sovereignty every day in France: men's desire to rule and their equally powerful drive to be free.

The crowd outside her carriage cheered louder than usual. She winced before searching the platform for the next victims. The executioner called out, "Charlotte Corday, guilty of the crime of murder!" The crowd jeered again, and the executioner continued. "Murder of our own Jean-Paul Marat while in his bathtub."

Catcalls carried across the throng to Scarlet. They liked this new murderess, yet they still condemned her. What was the difference between her private taking of life and their very public one? Robespierre would say it is the rule of law. He legally sent people to their death.

In truth, Charlotte's own efforts to cleanse France of a mad, bloodthirsty dictator only created a larger problem, for Jean-Paul Marat's death increased the power of Robespierre and Saint-Just, proved their point that if they did not legally cleanse the populous, the masses would do it for them.

Scarlet closed her eyes and tried to shut out the sound of the blade falling. Another brilliant woman lost from their land, such a tragedy when they were in great need of the bright souls who could lead France to a better place.

Scarlet sat back on her carriage bench, again willing the crowds to disperse so she could all the sooner be admitted to see Marie Antoinette. She knew the Seamstress would be tasked with stitching the lovely queen's name into the folds of lace. She had seen the paperwork; while Robespierre studied her intricate stitching, she had scanned the list. She knew she could not neglect to stitch it. Robespierre would likely wish to see her handiwork himself. Marie's escape must be planned immediately. It was for this reason Scarlet had returned to France as soon as she did—home for barely a moment to gather important pieces of her costume, paperwork, and other items for the league. *And to see Matteo*, she reminded herself.

Her heart paused in painful recollection of Matteo's expression, pleading with her for a moment of her time, to explain. She would have relented, would have listened to him that night had her own need to return to France not been so urgent. Time had lessoned the sting of his disloyalty, and she felt ready to listen, doubting her own rash decisions.

Except here she sat in France, yet again. She ran a finger along the wood-framed window of her carriage. She would have time enough in the future to mend things—or to discover just how much of a traitor and liar Matteo had become—after the royal family, including the *dauphin*, was safe.

She had tried to think of any excuse for Matteo's name to be on the denouncement papers, and she was willing to give him some leeway, to hear him explain, knowing he could have been framed. But secret trysts with Éléonore she could not excuse. She had heard Éléonore with her own ears. Great sadness escaped with her sigh. *Thoughts for another day*. She focused again on the challenges ahead.

With King Louis XVI already beheaded, it was only a matter of time before the others followed. Only the *dauphin* had a small measure of protection. The Austrians and her own Prince George expressed significant interest in his well-being and protection. The new French National Convention carefully assured these neighboring foreign powers of his life and health.

But time did not befriend Scarlet these days in France. Loyalties switched as quickly as the tide. She remained uncertain they could get the queen and her children out of France before it was too late. They had to try.

As her conveyance at last pulled away from the crowds of *La Place de Grève*, she thought about the last time she had seen beautiful Marie. Her violet dress had fallen in waves from her petite frame to the floor. Layers of lace fell from her décolleté, and her waist had been cinched so tight Scarlet wondered if she could eat.

The woman reigned as the decade's most brilliant fashion genius, and Scarlet had copied, from Marie's earlier modes, many of her own outlandish designs. But Scarlet knew that for Marie, it was all a façade, a farce, something to draw attention to herself, to win the people's love. As much as they hated the queen's excess, the people gloried in the image she portrayed, proud of their monarch. It was her beauty and elaborate hairstyles and gowns that had attracted the *sansculottes* in the first place. They loved to catch sight of her and bask in her beauty, many thousands gathering at any rumored sighting.

Marie had quickly lost their approval, however, with her excesses in spending that excluded the general populace. Her idyllic, whimsical, miniature farmland retreat, the *Hameau de la Reine*, had angered them all the more; the rumors of her lavish parties and succulent desserts stirred them into a mad frenzy. Her excesses became criminal and their bloodthirst all the more real.

Still, they executed King Louis XVI first. And according to the denouncement lists, Her Majesty's turn would arrive any day. In watching Robespierre's confidence, his exuberance at adding her to the list, Scarlet had realized with cold dread that he now felt his power complete, even greater than the queen's.

***

Captain Clough surveyed the arrival of fifteen unmarked trunks to his ship. From his lookout up top, everything appeared to be moving forward as it did every day. Nothing indicated anything out of the ordinary, especially not something so out of the ordinary as the arrival of the royal belongings of Marie Antoinette and her children. The cats, though a regular occurrence on the docks, provided the most cause for suspicion. The contact from the Pimpernel's league had insisted on the cats. Therefore, someone had arrived in the dead of night with a few of the creatures and placed them in a locked cabin below deck. Were anyone to pay close attention, the delivery of fresh fish and bedding for the lovely creatures would have raised an eyebrow.

The captain shook his head. His heart went out to these French. But if not for the money, he never would have agreed to such a plan as this. As his gaze flitted over the docks, he found nothing amiss, no suspicious figures counting trunks or anything of the like. With any luck, he would arrive on the shores of Maine with a group of lovely new houseguests and furniture and clothing from the palace.

The trunks had come from Marie—some royalist sent them along. But the furniture he had purchased himself off the streets of Paris. As soon as the family had been imprisoned, their home was ransacked and everything in it sold. Captain Clough prided himself on his rescue of several valuable pieces.

His ship, *The Sally*, would be ready to depart by nightfall. The longest they could delay would be until the morning tide, with or without the extra passengers. If the local revolutionaries got word that he was a royalist helping to free Marie Antoinette herself, he might never be able to trade in the city of Paris again. Satisfied that the trunks had been loaded properly and without any undue interest, he retired to his cabin for an afternoon nap before the potential sail at dusk.

Chapter Twenty-Three

MATTEO STEPPED DOWN THE LOADING platform, off the boat, his legs buckling under him for only a moment while he accustomed them again to land. A great smile filled his face as he took deep breaths of French air. To his left, an American vessel, *The Sally*, sat docked with a new flag of red and white stripes, a white circle of stars on a patch of blue in the corner. Wind gusting about him, Matteo searched the shipyard, dusk arriving with him. He hurried toward a waiting carriage, satisfied that, as of yet, his arrival in France had gone undetected.

Handing a small trunk off to the waiting coachman, he climbed into the carriage with instructions for the driver to hurry to the first inn. There, he left express messages in the hands of a courier for all the remaining people on Éléonore's potential denouncement list. As he had before from England, he told each family to leave France immediately. Then, with a great sense of urgency, he gave the coachman the directions to Potier's country home.

Arriving two hours later, he checked his pistols again and put a hand on the sword at his waist. The carriage slowed to a stop. Before the wheels stood still, Matteo's feet touched the soft earth, and he made his way in the darkness of night toward the light glowing in an upstairs window. Dark tree branches stood out against the moonlight sky. Shadows moved all around him, and an uneasiness grew in Matteo's chest. Foolish to come alone, he reviewed his plan of escape: enter unseen, gather the household, and leave as quickly and quietly as possible. Not a very detailed plan, his lack of preparation caused every noise to take on a menacing tone.

The front door creaked open at his hand, and he peered inside, taking note of an unnaturally quiet home. The Pimpernel's petition came to him.

Trust us. You must trust us.

Matteo shifted his weight. So great was his unease about entering the home that he began to turn around on his heels and head back down the front stoop, but the sight of a familiar cloak hanging on the hook near the door stopped him. Potier's hat hung above it.

Warmth filled Matteo. How he missed his dear friend. Surely all would be well, the man reading upstairs in his bed. Soon he and his family would be safely tucked in Matteo's hired carriage and then on their way to England. With those thoughts to encourage him, he entered the home, making his way around furniture in the darkness.

Upstairs, one glowing, flickering light spilled into the hallway. Uneasy enough not to call out, he made as little noise as possible approaching the door. The room appeared empty, light coming from somewhere on the other side of the door. His feet moved forward while his heart and mind questioned the action. Two additional steps into the room, and the door slammed shut behind him, the lock clicking. He spun, grabbing for his pistol, but a solid thump hit his head and the world began to blacken around him. As he slumped to the ground, he tried to draw his sword but fumbled and hit the floor before he could manage it. A blurry form of the French tricolor cockade came into focus and then faded to complete darkness.

**

Scarlet's visit with Marie had been bittersweet. It was lovely to see her old friend and fashion consultant but painful to see her reduced in such an obvious manner. Her small frame had turned wiry, lacking all of her former buxom curves. Her thinning hair under the wigs, unnaturally gray, showed an age that should still be a few years in coming. But Marie's gratitude and relief in behalf of her daughter motivated Scarlet to keep working, even now, sitting with detestable Pauline and Claire as they planned who would deliver the denouncements to the guards.

"Robespierre's note said our personal delivery to the guardhouse is not secure enough. He wants to see the list himself." Pauline's eyes slanted. "I feel like he is spying on us."

Claire added, "I hear he's getting suspicious. Guards say they never find the people on our lists."

Pauline scoffed. "I say the guards are being lazy. There is nothing wrong with our lists."

"Well, it's a problem when the neighbors claim the person never lived there, ever." Claire crossed her arms.

Both ladies turned to Renée.

She placed another sheaf of paper into the fire, watching the flames devour it. Her brow wrinkled and her voice wavered as she said, "I don't know, ladies.

I don't know." Her lips curved downward and she dropped her face into her hands. "What can I do if the people aren't where they're supposed to be?"

Claire moved toward her, placing an arm around her shoulders. "I don't know, Renée. It just doesn't look good, that's all. We could be in a lot of trouble."

Pauline stepped toward them and crossed her arms. "Well, we're not going to be. Marie Antoinette is on this list, and everyone knows where she lives. Now, let's hurry and get it pinned on me."

Claire turned to face her. "Pauline, I always deliver the lists."

Pauline's eyes flashed. "This list goes to Robespierre himself. It is only natural that I, the president, should present it."

"I don't see what that has to do with anything. I brought Renée here, didn't I? I helped create the Seamstress."

Pauline shoved Claire aside and stepped in front of Scarlet. "It doesn't matter, Claire. I'm wearing the list this time, and I want the list as close to *this* as possible." She ran a finger along the top ruffle of her gown, across her low and revealing neckline.

Claire, face red and mouth quivering, left the shop, slamming the door behind her.

Hands shaking ever so slightly, the Seamstress began pinning. She felt uncomfortable in the knowledge that, of a necessity, real names had been sewn into this particular lace. A copy of these names had been sent on to Simon so he could set in motion tasks and orders to bring them all to safety, but she could not help but feel great trepidation that her own tatting and stitches could be sending innocents to their deaths. Her mouth in a grim line, she continued her work along Pauline's neckline.

A large crowd of their women began to gather, and Claire's voice hung in the air, audible through the window. Today, they would again petition for a written constitution, a set of laws ensuring freedom. Their group wanted specific language for women included, particularly their right to vote and participate in governing bodies. Scarlet had to agree with their motivation. Sadly, misguided methods destroyed what good their intentions could have wrought.

Shrieks from the street caused her to jump, nearly poking Pauline with her final pin. A few women squabbled with each other.

"All finished. Please remove the gown. I will sew it up right here, and you can be on your way."

The women outside grew more and more raucous. Men had shown up, better-dressed, from some other part of town, and they were shouting in the faces of the Republic of Women. The encounter would need to be interrupted, or it would decline into a massive brawl. Scarlet shook her head.

Pauline noticed. "I'd better get out there."

"Yes, at least try to keep the noise down while I finish this sewing. We don't want to attract any further attention."

Pauline returned the dress and walked outside, joining her shouts with the rest.

As the Seamstress finished the last stitch, the noise of the crowd escalated to an unheard-of level. Her eyes flew to the window.

Oh no.

Once again, the tide of goodwill among the revolutionaries had turned and the sun had set on the Society of Revolutionary Republican Women. The Seamstress swallowed and took a long, slow breath. She should have predicted their arrest to happen even sooner than this. No one remained in the good graces of the committee for long, not even the committee itself.

They fought fiercely against their brothers in arms from days ago, all Jacobins working for the same goals, but that did not matter.

No match for Robespierre's army, most women succumbed to the force and strength of the soldiers. But Claire and Pauline and a small group of the others kicked and fought the best they could to avoid capture.

A rock broke through Scarlet's window. With a yelp of surprise, she flung herself to the ground, clutching the gown to her breast. Any delay in this lace reaching the eyes of Robespierre was a good one. She smiled from her vantage point on the floor.

The sound of boots entering her workshop hushed her breathing, and she lifted her eyes. Men stormed in through the door.

One guard bore down on the other. "We are to bring the women without harm."

"You try to detain them without harming them. They're vicious, they are. Take a look at that, will you? Teeth marks!" The smaller guard showed his arm to the others.

A pair of boots approached Scarlet at her place on the floor. "Ah, here she is. The Seamstress, I take it?" He peered down at her.

She nodded her head.

"We are to instruct you to hand over the list. He said you would know what I'm talking about."

She rose, dusted off her dress, and then handed the dress to the nearest guard. "Careful, there are pins."

He raised his eyebrows, looking over the gown, but said nothing.

"You will come with us. You are under arrest as a traitor to the republic." A different guard moved to her and would have tied her hands.

But she said, "No shackles are necessary. I come willingly."

They raised their eyebrows and moved to tie her up anyway. Wincing, preparing for rough ropes on her wrists, she widened her eyes when the men fell away and Robespierre entered.

"Citizen Robespierre." One of the men saluted him and stepped forward. "The women are being gathered at this moment. All is going according to plan."

"I see that, Marcos. Well done. The Seamstress and I have some business to take care of. Guard the doors."

The guards exited, and Scarlet felt her breathing quicken. Hiding behind the character and personality of the Seamstress, she cooled her features and allowed an appropriate amount of fear and deference to show. "The guards have my latest list."

He rapped on the door, requesting the dress from the guards. Fingering the lace in a reverential manner, he searched for each name. "I take pride in being able to read this, you know. It is so complex; it takes a practiced eye."

Scarlet nodded. "Thank you. You will find that it is complete."

Still studying the fabric closely, he said, "Someone uninformed would not be able to recognize the names. They would have to be clued in, told, to seek them out, and then, as I mentioned, have a practiced eye"—his voice lowered, menacing—"to discover the name of each filthy person." Venom punctuated his last few words. Eyes narrowed, he studied her. Even Claire's loud shrieking outside did not distract him. "Why are none of the people on my lists reaching the guillotine, Seamstress?"

She swallowed and stumbled on her words. "I—I don't know. We have tried to figure it out. Claire wears the dresses herself, and we deliver the message. Perhaps the problem comes from your messenger before the names reach me . . ." Her voice trailed off.

Robespierre's eyes, glinting and menacing, accused her of treason. "Impossible. At times, I dispense with the messenger and deliver the notes myself."

When Scarlet raised her eyebrows in question, Robespierre responded, "Of course. A little disguise, nothing too terribly complicated, and I can roam the streets myself with no one the wiser."

"I see. Then I don't know. I stitch the names, deliver the lists—"

He stepped closer to her. "And warn the denounced. There is no other explanation. As soon as I deliver the lists to you, the people disappear from France. So careless. If only you had let a few of them die, you would not be suspect."

Sensing she had no other recourse and that she would indeed be entering the prison this afternoon, she asked, "And what of the others?" She pointed to the women outside. "Must they also suffer from your accusations?"

Shaking his head in frustration as the noise outside escalated, he said, "They are guilty of their own crimes. Too overzealous, critical. Their actions would throw us into a massive civil war. We don't need division within when we are facing enemies from Hungary and others without." He motioned for the guards to enter. "Take her with the others. Place them all in a cell."

Shoving her along with them, the guards exited the shop and herded the fighting limbs and claws of the revolutionary women down the streets toward carriages and prison carts.

Chapter Twenty-Four

Before Matteo opened his eyes, his nose recognized he awoke in prison, or some other place where people slept in their own vomit. His head pounded from the impact that had rendered him unconscious. He winced, thinking of the obvious trap at Potier's residence. A trap he could have easily avoided had he placed even a modicum of trust in his friends, in the Pimpernel. Potier, obviously not in the home, could be anywhere. Matteo hoped he had escaped on his own and was safely concealed from the committee.

Matteo tried to clench his fists but felt the pressure of sharp iron bands too tightly clasped around his wrists. Yanking on the chains, his movement jerked to a stop when the hooks on the walls behind him held. The thick darkness allowed for no sight. Either the deepest part of night was upon him, or his cell had no windows.

Moisture from the damp floor seeped through his breeches to his skin. His head tipped backward in frustration, connecting with an overly soft wall, spongy. Matteo leaned forward instead, resting his head on folded arms across his knees.

What felt like hours later, a guard opened the hatch of a door, allowing some filtered light inside Matteo's cell. Four moss-covered walls surrounded him. Puddles and damp areas stained the dark and crusty floor. Mounds, piles of filth, marked the corners and explained the stench. The guard called to someone at his left and then swung the door open. Coming forward, one of the men unattached Matteo's chains from the wall, but left them tightly bound to his wrists.

Yanking him along, the guard said, "Come with me, ye scum."

Jerked to his feet, Matteo stumbled forward and then found his footing. "Where am I?"

"Shut up. Lucky you are—movin' up, swell. Were it up to me, you'd rot in here like the rest of the aristo scum."

Unsure if that was good news or bad, Matteo chose to be happy about any positive change in his accommodations.

"Seems you'll be getting a visitor this week—have to be presentable when that happens."

Matteo remained silent and followed the guard who jerked his chains forward unnecessarily every now and then. A visitor! Hope filled him and dulled the strain and worry about his present circumstance. He told himself a visitor could be someone dreadful from the Committee of Public Safety, even Éléonore herself. But it didn't dull the glow of fire that lit at the thought. Far worse than any visitor would be no visitor at all, no contact, to be forgotten in the depths of prison.

They moved into a better-lit area and walked through a maze of corridors, eventually entering one with windows that allowed a view of the courtyard. As he suspected, the tall towers and walls of the Bastille rose around him. At least they locked him in a place familiar to him. He pushed the memories of the Bastille storming aside.

Shouts echoed in the courtyard. Guards led a group of around fifteen struggling women across the open space toward the stone walls that encased his hallway. Their noise rose as they drew nearer. A small group of them fought each step, dragging feet and flailing hands. The guards' faces strained, and they grunted, pinning the arms of the women to their sides. Women prisoners, all of them—scratching, furious women.

One shouted, screeching in fury, "Let us go! How dare you throw us into prison! You would be nothing without us." Her black, sunken eyes were pits of darkness. Matteo shuddered at the look of her, midnight hair flinging about as she clawed and shouted, kicking and resisting across the stone ground.

A pretty, golden redhead followed behind, more docile, though a look of supreme confusion flitted across her face. And next to her walked a neat, proper-looking, clean woman with white-blonde hair. Something about her downturned face seemed familiar. He nearly stumbled when his foot caught an uneven dip in the floor. As he passed each window, his neck strained to get a better view. How did he know this woman? Fate smiled on him when they all converged on the same set of doors, the loud, raucous women entering while his guards were attempting to exit out into the courtyard.

"Make way, I tell you. The lot of you. Out of the way." Matteo's guard shouted at them, using his arm to shove the nearest ladies aside.

The women and their guards paid him no heed, intent on their own struggle.

Matteo's eyes searched the crowd, not seeing the white hair anywhere. Disappointed, he was yanked through the door, and he stumbled out into the open courtyard.

"Glad I am to be out of that mess. Witches, they are." The guard wiped his brow.

Movement from the shadows caught his attention, a sleight of hand just large enough for his eye to take notice and follow. His arms stiffened in shock. A stunning pair of green eyes stared out at him from their darkened corner. *Scarlet.* Her features, her eyes, under a mass of white-blonde hair, dressed in a French costume. His arms jerked in the opposite direction when the guard began to move. But his eyes drank her in as long as he dared.

Shouts from behind the doorway made her jump, and she ripped off her wig, running along the shadows toward a set of doors. She pulled a cap out from her bodice, and before the door shut behind her, she pulled away at the skirts she wore and placed the flat cap on her head.

His mind tried to make sense of what he had just seen. Scarlet. He could not be mistaken. Those green eyes could not belong to anyone else. Another pair of green eyes, wrapped in a dark turban, flashed in his memory. Scarlet. His rescuer in the turban, this white-haired beauty, and his wife, all the same woman.

His feet trudged along, but he no longer saw his surroundings. The note to Buckley: *I will follow our usual methods.* Her sudden disappearances, her friendship with Simon, her home in Paris. How was it that she had been in Paris right at that moment when he'd needed to escape the city? Scarlet never travelled to France; at least, he didn't think she ever did, not dressed as herself anyway—except in the moment of his rescue at her home in Paris. Perhaps she visited more often than he'd realized. Because here she was in France right now, dressed as . . . someone. He felt her eyes follow him as the guards dragged him across the open space and down another corridor from there. One quick glance over his shoulder proved she watched him still, leaning up against a doorframe, dressed as a young lad. His heart pounded in shock and disbelief at what he was seeing. He didn't dare turn to see her again, hoping not to draw attention to her figure, hoping she could escape.

But he couldn't make sense of it. What was she doing with those women? He knew she helped the Pimpernel from time to time. She always played it off as some big game. Just as she played off her fashion act for the members of the *ton*. And now she was dressed as a lad? What if everything about her was one big act? What if she were far more involved in France than she let on, even to him? He reviewed again all he could remember about the green-eyed turbaned woman.

The league had given her great deference. And when the plans changed, she had taken charge and the others had followed with a practiced efficiency. Could she head up this gang? Work closely with the Pimpernel himself?

Hot, fiery jealousy filled him, almost whiting out his eyes. The only other man who could be worthy of such a woman as Scarlet would be the Pimpernel—and someone of her brilliance would surely be attracted to such a man.

Was he the reason for her change in allegiance? For her coldness in their marriage? The despair that always weighed him down deepened into a heavy knot. How would he ever win back the affections of his wife if she were also enamored with the Pimpernel? What had he ever done of equal valor? Instead of saving his fellow Frenchmen, Matteo had cowered, dancing attendance on the English nobility, selfishly engrossed in pursuit of a woman, of winning her heart.

Selfish, foolish, man!

He could never regret Scarlet, but his heart burned in shame when he thought of the time he'd spent away from his homeland.

The guards stopped in front of a door, this one cleaner, in a well-lit corridor. A smaller window on the front of the door showed him a room with a straw bed, a tiny upper window, and a chair. Much improved indeed, and he felt grateful for the blessing of a chair to sit upon. They used a large heavy key to unlock the door, unfastened the bands around his wrists, and then shoved him into the room. The lock clicked when the door shut behind him.

Chapter Twenty-Five

SCARLET HID BEHIND A TREE, grateful her veil and headdress shielded her face from the cold misty rain. The guard delivered one white carnation to Marie Antoinette, wrapped in a note. Scarlet awaited her response, hoped she would understand the change of plans and prepare to leave tonight.

Blast Matteo. Why was he in prison? Why was he in France? An icy fear gripped her whenever she thought about him. Focusing on any other task had required all her mental faculties.

Potier and his family were safe. She had received word that morning. The guards, planted at the fake address, had merely been waiting for Matteo on the chance he showed up. Éléonore knew he would come, knew Matteo better than Scarlet herself did, apparently. The knowledge scraped at her fresh wound.

And now, as a result, she would have to exert all her expertise in trying to save his life. Again, she had a strong desire to shake him for his stupidity; his presence here had put at risk all the other operations in play, including this now-rushed attempt to free Marie.

Ironic. Simon's letter, explaining Matteo's arrest and reaching her mere hours after her escape from the prison, could have spared her the shock of seeing him there. Thank the stars Matteo had had enough sense to school his expression and emotion. But Scarlet had seen his eyes. Shock, confusion, realization, and betrayal. How could one pair of eyes communicate so much in an instant? But she had felt it all, almost in tune with his own feelings.

The wall behind her had kept her still and anchored as she'd watched him walk away in chains. Rushing to change costumes, she again silently thanked her modiste. Bless the woman. She should have run straightaway, through the outer courtyard door, but she'd had to peer out, had to see Matteo. After he had rounded the corner, she'd turned and run, exiting out onto the street soon after.

Once in that courtyard, it had been relatively easy to leave the prison. In the public parts of the edifice, many would not question the presence of a young lad, a street urchin or messenger. She had been blessed at Matteo's arrival with his own guards so that she could slip away in the confusion, because leaving a locked cell—*that* was a near-impossible feat.

Still, she cursed Matteo. Now everything about Marie's rescue must be rushed—Marie, who, with her daughter, stayed in an entirely different prison with much tighter security, *La Conciergerie.*

Its walls loomed above her now while she waited for the queen's response.

And worse, she had to bribe the guard, a man she knew little about, to deliver the flower for her. Taking far too many risks, more than she ever took, Scarlet stood in the darkness, waiting for word. Movement drew her attention to the shadows. She crouched lower, holding her breath as a man tromped toward her, not hiding the sound of his boots on the pavement.

"Mademoiselle, she sent this out for you." He held out a slip of paper.

"Thank you, Enzo. Here is another something for your troubles." She offered a small bag of coins. "It means so much to have this last communication with my dear friend. Bless you for your kindness." Scarlet lifted her veil and wiped a tear from her face.

Enzo stood up taller and said, "You are quite welcome. She's a lovely lady, really. Kind to all the guards. If only she had lived a better life before now."

Scarlet nodded. "Thank you again, dear Enzo, and for your service to France. I suspect I'll come knocking shortly."

Waiting until he tromped away again into the shadows, she unfolded her missive. Marie had responded with pin pokes in the parchment. Adjusting her location to a moonlit patch on the street, energy coursed through Scarlet at the words, "I'll be ready."

A great breath of relief lessoned her tension, and she rushed to put the rest of her plan in motion.

Fifteen minutes later, she rapped on the door to the tower prison, dressed in the deep gray color of mourning, large hoops holding out her voluminous skirts. A sheer veil covered her face.

The guard opened the small square hatch and asked, "What do you want?"

"Oh, my kind sir. It is just I, Lady Scarlet Cavendish, emissary for Prince George himself, here to see my dear friend Marie again. I was here earlier in the week, you might recall."

She held her breath.

"Enzo! Do you remember this woman? Says she's from Prince George."

Enzo peered out at her, and then the door opened. "What's your business here again? You were given one visit; that is all."

Scarlet's voice pleaded, and she wrung her hands. "I know, I know, but I forgot to tell her just one more thing, and as we all know, she may not have long to live on this great earth of ours. Oh, please, might I have another moment with her?"

Enzo grunted and let her pass. He winked at her.

She reached for his hands, squeezing them, slipping him another small bag. "Oh, thank you! Thank you, my dear French friends. You are all that is goodness."

He pocketed the coins. "Five minutes. That's all you may have. We will knock on the door when you must leave."

The corridor stretched out, long and dark. For a moment, a deep foreboding filled her as she considered the finality of such a walk: long, sterile, and eerie.

When Marie's prison door opened, the woman ran to her, flinging her arms around Scarlet. "Thank you for coming! Oh, thank you, *mon amie*."

They heard the door shut behind them. Scarlet pulled her to the corner where no guard could see them. "We have no more time. Quick! Put on my things."

"What about my daughter? How will she escape?"

"But my dear, it will be simple." Their whispers fluttered into the darkness of the prison like the whoosh of butterfly wings.

To the guards outside, Scarlet hoped, they sounded as the words of a final goodbye. They rapped on the door. "Two more minutes!"

The women hastened, working as quickly as their fingers allowed. Marie gasped when she saw knives sewn into Scarlet's underclothing.

"Hush now."

When the men opened the door a few short minutes later, a very solemn woman exited, her large skirts billowing around her. She spoke not a word, hiding behind her veil, wiping tears and mourning the soon to be dead. Nodding to the guards as she passed, she stepped regally past them, a handkerchief at her nose.

Showing a rare form of decorum and respect, they let her out into the night with equal solemnity. Shutting the door behind her, one of the guards said, "I liked that one. Felt like she'd care for my own mother, she would."

The others guffawed in great heaves of laughter. "Gone soft, have you? Take care of your mother, indeed! She's aristo, as aristocratic as the rest, just lives in England; and word is, we aren't supposed to touch her—protected by her prince."

Another grunted. "Let's have a look at our bird in the tower, shall we? Do you suppose she's up and crying?"

They opened the hatch, taking turns peering into the room. Marie sat in the corner, face in her hands, her body shaking with sadness.

"Marie!" one of the men barked.

She turned from them. "Have you no shame? Leave me to my sorrows."

Satisfied, the men returned to their cards down by the entrance.

***

The veiled woman kept up her subdued pace and regal stature across the dark square and down an alley to the next cross street. A carriage door opened for her, the footman bowing. "Lady Cavendish."

She stumbled a bit as she climbed the steps, reaching for the footman's outstretched hand. After the door closed, she lifted her skirts. "Marie-Thérèse, are you all right?"

"Yes, Mama," a quiet voice answered. A young girl, small, emaciated, crawled out from under the gown and sat as closely as she could next to her mother on the carriage bench. Her tiny frame had crouched carefully and tightly to her mother's legs so that she would not be noticed.

"You were so brave. I am proud of you, *mon ange*. Now, sit close and be so very quiet."

The child nodded, brown eyes wide, her body trembling. Even at thirteen, she seemed young.

They rode through the streets of Paris, heading out and to the west. Simon handed over Scarlet's papers without incident, Marie-Thérèse again hidden beneath the voluminous skirts.

Once they left the streets of Paris behind them, Marie Antoinette relaxed against the carriage seat cushions, and her daughter rested her head in her lap.

Their driver opened the hatch above. "We have a two-day journey in this carriage, Your Highness. We will stop as little as possible. A basket rests on the floor with food and drink. Might I suggest you use this time to get some rest?"

Her voice quavered. "Thank you, ever so much."

"The Pimpernel will always do his best to see that innocents are saved. Your ship awaits at the port *Le Havre*. *The Sally* will sail at the earliest tide upon your arrival."

"Where is our destination?"

"Maine, Your Highness. The family Clough is ready to receive you there."

She nodded.

"And he has been purchasing up your things. I believe he even has your dressing table loaded on his ship, as well as your cats."

She brought a hand to her throat. "I don't know what to say. Bless you all for this wonderful act of mercy." She wiped away a lone tear from her cheek.

Marie-Thérèse reached for her hand. The two adjusted themselves for the greatest comfort and closed their eyes, hearts filled with hope for the first time in many months since the death of dear King Louis XVI. One small, sharp worry persisted, but Scarlet had assured her that her young Louis, the *dauphin*, now rightful king himself, would be spared also. The horses raced through the darkness toward the sea.

Chapter Twenty-Six

How had Marie Antoinette endured prison day after day? Scarlet fought her own restlessness, reading stories to a wad of pillows wrapped in bedding. Just a few more hours and the rightful monarch would be on board *The Sally*, and Scarlet could make her way out the window to her league below. If she must, she would make known her disguise, calling on her closeness to Prince George, but they might send her to the guillotine anyway; or, if they let her go, she would no longer be safe in France as Scarlet Cavendish. With any luck, she would hear the sound of rocks on her windowpane that very night and escape.

So far, the plan had worked just as she hoped. She turned away from the guards at mealtimes and found it easy to play the part of the lovely Marie, doting on her daughter, Marie-Thérèse. No one the wiser, her only danger had been a slow death by monotony.

Shouts from downstairs distracted her, as well as the clanking of metal and the sound of hooves on the cobblestone. She entered the main room of her two-room domain. Outside the door, loud hurried footsteps in the hallway rushed toward her.

When Scarlet recognized a shrill female command, she pressed her lips into a fine line and commanded her clenched fists to relax. Checking that her blades were still fastened to her bodice, she turned around with just enough time to face Éléonore head on, chin high.

"Oh, my dear Éléonore! How lovely of you to visit." She held her hands out in welcome, reaching for a quick embrace.

"Dispense with the pleasantries. We've come to arrest you."

Fanning her face nonchalantly, she said, "Arrest me? Don't be silly. As you can see, I am already in prison. And what is my crime? Playing nursemaid to the queen's lovely child?" Stalling for time to create an escape plan, she couldn't resist a bit of fun with the excitable Éléonore Duplay.

"For aiding in her escape. The former queen herself *and* her daughter left here two evenings ago, with your assistance."

Scarlet put on her most confused expression. "But how can that be? I've been reading stories to Marie-Thérèse these past several hours and all day yesterday. Just ask the guards. I feel it is all I ever do." Turning a pleading look to Enzo, she batted her eyelashes.

Enzo stared down at the floor with such a look of guilt, Scarlet knew how she had been discovered.

He stuttered, "She does do a lot of reading, citizen."

"Oh, shut up." Éléonore turned to the next room, walking briskly. "I will show you what you have been reading to, Lady Cavendish. I find it suspect that you are so very daft."

Scarlet followed Éléonore into the bedroom, mind spinning with possibilities for escape. When the bedcovers were thrown back to reveal cleverly placed pillows, Scarlet shrieked in shock. "But where is my little *ange*? Where is Marie-Thérèse?" She turned to the guards. "What have you done with her? Stolen her while I was sleeping?"

Grasping on to Éléonore by the shoulders, Scarlet gave her a little shake. "You must find Marie-Thérèse. Her Majesty will be so worried. I was to watch her carefully, read to her, and not let her up from bed because she was so very tired, recovering from a lung illness, I believe . . ." She raised her hand to her mouth. "Though I found it curious I heard no coughing. I have thought several times, if there is a lung disease, shouldn't there be coughing? I dared not wake her at the time of my thoughts, hoping she would rest well and be recovered before her mama returned—"

Éléonore reached out and slapped Scarlet's face, stopping her speech.

Scarlet prided herself that she did not flinch. Instead, a small smile played on her lips. Her ridiculous nonsense had probably carved years off Éléonore's life.

"Her mama is not returning! She is captured and on her way to the Bastille, where she will spend her last twenty-four hours and then be promptly executed."

Scarlet's heart may have stopped for the longest two seconds of her life, and then it commenced to pounding painfully in her chest. "No."

The responding shrieking laugh grated through Scarlet's head, leaving pain in its wake. "Oh, yes. Yes! Thought you were so clever, did you? Thought you could free the former queen of France? What kind of numbskulls do you think we are? As soon as I discovered your visit here to *La Conciergerie*, I knew something was afoot. It did not take long to find your carriage at the docks. Perhaps she would have set sail?" Éléonore's laughter tore at Scarlet.

Some small modicum of reason remained and helped her keep up her charade. "But the man told me she would return for her child . . ."

Shaking her head, Éléonore pointed a long bony finger in her direction. "Stop with the nonsense. Enzo has provided evidence against you: bribery of one of my most loyal guards, notes to prisoners, plans of escape. I have all the proof I need to throw you in jail and ensure that you never see the shores of England again, emissary or no."

"Prince George would not take kindly to that. If I do not return by a certain time, you will be hearing from him."

"If your head is already in a basket, I am unconcerned about whatever he might say to me." Waving her hands, she said, "Guards, arrest this woman." Then she leaned closer to Scarlet, resting a hand on her arm. "And Lady Cavendish, or should we say, Comtesse Durand, you are also guilty by marriage to a traitor. Marie Antoinette's head will roll early, as soon as possible. She has you to thank."

Scarlet's heart still performed unnaturally in her chest, and she willed her feet to move, but they would not. All senses dulling, she slipped into an emotional blackness. She fought the despair. What could she do? Surely there was something. But a thick blanket of nothing came to mind. No brilliant plans, no creative turns of phrases. She felt like the dead, as cold and silent as a fish. Another life slipping through her fingers . . . and Simon. A sliver of panic rose at the thought of losing Simon. Not knowing what else to do, she followed the guards out the door without comment. They marched down the hallway and into the night.

Once inside her carriage, Éléonore addressed Scarlet from her window. "We will take you immediately to Robespierre. He has some words for you before you will be thrown to your fate amongst the others in their cells at the Bastille."

Back to the Bastille? A flicker of hope reminded her Matteo was also in the Bastille. Did she not plan to go in after him at any rate? She was not without friends there.

But Marie. Her escape had fallen apart, every moment worse than the last. When Scarlet slowed, a guard nudged her forward gently but insistently.

Outside, under the night sky, she recognized a familiar sound, a dove cooing, but it did not fully register as important. Three steps later, it sounded again, and she almost stopped abruptly as some sense returned. The sound of a dove. She fought to hide her smile and then whistled three times in return.

"Be quiet, you." A guard held up a handkerchief, threatening to use it as a gag.

Scarlet's eyes scanned the night. Could that be her signal? Perhaps Simon remained free. Subtly, her eyes flicked to every corner in the darkness around her. Who would be here now, if not Simon?

The only carriage now out of sight, Scarlet shook her head at the ridiculous situation. "Will you be walking the distance with me?"

"No talking."

"Oh, come now. No harm in her knowing," Enzo interceded. "We aren't going to the prison straightaway."

"We aren't?"

"No. Seems you are wanted elsewhere first. Robespierre waits in a home nearby."

Yes, they had mentioned. Fear tightened in her gut. He would recognize her as the Seamstress and all ability to reason or bargain with the man would be lost. Any connection with the prince would mean nothing. Another sound of a dove filled the alley near her to the right.

Stepping out of the shadows from their left, a young boy approached.

"Sir. Might I have some help, please?"

"Be on your way, lad. You have no business being out at this hour, and we've no time for you. Now, be off!"

Abelino burst into tears. "But I'm so hungry. Please, have you a bit of bread? My mama is near starving she is, expecting a baby."

Scarlet found herself moved, even knowing she witnessed a deception. Such a clever lad. She waited, alert.

"Stop the racket, lad. Now, be off!"

Abelino only cried louder. Soon his sobs turned into wails, and he fell to a heap in front of them.

A group of people stepped into the light from the alley on their right.

"What's this here?" A tall and bony woman moved forward at the head of the group. "What's the matter, lad?"

A pause in the wailing brought a welcome quiet to the streets. He said, "He won't give me no bread, he won't. Not even for Ma. And I know he's got blunt in those pockets of his."

More people joined behind the woman, crowding.

The soldiers inched closer to each other, perspiration forming on Enzo's forehead.

She searched the crowd. Except for Abelino, she didn't recognize a single person.

He took to crying again. "I'm just so very hungry. Doesn't anyone have a bite for my family to eat? Or a coin?"

A burly man stepped forward. "Come now, I think you should help the lad."

Others pressed in behind him, their faces menacing.

Abelino opened his eyes wide, full of innocence and angst.

Scarlet turned her head downward, eyes searching the stone ground, hand over her mouth to stop the grin. This child was a natural for the stage; she should have employed him long ago.

The soldier fumbled about in his pockets. But as he patted down each one, he shrugged and said, "I don't have anything to give you. Now, run along."

A guard from the rear of their group called out, "Do you think it's our job to feed you? You mangy lot. Go feed your own. Be off! We have important work to be doing."

Abelino took to wailing again, even louder than before.

Scarlet shouted in dismay when the soldier's backhand sent Abelino tumbling to the side, toward the crowd.

"I said, get out of our way."

Enzo mumbled, "You shouldn't have done that."

The crowd surged forward, rushing in upon them. In short order, the guards were tied and sitting in the dark shadows of the alley, bruised and beaten, while Scarlet and the others ran in the opposite direction of her initial walk. Abelino joined her in the midst of the group of people and reached for her hand.

Her heart warmed. What a brave and brilliant child, and yet still so young. "You were amazing, my friend. And I'm looking forward to meeting everyone else. Many thanks are in order. And there is much to be done, tonight, if possible, and into next week if we are to save those who are dear to me."

His small hand squeezed her own. "We are almost there."

They turned down a side street and then poured through a door, pushing back into a small apartment until it accommodated them all. A stout, cheery woman greeted the few closest to her and then lifted her head, including them all. "Tea is on, and I have a bit of cake, if you'll be patient."

Someone in the back of the crowded space called out, "Should've had Lucien drop some by from his bakery."

Two buxom ladies chuckled to each other, nodding.

"Holding out on us, he is."

"Did I know we'd be about the task of rescuing tonight?" The man named Lucien held his hands up in a good-natured surrender.

"Quiet down. Let's hear what the lady has to say."

All eyes turned to Scarlet.

She cleared her throat. "I am at such a disadvantage. I don't know who I am to thank for such a brilliant rescue. And yet, I do thank you, with all my heart." Her voice caught and she brought a hand up to her mouth. "You see, I was about to give up." She shook her head and her eyes found the floor as she struggled to continue, her throat aching from the lump that had formed. "I have never been so low." She blinked back tears, and her eyes travelled the room, looking into their faces.

"What could we do *but* help you, my lady? When we heard that the very person who saved my dear Daniele—" A towering, broad man squeezed his eyes, fists pressing into them.

"And my Juliet."

"And Henri."

They each called out a name until everyone had listed a few.

Scarlet searched their faces. "The shop owners? Are you shop owners?"

A woman called out, "Some of us are now. We took over the shops left abandoned when the committee would have sent them all off to prison, except that you saved them."

They spoke of the shop owners who'd recently travelled to England on her ship. The Seamstress had rescued them all on her last trip to France, just days before.

"Saved my sister, you did. I'm not nearly as good at keeping shop as she was, but someone has to keep it going. We are hoping there'll be something to come back to when this mess is all over."

A small-framed man rested his hand on Scarlet's arm and said, "If it weren't for you, there'd be no point now, would there? It is we who are thanking you." He squeezed her arm for emphasis, his eyes misty with unshed tears. "Now, what do you need us to do?"

Scarlet's heart filled with wonder and gratitude. She had witnessed good people rise to help during the worst tragedies. And here they were again. It warmed her. She had one more question. "But how did you even know I was in need?"

A cheerful mumble rolled through the group, with a few chuckles and fond glances in Abelino's direction.

He blushed and said, "I told them."

"Ran from home to home, he did, pounding on our doors as if the darkness were after him."

Scarlet tousled his hair. "Thank you," she whispered.

He held his chin up and nodded at her.

The group responded in laughter, and then, a few at a time, they quieted, eyes on Scarlet.

She swallowed, unsure yet how to proceed but grateful for a new league of helpers and, though short, the blessed gift of time.

Her thoughts turned to Matteo, and she knew her safety amongst these lovely rescuers was short-lived.

Chapter Twenty-Seven

FILLING HER LUNGS WITH AIR and then slowly releasing it, Scarlet raised her hand to the door of the Bastille and gave it a sharp rap. The shop owners would be none too pleased, she knew, a note lying on the baker's table the only evidence of her return to the prison.

But they and Abelino busied themselves with their own tasks, a plan which she prayed would free her dear Marie and ensure the safety of the others who shared her denouncement list.

But she could no longer continue in the planning, not when Matteo still remained behind the stone walls of the prison before her. Her throat tightened at the thought of him. As ill-thought-out as her current actions might appear to be, what other choice did she have? Traitor or no, Scarlet would stay in prison with him, die with him if she must—but her plan was to free him. She swallowed. *Somehow.* With any luck, the same measures she took to help Marie and the others would benefit Matteo as well as herself.

The hour late and the street lights dim, the answering guard squinted at her. "Eh, what do you want? Be off with you."

"I seek an audience with Robespierre."

"An audience with Robespierre, she says." He turned his head to call to the man behind him. "This little slip of a thing seeks an audience with Robespierre."

The other guard's head peered around the edge of the great door, eyeing her with amusement. "Most don't seek him out. If he needs you, he'll find you, make no mistake."

She threw back the hood of her cloak that had shrouded her face. "But I come on official business from England, as emissary from Prince George himself."

They eyed her for a moment, hesitancy showing in their eyes, and then laughed in her face in great guffaws, spittle hitting her forehead. "In the middle of the night? With no carriage or anything to drop you off?" The first guard shewed her away with his hands. "Go back home to your mister."

"Maybe she doesn't have a mister. Is that it, miss? Hoping for a little attention this evening?"

Scarlet's toes curled in disgust. She would get nowhere with these brutes. Realizing she had overestimated their innovative acuity, or even their base intelligence, she changed tactics, knowing she risked a night in uncomfortable circumstances, but it couldn't be avoided.

The guards, leering, opened the door wider, beckoning for her to join them.

She straightened her spine. "No, gentlemen. I would not seek your company under any circumstances. Now, perhaps if you would tell Robespierre that the Seamstress has arrived, we can get somewhere with this."

The nearest guard sharpened his gaze and grabbed her arm. "The Seamstress, you say? Are you her?" He shook her a little as he searched her face, his own menacing.

"As I said. Now, please unhand me." She tried to peel his grip from her arm. "I'm here to speak with Robespierre."

"Oh, you'll see him, all right, on your way to the scaffolding outside."

Their low laughter chilled her, but her courage burned brightly. "If you could just tell him that I am here . . ."

The guard pulled her in through the door, hand gripping her arm tighter. "We'll tell him in the morning. First, it might do you some good to spend a night with the other aristo scum and traitors." He dragged her behind him, deeper into the prison. "Because of you, I was sent to solitary with the rats! Thought you were so clever, turning in false names. Guards searching into the night for people who don't exist." He shook her arm and picked up the pace. "We'll see how clever you are now, won't we?"

They continued on a swift march through the many converging passages in the Bastille. Her arm bruised beneath his fingers, but she concentrated on moving her feet quickly enough under her skirts to keep up with him. She had not predicted such an angry reaction from the guards at the gate, and she hoped they wouldn't forget about her in her cell for too long.

The prison hallways darkened the farther they walked, and the air grew staler, the ground softer, and the noises behind doors more desolate. Low moans and cries escalated as she approached doors, and then faded behind her as they hurried past. At length, they drew near the farthest door down a long hallway of hopeless noise. The guard pulled out his keyring, opened the door, and pushed her inside without another comment. Before he could close the door all the way, she called out, "Miss Duplay will reward you for my presence here. She will want to deal with me herself."

The guard grunted and shut the door in her face.

Rot and stench hung in the air. Reaching for her handkerchief, she held the white fabric up to her nose and mouth, but it did little to prevent the odor from overpowering her. The attempt not to breathe brought on dizziness. As she turned to face the room and allowed her eyes to adjust to the blackness, she leaned back against the door.

As she searched her new surroundings, dark shapes sharpened in her vision to become bodies, many other people who had claimed a bit of dirt to sit or lie upon. Very little space remained for her body to join them. Still too dark to see into the corners or much farther into the room, she stepped two feet to the right and made to sit down, but her foot nudged something soft. "Oh, I'm sorry." She stepped back in front of the door and gingerly lowered herself to the ground, leaning her back against the wood frame. Alert, she tried to distinguish outlines of people.

The room must have quieted when the guard opened the door, because now that she had settled, small whimpering noises, rustling, and motion along the far wall startled her. A gentle cooing sound followed, and the tones of a comforting female voice soothed.

Adjusting her handkerchief, she gagged as the full strength of the smell in the room entered her nose. Human waste, vomit, body sweat, and stench of many days without washing all assailed her, but more than that, illness, possibly death and decay. Her eyes scanned the room again, attempting to make out a clear image.

The sound of retching followed by the contents of someone's stomach hitting the ground sounded to her right.

"Are you ill?" Her small voice carried.

No one responded.

She nudged the person immediately to her right. "Excuse me, will we get light enough to see, in the morning?"

Waiting without success for a response from anyone, she leaned her head against the door and closed her eyes.

At length, after many hopeful attempts throughout the night to see the light of morning, she opened her eyes again and gray light filtered in through a grate on the upper wall. Adjusting her legs and shifting her weight, she waited for feeling to reenter her lower extremities.

The sleeping forms of the very ill lay about the room. Some had caregivers, allowing their laps as pillows, but most rested heads or even cheeks on the filthy floor. "Oh, you poor dears." Her voice was just a murmur.

"I'm afraid we are all very ill, or soon will be." The soft form she had nudged shifted, and an older man struggled to sit up.

Scarlet immediately rose to assist him and felt heat from his body through his clothing. "Oh, sir. You have a fever."

He chuckled a little, which turned into a great fit of a hacking cough. When he finally regained control, he leaned his head back against the wall and took in great, rasping breaths of air. "Yes, I've had the fever for two days now, many of the others for longer."

"What can be done? How may I assist you?"

He turned to her, and she recognized a familiar twinkle in his eyes.

"Do I know you?"

"It's difficult to tell in the dark, but you do seem familiar, remind me of the wife of a dear friend." He inclined his head to her, as if in a bow. "I am Antoine de Gramont."

Her heart pounded, and she said, "Antoine VII? Duke of Gramont?"

He turned to her, his body weak but his eyes alight. "Could you really be? You are not Rupert's wife, Scarlet?"

"Oh, Antoine! I am." She leaned into him, squeezing his weakened frame to her own. Tears wet her cheeks. "But you are alive. I heard they had taken you, one of the first. We all thought you dead."

"Scarlet, my dear friend. It is you. God has answered my prayers for a bit of sun in my last days on earth. But I pray you are an angel only and not really before my eyes." His head turned away from her, and he began mumbling to himself.

"Antoine." She shook his arm.

He turned back to her. "Oh, Scarlet, there you are. Perhaps I shall see Rupert today, no? Shall I deliver a message from his wife?"

A sob caught in her throat. "Yes. Please give him my love." Her eyes searched his face, memorizing what she could see in the dark. He and Rupert had been dear friends, Antoine spending a full summer three years past at their estate with his family. She had been devastated to hear of his capture and sudden death, one of the first, and England had reeled from the atrocity of it all. Soon after, she and Simon had created her league and planned their first rescue, always regretting she had not stepped in sooner to save dear Antoine.

Antoine's breathing fell into a rasping rhythm beside her, his head tilting to the side and bobbing forward now and then. She moved closer to him and pulled him toward her, resting his head on her lap.

He sighed, and a small smile played on his lips before succumbing to a deeper rest, his breathing shallow but steady. Grateful she could provide some small comfort to Antoine, Scarlet leaned her head back against the door again, watching the others.

Chapter Twenty-Eight

MATTEO'S PEN HASTILY SCRATCHED ALONG the small slip of paper he had found hidden underneath his bowl of porridge. Comforted in knowing that some in the prison befriended him and were loyal to the Pimpernel, he wrote all that he knew to Simon, answering his questions and hoping for an easy escape solution.

He stared again at Simon's letter. Evidence of Potier's safety and that of his former neighbors and friends shamed him for his lack of trust. Everyone around him behaved with much better bravery and decorum than he, it seemed. He must improve, better himself, prove to Scarlet his worthiness.

The next lines intrigued him. The queen was expected in the prison today? She had previously been imprisoned at *La Conciergerie*. If they moved her, something had changed, and it did not bode well for her safety.

His mind scrolled through all the information he had learned about the Bastille's day-to-day management. A new idea began to form, simple, obvious even. He scratched a few more lines to Simon. He wouldn't be able to do much himself, and they had little time, but the league should be able to get everything in place. His plan was a bit gruesome, but if they carried it out just as he described, they would free the queen in the next few days, if possible.

A rap sounded at the door; four brisk taps—Abella, the food wench. He could only guess the horrors she witnessed every day, poor soul. He vowed to rescue her when he left.

He gently greeted, "Hello. I am almost finished."

She nodded, scared eyes searching the room, darting from corner to corner, though surely she knew he was alone in the cell.

He folded the paper, mimicking the missive he had received, and hid it carefully again beneath the porridge. "Thank you. You are an angel of mercy."

Her large soft eyes turned to him and glistened. A small smile played on her lips, and then she studied the floor.

He tipped his head, trying to once again cross her line of sight. "Might I ask you a few questions?"

She nodded and dared another glance up into his face.

"How many servers like you are staffed in the kitchen?"

She thought about it and shrugged.

"How many work with you in these hallways?"

Her small voice almost faded into the stone. "Two, sometimes three here on the north side."

He reached forward to finger the fabric on her dress at her shoulder. She flinched and stepped back at his touch.

He pulled back is hand slowly. "I'm sorry. I am curious about your clothing. Do you all wear the same uniform?"

She shook her head. "*Non.* They gave me this, but everyone's are different." Her face paled, and she held her stomach. "*Vêtements des morts.*" Her barely audible whisper stung him, sending a chill reverberating through his bones.

Clothes of the dead? For a child.

She started backing out of the room, tray in hand. "I need to get back. They whip me if I take too long."

"Yes, of course. One more thing I must know. Tell me, do any prisoners die in the prison?"

She swallowed twice. "Yes."

"I am sorry to dwell upon the sadness of death, but what do they do with their bodies?"

She knew, and she told him.

"Thank you. Bless you, my dear friend." He waited until the door shut behind her before clenching his shirt in his fists. He tried not to think what she left his cell to face. How could they treat her, a young girl, so? Surrounded by the wails of the terrified, wearing the clothes of those recently executed, the child had little good to inspire her; and yet she took great risks inside these walls, undoubtedly saved many and surely brought hope to many more. An angel, not yet departed, but all the more real for it.

Four days passed, and he wondered at his supposed visitor. The notes continued from Simon, and hope lightened Matteo's time in the prison, which otherwise would have filled his life with darkness. His yearning for sunlight could not be quenched, challenged in strength only by his desperate need for Scarlet.

Simon had been silent in her regard. Matteo's assumption that she had escaped the prison and was now waiting for him somewhere kept his heart alive and his mind active. A person could quickly lose his lucidity in such a place otherwise, with nothing to incite or activate productive thought. By a strict force of will and the many plans and communications from Simon, he was able to stave off the awful restless insanity that often infected those in dark, solitary confinement.

Abella's visits were also a balm. He had communicated to her his plan to rescue her from this place.

Her first worry, the first question to come out of her mouth? "But what of the others who come after? Who will help them?"

***

Hours into the third full day locked in her prison cell, Scarlet heard Antoine's last breath, his head again resting in her lap. Her tears fell onto his face, but they were not full of sadness. A profound peace filled their small patch of ground, and she breathed out in relief that his suffering had ended. Shaking her head in weak frustration that a good man had been allowed to suffer so, she then bowed it in a prayer over his life, his family, and his estate, sending him off in peace and love.

Moments after she shifted her body and gently laid his head on a slip of fabric, voices in the hallway reached her ears. Éléonore's shrill tones were, for once, a welcome sound.

"No harm is to come to her. We mustn't upset relations with England. She will live for now, but I have my own plans." Her laugh, loud and menacing, was just outside their door.

A wave of dizziness overpowered Scarlet's vision as she stood. In the moment the guards opened the door, she nearly collapsed to the ground but steadied herself against the wall, slowing her breathing. Her head pounded, and her hands felt clammy.

"Overwhelmed by my very presence, are you?" Laughing again, she pointed to Scarlet. "See, she can barely stand. Take this sorry excuse for a woman and follow me. We have an appointment with *La Guillotine*."

The guards reached for her to roughly drag her along, but when her knees wobbled and she almost collapsed, each stood at her sides and half-walked, half-carried her, following Éléonore back down the hallway. She clucked her tongue. "You think you are so clever playing at disguise. But I have found you out."

Scarlet hardly noticed their surroundings; her mind was wrapped in a confused, circling nightmare. After what felt like a breath or two, she stood blinking in the sunlight on a platform in front of *La Guillotine*. The sun cleared her fog, and she recognized her place of honor as the stage for visiting dignitaries and Robespierre himself to watch the beheadings. The rhythmic drumming of the crowd and the wailing of the prisoners in carts brought bile to her throat. She leaned to the side, retching only air, and used her now dirty and soiled handkerchief to wipe a bit of saliva from her mouth.

"Hold her up. She must watch this," Éléonore called from behind.

Fingers of alarm began to spread through her core. She searched the prisoners for Matteo's dark hair. Her anxiety heightened the longer she looked. Then a great cheer rose up in the crowd, and Robespierre himself walked out onto the platform.

He held his arms out toward the people, and they quieted. "We have long fought the system of government here in France."

The crowd responded with a shout of death.

"We tired of the elaborate clothing of the aristos when our children had none. Tired of the carriages and equipages tearing through our streets, running us down, while we walked without shoes. And why was the food scarce from our tables?"

The crowd stood in a frenzied, crying mass.

"Because the wealthy ate it all and then taxed us for their privilege."

The crowd, becoming angry, shook their fists and snarled, shoving each other and seeking for a wealthy person to blame.

Scarlet stepped back away from the edge of her platform.

"But we are almost finished. France is almost cleansed. Only a few remain, and today, I bring you a great victory! I bring you one of France's worst problems, with her finery and her parties and her waste and her food!"

Scarlet's heart rose to her throat. "Oh no. Oh no." She searched the lines of people, searched the carts, looked among the guards.

Robespierre continued. "Thanks to our gracious Seamstress,"—when he pointed in her direction, the eyes of every person in the crowd turned to her, and she stood frozen, not daring to make even a change in facial expression—"we bring you today, Marie Antoinette."

The shouts of the people filled Scarlet's head, slammed through her ears, and ached all the way into the center of her soul. Then, at the edge of a group of prisoners, three guards stepped forward, shoving aside the crowd in their way, and led her lovely friend Marie forward through the crowd of people, who soon learned to part and make way.

Tears filled Scarlet's eyes. She was not close enough to see facial expressions or really to make out any of her features, but Marie walked regally, with head held high, slowly, gracefully, through the crowd of jeering, cruel bystanders. She stepped carefully up onto the stairs, circled around, and stood before the square. How changed she seemed! Gray strands of stringy hair fell down around her shoulders midway down her back under a white wig thrown, tilted and haphazard, onto her head. Her frame, instead of round and buxom, had become sharp and emaciated. No finery, cheeks sunken, she hardly looked herself. If Robespierre had not announced her, Scarlet would not have recognized her friend.

Scarlet shook her head, waving her arms. "No, no. I do not denounce her. It is a lie." Her eyes not leaving the slender form of her friend, Scarlet willed her to understand. Never had she felt so helpless in the face of need. But even as her mind scrambled and she exercised every available possible option for rescue, she could not summon anything useful.

And then Robespierre indicated they were to begin, the crowd growing ever restless. Marie was forced onto her knees, her head placed chin down onto the semicircle carved for that purpose, and with a swift release of the rope, she was gone.

Scarlet collapsed into a heap on the platform, and the world went black around her.

Chapter Twenty-Nine

MATTEO'S HEAD HIGH, HE PACED off his energy. Today he would escape this place, find Scarlet, and work together with her to put an end to the terror in France. The plan was in motion, including a brilliant rescue of Her Majesty, Marie Antoinette. Within moments of preparing himself to leave the cell, his door slammed open and a sobbing, hysterical Scarlet was thrown in to him, landing in a heap at his feet. Immediately he reached for her, pulling her trembling, heaving body into his arms.

"What have you done to her?"

His cry went unheard. His cell door had already closed. Sitting in his only chair, he cradled her, hugging her to his chest. Her frame was much thinner, her lips dry and cracked. "There, my love. It is I, Matteo." He lifted his tankard of water and wet her lips.

She swallowed eagerly and then rested her head against his chest. "I wish to sleep."

He whispered endearments, rubbing her back and running his hands through her hair until she quieted and the time between her shudders lengthened.

Eventually, her breathing evened and slowed, and he could tell by the new rhythm she must be asleep. Sadness pricked him at the reminder of his, as yet, unfamiliarity with her sleeping frame, but he pushed that aside and went about the task of checking her for any obvious injuries. Without disturbing her position or closeness to him, his eyes travelled over the limbs he could see. She seemed physically unharmed. He adjusted his body and his arms so that he could withstand many hours holding her while she slept, and then he closed his own eyes, enjoying the rise and fall of her chest and the feel of her heartbeat.

His mind worked through the plan. How would they accommodate her escape? He reviewed scenarios and options, questioned, and studied. There had to be a way to free her as well. If Simon had not already been apprised, he would need to know as soon as was possible. He hoped it was Abella who brought the food at supper. He guessed she would come in a few more hours.

After a good long rest and all of Matteo's limbs beginning to feel numb, Scarlet stirred in his arms. She gasped in a sharp breath and opened her eyes. Making a slight whimpering sound, she whipped her head around to face him, tensing. Then, making out his features, she fell back against him, breathing out in relief. "Matteo."

"Yes, I'm here."

She remained quiet for a moment. "How long have you been here in prison?"

"I don't know exactly. I may have missed count at the beginning, but I think it has been seven days."

She nodded. "That sounds right. Have you heard from Simon?"

"Yes."

"Good."

She seemed to be calculating, clearing her brain, trying to make sense of things. He didn't know how soon he could begin asking the flood of questions that came pouring into his mind. When he acknowledged one, another one came crowding in on its heels. He had never seen her so visibly tortured, so emotionally distraught. A part of him greatly feared a return of that pain to her by asking the wrong question.

Instead, he tried a statement. "I saw you."

"Yes."

"You escaped from the prison?"

"Yes."

"But you are back?"

A great sigh of air left her lungs. "Unfortunately."

When her face turned up to his, her eyes inches from his own, his breath caught at the great sadness they reflected.

"I thought it was a good idea to come for you, an official visit of sorts. But the guard knew the Seamstress, and he . . . he . . ." She stopped and covered her face with one hand while she tried to compose herself.

The dull ache in his chest sharpened. "What can I do?" Anything he could do to relieve the pain on her face, he wanted to spend all his energies doing.

She shook her head, took two deep breaths, and continued. "Marie died today, earlier than planned, before we could save her. Because of me."

"Who? The queen?" That could not be true.

"He ordered her execution, called for her to be brought out so I could see it for myself. So altered I did not recognize her. But she walked out, head held high, a queen to the end."

Something sounded wrong. That had not been the plan. She should have been passed out, carried by the guard. A new anxiety gripped him. "You saw it? Saw her . . ."

"Yes, I did. My dear Marie. I do not even know how her daughter fares. I have failed again. Matteo, I cannot go on. It is too much." She curled into him, bringing her knees up to her chest, and closed her eyes.

"Surely it is not your fault. You take too much on yourself. Please, Scarlet, do not blame yourself for this."

But she would not respond. She kept her eyes squeezed shut, and after a moment, her body began the restless twitching of the unconscious. Sleeping again. He pulled her closer to him. Something seemed terribly wrong with her. She felt unnaturally warm. He cradled her the best he could while his mind raced with possibilities. If Her Majesty walked out, unassisted, then it was possible she did in fact lose her life to *La Guillotine*. Restless, crazed images and thoughts flashed through his mind, bringing with them a rush of worry and a racing heart. He wished for the evening meal to come and with it some information from Simon.

He studied Scarlet: her hair, the graceful turn of her neck, the slight pink on her cheeks, the three freckles on her nose. Always his balm. He felt his mouth turn up in the grin of new love while he watched her sleep, her chest rising and falling in soft little breaths.

The room began to warm, or he did, with another body pressed against him. And soon, the clothing between them felt wet with perspiration. Drops collected on his forehead and he longed to wipe his face before they dripped onto his precious wife, but he daren't disturb her.

She shifted in her sleep and smiled. "Matteo," she mumbled and turned to his chest.

A great happiness and relief filled him. Something about that gesture—turning to him, even in sleep—warmed him and gave him great courage. Whatever it was she desired, he would be at her side. His grin widening, he squeezed her closer to him, tilting his head to watch her face.

"And now I might be ill at the sight of you." Éléonore's shrill voice grated his nerves, and Scarlet startled in her sleep.

"Have a care, Éléonore, and do be quiet." He scowled at her.

She slammed the hatch on their door shut and ordered the guards to open the door. Matteo braced himself.

Her hips swiveled as she walked. Once she was completely in the room, she ordered the guards out. "But leave the door open, please, the stench is overwhelming." Holding her nose under a handkerchief, she cackled a horrible screechy laugh.

Scarlet's eyes fluttered open. She watched Matteo's face. "I thought she was just interrupting my dreams. But here she is."

He nodded.

Louder, she asked, "Is she dressed as dreadfully as last time?"

Not even bothering to hold back his chuckle at his wife's superb humor, he turned his head to Éléonore, allowed his eyes to travel from her feet to her hair, and tilted his head to the side. "I don't know. I'm not the best judge, but I'd say worse. Or she has some kind of costume today, I don't know."

Scarlet eyed him, refusing yet to look at her. "Costume, you say? Is there a ball? A masquerade? Oh, Matteo, we must attend."

"Hmm. No, not that kind of costume. You'll have to see for yourself, to be sure, but I do believe she's going for a certain look here, a tone, as it were."

"Oh, if I must. My fashion expertise is needed everywhere, I tell you. French prison is a first, I must admit, but . . ." She turned in his arms so that she faced Éléonore. "Oh, dear, you are right. Dreadful; worse even than the last we saw her." Scarlet moved her hand to her mouth and shared a look with Matteo before turning back to Éléonore. "Prison officer."

Éléonore snapped, "What?"

But Scarlet turned to Matteo as if she hadn't spoken. "The words you are looking for, her costume. Prison officer."

"Well done! You've hit upon it precisely. That's the tone. Black clothing, sickly pale skin, glinting evil eyes—"

"Enough! I have had enough of the both of you!"

They each looked into the face of the other in turn and began giggling, then laughing, and then holding their stomachs with hilarity at Éléonore's rage until she turned and walked out of the cell, slamming the door behind her.

"Hmm. Perhaps we should not have done that." Matteo's nose almost touched Scarlet's as they looked into each other's eyes.

The hatch on their door opened again, and Éléonore's squinty eyes glared at them through the grate. "Do you think I am so stupid? I have figured you out, Comtesse." She spit the word out as though it were vile to her. "Oh yes, I recognized right away who you are. Parading around as this Seamstress person, aiding that vile Pimpernel. There will be no dinner this evening. Your comfort does not concern me. Your lives are worthless, except for the slightest chance that your presence will attract the Pimpernel. I will return in the morning before breakfast, and we will see how things go. If your humility has not returned, we will withhold food again until I see a better demeanor from the both of you." The hatch shut, and they heard footsteps, hers and the guards', walking down the long corridor outside their cell.

"Quickly, while we have time, let me have your jacket." Scarlet stood and then faltered, her legs giving way beneath her.

"Scarlet! You must drink something." His arm around her waist kept her standing.

After she had several sips of water, she began contorting at all angles, reaching up and under the skirts of her dress.

Matteo was immediately distracted by her lovely ankles and petite little feet.

She stopped and smiled. "Would you mind averting your eyes?"

He turned his back, embarrassed that he had been watching her and chagrined, frustrated, and impatient that as her husband, he did not know every part of her intimately. Back still turned, he held his jacket out to her and felt her relieve him of it.

"You may turn around."

Mouth gaping, Matteo took two steps to get a closer look. On her lap were three knives, a small sewing satchel, and a long pouch that he guessed she wore, moments ago, strapped to her leg. "Brilliant. Charming, beautiful, and a prison escape expert."

Scarlet's small smile was her only response while she quickly and efficiently began ripping at the seams in his jacket sleeve. "I had to give up the pistol when they searched me at the gate."

"Really? You had a pistol hidden about your person?"

Her lovely laughter warmed him. "No," she teased, and he loved her all the more for it.

Shaking his head, Matteo sat beside her on the bed. "And my jacket?"

"I'll be concealing two of these knives in your jacket sleeve. But be careful. Robespierre has one also."

"How could you know . . ." His voice trailed off. A part of him knew he would discover more by plain observation than she would be willing to divulge through conversation.

But she surprised him with a response. "I sewed the pocket for him. When you saw me against the prison courtyard wall, I was dressed as the Seamstress, a . . . person I pretend to be while I am here, and Robespierre needed hidden knife pockets in all his sleeves. But I included something extra, so if he uses his knife against you, it will be his downfall."

He waited for her to further explain, but she said nothing more, her fingers moving swiftly now as she created a place for him to hide a knife.

"So, you had a cover . . ." He watched in silence as she finished one sleeve, slipped the knife inside, and then began work on the other. "You are really quite brilliant."

She smiled and kept working, eyes squinting in the dark, leaning to the side to place her stitching in the small patch of light that filtered in through the rectangle opening at the top of the wall. At length, she finished the other sleeve and then held out the jacket for him to put on. "Practice accessing the knives. If you shake your arm down just so"—she demonstrated with a sharp shake of her hand in a downward motion—"the knife should come forward into your hand. If that doesn't work for you, use the opposite hand to grab it. Figure out what works best, and become accomplished at it."

He nodded and immediately began shaking his arm, trying to summon the knife into his grip. On the first try with his left hand, he felt the knife handle fall into his palm. Smiling victoriously, he held it up for her to see. Then he carefully returned it to the pocket, the point of the blade entering first.

They needed to talk, about so much. Since she seemed reluctant to do so, he could begin at least with some of the more urgent matters. "About Éléonore—"

"I don't want to hear about Éléonore. I've had enough of that woman and her loathsome ways. Friend of yours or not, I cannot abide—"

"She is no friend of mine, Scarlet. Please, hear me out." He waited.

Her face pinched, wary, but she nodded.

"I have been enduring her intrusion into my life since I was a child. When we were younger, we played together, at first because my father impressed upon me the need to be kind, but then I took a liking to the adventures we would have together. We made use of servants' hallways and the tops of trees and the dark of the woods to sneak around and creep up on people and act as the protectors and saviors of France. As youth, we would pretend to lead out in a revolution for freedom.

"But very shortly upon leaving my childhood, she became a dangerous burr, and I have lived in wariness of her temper and under the thumb of her goodwill until you rescued me, not just from France but from her clutches. That moment in the cabbage cart? I felt free for the first time in years."

He searched her eyes, trying to show his sincerity, seeking a place inside her heart that would understand. "She has threatened my closest friends, implicated me in their deaths, threatened and blackmailed me at every turn, imprisoned me—twice now—and ordered my execution. I have absolutely no feelings of any positive nature for the woman and in fact constantly battle the evil thoughts of wishing for her death.

He knelt in front of her, holding her hand in his own. "Please, Scarlet, I thought you of all people would understand and not become one of the many voices accusing me of some kind of alliance with her." He needed her to understand. It had suddenly become the most important goal of his existence that she believe him and know where he stood with Éléonore Duplay.

The lines on her forehead softened. "Of course, Matteo. I should have seen it. When you say it like that, I see that for you to still harbor any kind of good feelings for the woman would be the most ridiculous thing in the world." She reached forward and placed a hand at the side of his face. "I am sorry for ever thinking it of you. Might I ask you to clarify for me a few things?"

His heart filled with hope. Would he finally understand whatever chasm had come between them?

He nodded. "Of course. You may ask me anything."

"You said she implicated you in the deaths of your friends. Did she, in fact, sign your name?"

He grimaced. "She did, but it is worse than that. She produced evidence against them in the form of letters I wrote."

"You wrote?"

He sat on the straw and dipped his head into his hands. "Yes. As youth, we began our own letters of denouncement, taking down as evidence all unjust treatment we saw around us. Years before the committee even thought of it."

"But why did you do this? What did you hope to gain?"

"It began, for me, when the de Moliers refused food to a starving child. The poor thing could hardly remain standing, so weak she was. She held out a shaking hand and asked for a bit of bread while crouching outside the bakery. The comtesse barely took notice and shooed her away to clear the path for her daughter behind her. The child was knocked to the ground in the process and did not move."

Scarlet's face lined with sorrow. Her hands gripped the fabric of her dress.

He marveled at her obvious love for his people. "I ran to her, carefully lifting her to my arms, but weakness had overtaken her body. Rushing to the apothecary down the street with the child still in my arms, I called to anyone inside. The man behind the counter said she needed water, and he also gave me a tea to have brewed for her.

"Not knowing where she belonged, I brought her home with me. The servants had compassion for her and we all did the best we could, but we were too late. She passed away in my home that evening." The memory of her small and helpless frame still burned at the back of his mind. When he closed his eyes, he could see her on the back of his lids.

Scarlet reached for his hand. "You are a good man."

"I felt angry, sad, devastated, and angry again. I blamed the de Moliers. Then I blamed everyone around me for their rich lifestyles, their wasteful spending, their ignorant walks in life. It soon became everyone's fault an innocent child had died of starvation. Every new dress became a month of meals stolen from a poor family. With excess all around me, I soon became a very bitter and unhappy youth."

"I can easily see how this would have ruined the peace of a goodhearted soul."

He shrugged. "So I began a journal of sorts. It helped my peace of mind. When I saw an injustice, instead of letting it fester and destroy my happiness, I reported it in my journal, wrote a letter about it as if to a rule of law, and it worked. I felt better."

She eyed him thoughtfully. "And because of it, your soul was spared the devastating damage from bitter, resentful wounds." She turned his hand over in her small ones and began tracing lines on his palm, thoughtfully, carefully, her brow furrowed. "And Éléonore has this journal?"

He nodded. "Yes. And has already denounced a family because of it, using my observations as evidence against them."

"Have you warned the others?"

"I sent them letters the moment I heard her plans, and I have enlisted the aid of the Pimpernel." He paused, waiting for her reaction when he mentioned the man. Seeing none, he continued. "Simon has informed me the families are all accounted for and safe."

"Potier as well."

He blushed in embarrassment. *Did she know the details of his own capture?* "Yes, long before I showed my sorry face to rescue him, he had been safely on the road and away from any danger. I should have trusted, listened, but I felt so alone, unheard. I couldn't bear another moment waiting around in safety while my actions were possibly putting people to death."

She squeezed his hand. "I would have done the same."

He turned to her, eyes widened. "You would?"

"Without a doubt. I am sorry for not understanding. We should have involved you from the beginning." She shrugged her shoulders. "I only hoped to spare your life. Yours is particularly at risk here, you know, and we worried your presence would endanger the mission and yourself."

He did not know how to act around this new Scarlet. She was the same as ever and yet different. He could also sense a new delicate thread holding her together; somehow he knew that thread wore ever thinner and that as strong as she appeared, her growing fragility could easily break, and at any moment.

But he had to understand. "You were so different. Our wedding night . . ." He almost winced when he said it. Dare he bring it up?

"I should have talked to you, asked you, but I didn't know what to do, and I was off to France the next morning." She paused and then smiled sheepishly, possibly trying to cloak a hint of vulnerability. "So, you weren't secretly meeting with Éléonore?"

"I was."

Scarlet moved backward on the bed, leaning away from him. A new fear entered her eyes. "Matteo?"

"She blackmailed me. Threatened to use the journals and letters against innocent lives if I did not try to help her track down the Pimpernel. Demanded meetings and attendance at parties with her, all the while using me as her spy. And then the prince asked me to watch her, keep her away from as many as possible. I didn't know where to turn for help, so I kept her happy, giving her nothing, until one evening I had had enough and told her to leave me alone. The next day I sailed for France myself." He dared a look at her face and was taken aback by the joy that shined in her eyes.

"Oh, Matteo, I am so sorry. How I have doubted you, mistrusted."

He stood and pulled her to her feet in front of him. "You were worried I was having secret trysts with Éléonore, romantic trysts?"

A deep rosy blush filled her face, and she closed her eyes against the pain, easily discernible there, and then nodded.

He longed to kiss her closed lids. "No, no, my dear. I can see how you would have thought this. Éléonore did her best to lead many to believe such a thing was happening between us. You are not to be blamed. But let me reassure you now, my dear Scarlet. The moment I first saw you at my rescue, dressed in your finery at your home in Paris, I became lost to all other women. You are the answer to the longing of my heart. I cannot feel whole without you, and no other could ever stand in your place."

Her eyes glowed with happiness as she watched his face.

He chose his words carefully, trying to explain the depth of his sincerity. "And further, I made promises to you. I do not take my wedding covenant lightly. I pledged myself to you. I will honor, protect, and be loyal to you until the last breath of my life. Your happiness is my everything, the very purpose that I breathe. Please know I am your constant. The one thing you can count on, forever."

She wrapped her arms around him, squeezing him, hands stretched around to his back as far as they could reach. His heart overflowed with relief, joy, the pure happiness of being alive with Scarlet, who loved him. The world forgotten, he held her, loved her, and swayed in place, lost to anything but the feel of her body pressed up against his, her heartbeat pounding near his.

She tipped her head back and up, her lips seeking his. He covered them with his own instantly and felt the comfort of the home fire transform to a blazing white-hot brand, singeing him to his marrow. His body burned with recognition. Scarlet. She filled him, completed him. Every movement of her hands as they ran up his chest and across his back left burning trails of awareness. His wife. Her lips hot, her flesh searing, he pulled her closer, pressed her more insistently against him. But her cheeks felt clammy and something registered; some sense of logic returned. "You're too warm."

"Mmm?" she mumbled against his lips.

"Your skin. It is so warm, scalding." He brought a hand up to her forehead. The heat from her head nearly scorched him. Panic chilled him. "You have a fever."

Her body began to tremble, to shake and shiver. "I do feel unwell of a sudden." Her teeth chattered. "And so cold." Her arms pulled inward and wrapped around herself. He pulled her closer to him again, rubbing her back to warm her. She wiggled under his palms. "No, that almost hurts. Just hold me." She swayed on her feet. "I need to lie down."

And then he lost her. Eyes rolling back into her head, she shut them involuntarily and collapsed in his arms.

He rushed her to the straw and laid her down, covering her with his jacket. He again placed his hand on her head, and she felt even warmer than before.

He ran to the door, pounding, shouting, and desperately calling out, "Please! She is ill. I need help. Please. Come quickly."

He rushed back to Scarlet and held her hand. Trying to remember his childhood illnesses, his mind searched for ideas to help her feel more comfortable. He knew he must immediately loosen her stays and remove some of her clothing layers. But she shivered in cold. She would be miserable. Her skin felt so dangerously, unnaturally hot that she must be cooled down. He longed for his dear housekeeper. She had nursed him through many an illness and scrape.

A noise at the door distracted him. The key turned in the lock, and Abella's head peered in at him. She entered quickly, carrying two tankards, and shut the door behind her.

"Abella. Praise the heavens it is you. She is ill with fever."

She took two steps back. "The plague?"

Matteo frowned. "I don't know. But I have to help her. Do you have water?"

She nodded and brought forward the tankards. "Miss Duplay said no dinner, but she didn't say anything about drink. So I brought the water."

"Again, you are my *ange*. I wonder, could you help me with her dress? Her stays and things?" He didn't want to invade her privacy if at all possible.

Abella hesitated for the briefest of moments and then nodded.

When she had finished loosening Scarlet's stays and removing some of the petticoats, Matteo asked, "Could I trouble you to get us some different clothes from the coffers used to clothe the staff here?"

"You want the clothes from the dead?" her eyes were wide and questioning.

He swallowed and then nodded. "I do. She will need something less confining, simpler, to wear, and I too would love a change of clothing." And the new clothing was their only hope of escape, if he could still manage it with a feverish and unconscious wife.

Abella nodded. Then, reaching into her pocket, she brought out a folded slip of paper. "I almost forgot to give you this. It came today."

Snatching it up gladly, he grinned at her. "News. Let us pray it is good news."

Reading it quickly, his eyes scanning the page, he frowned and crumbled it in his fist. "Marie is lost to us." He squeezed the paper in his fist until his knuckles turned white. The king and now the queen, stripped from their throne and murdered. How could this happen to his dear France? He leaned over Scarlet. "I wish you were awake to hear. Simon got her to the docks, the ship in sight even. So close they could taste the sea. Then Éléonore's men ripped her from the carriage. Simon was able to escape. They let him go, thought him a hired driver. We have that to be thankful for, at least." He turned to Scarlet, but her eyes were still closed and she had begun tossing about. A moan escaped her lips.

Matteo ripped a piece of petticoat, using it to dip in the water and wipe her face. Breathing air lightly onto her skin to cool her, he left the fabric on her forehead, hoping to draw out some of the heat. He fanned her, re-dipped the fabric when it lost its coolness, and then reapplied it. So lost in his ministrations, he almost didn't hear Abella quietly close the door behind her as he began a nightlong vigil to cool Scarlet and lessen the effects of her fever.

Chapter Thirty

SCARLET'S MIND REFUSED TO FOCUS. She ran, lungs hurting, underbrush scratching and pulling at her dress. Her short, eight-year-old legs not covering much distance. Her heart sank when, in her dreamscape, she recognized her family's Spanish villa.

Aware she dreamt but unable to awaken, she tore through the bushes near the front door, rushing around to intercept the callers. But they pulled forward in their carriage just as she remembered. In a moment, her brother would come. Expecting him did not stop the startled pounding of her heart when a hand reached out and pulled her backward into the shadows.

"Be very quiet. Don't move." Trying to protect, her brother sounded more harsh than usual.

"But what is going on?" Her small voice sounded frightened and unsure.

"They've come to get Father. Because of his books."

"Come to get him! Will they take him away?" Her heart pinched and shrunk as fear came to paralyze.

"I will stop them. You stay here." His ten-year-old frame broadened about an inch as he inhaled and braced his shoulders. "Stay here. Promise me."

She nodded, her tiny voice whispering, "I promise." But her adult self, witnessing the dream, screamed out in desperation, "Don't do it! Don't, Nicholas. They'll get you, and you'll die. You will all die." Frozen, unable to escape her new torture, she couldn't look away from the horrors that followed.

He left the cover of the brush.

Voices from inside the house grew louder. Her father shouted, her mother pleaded. Feet struggled and shuffled in the dirt just beyond her hiding place. Her brother rushed forward as the men shackled her parents. But Nicholas's well-aimed kicks in their shins did little to stop progress toward the carriage. His fists pounded their lower backs. The determination on his face was as impressive to

Scarlet now as it was horrifying to her then. Finally, one of the men tired of him and struck him to the ground. A trickle of blood ran down the side of his face.

"No! Leave him alone." Her mother's voice tore through Scarlet again as she recognized the desperation in it.

"He'll have to come with us." The leader jerked his head toward the carriage, and his partner moved to pick Nicholas up.

Scarlet felt her younger self struggle, saw the indecision, saw her feet move forward to reach her brother. Her adult subconscious urged her on, begged her to move. "Go, Scarlet! Run to him. Cover his body with yours. Drag him away. DO SOMETHING!"

But young Scarlet backed up, cowering.

They tossed her brother's unmoving body into the carriage with her parents, and then the horses started moving.

Running out into the street, shouting and calling, she watched after them, her mother's tear-streaked face turned to her out the back window. Young Scarlet waited until the carriage rounded the bend, and then she fell into a heap in the dirt.

Sorrowing with that fallen little girl, her adult mind recognized for the first time the futility of any eight-year-old assistance. Throughout her life, she had blamed herself for cowardice. But now, decades later, a small measure of healing comforted the edges of her wounds, working its way inside. Although her heart still grieved and she could not yet quiet the searing guilt, forgiveness had begun and, with time, would make itself known to her destructive self-recrimination.

The dream closed around her, and Scarlet rose up through a dark tunnel into a blinding light. Squinting and turning her head, she tried to protect herself, but a voice said, "Look."

She shielded her eyes and tried to see into the light. Nearly blinded, she saw nothing but white until she focused and saw through it. There she saw Marie Antoinette, with her daughter, dressed in white. Marie smiled. "I live."

Relief, joy, filled her. Marie—yet alive.

But then Marie's clothing changed, and Robespierre's laugh sounded from Her Majesty's lips. Wearing her dress from the execution, she marched forward on the guillotine platform.

"NO!" Thick, warbling dream silence enveloped Scarlet's shout. Helplessly, she watched Marie again fall prey to the knife.

Marching after her in a clown-like manner, the DuPonts followed her, and each of their children lost their heads; even the toy horse took a turn at the guillotine.

The de Moliers watched on, shaking their heads, and taunting, "She saved us and not you."

"No. No, stop, please!" Unable to stand the pain, she sought the further darkness below, and she felt herself sink into its blessed coolness.

***

She tossed around, arms flailing, knocking against him as he lay beside her. He rose and placed a new piece of petticoat on her forehead. She did not feel any cooler to him. Her fever raged as strongly as ever.

"No!" she shouted and crouched into a ball.

"It's all right, Scarlet. I'm here. You're safe." He added quietly, "For now."

She rolled, turning into him, and buried her face in his chest. He gently stroked her back and ran a hand down her hair, murmuring soothing sounds.

She snuggled closer, and his heart warmed, but it could not dull the worry that grew in his chest. A tight knot formed there, and he could not relax the muscles in his neck and back. They must make their escape, and she showed no signs of improvement.

"Robespierre. His yoke. His collar." Suddenly her eyes flew open and she grabbed his shirt with both fists, trying to shake him. Crazed eyes searched his own. "Cut his jacket at the neckline, and you'll live." She fell back onto his arm, eyes closed.

Éléonore's shrill voice sounded in the hall. "Wait outside."

Their door opened, allowing minimal light from the hallway to enter as well as a welcome feeling of fresher air.

"Isn't that lovely? The marriage bed."

"She's ill, Éléonore. She needs a doctor."

"I care not for her health or your happiness. You are still alive for one reason." She held out a piece of paper and brought out ink and a quill. "You will write a letter to the Pimpernel."

He carefully pulled away from Scarlet in the straw and stood up. "How will you get it into his hands? Have you discovered his identity?" A dread-filled hope entered his mind at the thought. Could he get a message to the man through Éléonore? But if she knew his identity, how long would he live?

"We have ways of getting information into his hands."

Relief filled him. Reaching for the quill, he said, "I don't know what you are trying to accomplish. He is as elusive as any human. You will never capture him."

"Just write. Tell him something that will convince him of your danger. Tell him she dies if he does not come."

A sick ball of jealousy tried to disturb him. He pushed it away as well as he could, but a tendril of worry remained, and his brow wrinkled as he wrote.

Éléonore's laughter jostled Scarlet in her sleep and grated on Matteo's last nerve.

"Jealous, are you? Worried it would matter to him? Your imprisonment brings me more satisfaction than even I predicted." She leaned over him exultantly, pointing to his paper. "Write. Convince him he needs to give up his life for you, for *her*." She stood back a few paces, watching. "If he doesn't come, she will die. First her, then you."

Considering her, his eyes narrowed. "You have changed so much that I do not know you."

She waved her hand impatiently. "Write. I care not for you or your thoughts about my person." A nervous agitation defined her movements. As she lowered her hands again, they trembled.

"What will happen to *you* if this plan fails?"

Her eyes opened wide and she swallowed, staring at him for a moment before relaxing again. "It won't."

***

Hours later, Abella opened the door, carrying dinner, fresh water, and a sachet of herbs. "*Maman* says to try to get her to drink these herbs. I found you a bit of hot water."

Holding out a separate tankard, she indicated he should put the herbs inside to steep.

Overcome with gratitude for any small thing that could help Scarlet, he rested a hand on Abella's shoulder. "Thank you."

She did not flinch at his touch. "Here is a satchel with your clothes. Another note sits at the bottom. Tonight—during the dinner hour—we will leave then."

"Why then? She is still too ill. How will that appear if I am carrying her out?"

"It cannot be helped. An execution is planned—someone close to the committee—and the prison will be light on staff and guards. They've been given permission to watch. It will be our best chance."

"Finally, a viable plan."

Watching Scarlet carefully, he said, "And perhaps she will be well enough." Abella closed the door behind her, the silence of no accompanying clang of the lock not registering in Matteo's mind.

Chapter Thirty-One

SCARLET'S BREATHS MEASURED THE PASSAGE of time for Matteo. Two hundred later, he felt as though he would melt into the floor, his mind as soggy as the mossy concrete.

Continuing to mumble incoherently, she showed no signs of improvement even though he was able to get her to swallow a good amount of the tea from Abella.

"No click. No click in the lock."

"Hmm?" She had mumbled all sorts of things since the start of her fever, most sounding as though she were in the gravest danger or deathly worried for someone.

"No click. No click."

"Thank you, my dear. Try to rest."

His mind planned while lying beside her, curled around her body. Life for himself, life for Scarlet, could be remarkable, filled with joy and happiness. But what peace would they have while France suffered? He knew that neither he nor she would be able to rest until peace again returned to his homeland, until some semblance of order in their government could be trusted to care for its citizens.

She snuggled into him again, and a supreme sense of protective care filled him. She led a dangerous life, one he did not fully understand. Watching her struggle with this fever, unresponsive, everything faded when up against his greatest desire, above all else, to see her eyes, staring, coherent, back at him. He wanted her to live. He wanted her well. The reality that he could not live if she perished sharply impressed upon him, a brand of sorts. He could not endure the knowledge of her in harm's path again, not without his presence beside her. Whatever her mission, he would aid it. Even if she went to assist this Pimpernel, whoever he was, even if she truly loved him.

But first, they would have to leave the prison. He knew Simon would do his part, knew if they could but exit the outer prison doors, they would be as good as home in England. With any luck, they would all meet in the courtyard. Everything was ready. Just the passage of time stood between him and his efforts to leave this cursed place. He prayed they could reach those doors.

The clothes Abella had brought fit. They were tan, nondescript workers' clothing, large enough to conceal his jacket beneath. Like many in France, once out of the prison, they would blend in beautifully. And here in the prison, hopefully they would look just like any other staff, tasked with running dinner to all the many rooms.

Now, he waited. Waited for the hours to pass, waited for Abella to come and unlock their door, waited for Scarlet to wake. But awake or asleep, he planned to walk out of the prison with her tonight.

He shifted, waking from a doze. With no way of actually knowing the hour, his prison sense had developed somewhat and his stomach rumbled, indicating that dinner should be on its way. But where was Abella?

He extricated himself from Scarlet's arms and went to the door to listen. Silence. Anxiety welled within him. All the possible reasons she had not yet opened their door crashed into each other in his brain, increasing the tightness in his chest.

"Click." Scarlet shifted on the pallet.

Using his finger, he tried to push open the hatch window on the door. Stuck, locked, it wouldn't move. His frustration growing, he pounded on the door, shouting, "Hey! Dinner! We are hungry in here."

Silence filled the hallway. With his ear to the door, he couldn't detect any noise at all. Pacing back and forth in the cell, his mind spun with possibilities. He could think of nothing to do but wait. Longer. Kicking at the door, he then pounded it with his fists. Rattling in its frame, the door jiggled and then bounced back toward him, opening a crack.

"What?" Amazement and wonder filled him. The door was unlocked. Abella had left the door unlocked. Sheepish, he grimaced at the lost time spent counting breaths. Moving quickly to Scarlet, he gently picked her up and placed her over his right shoulder. "I'm sorry for this."

Opening the door quietly, he stepped into the hall, carrying their tankards and a tray used for food with one arm, the other holding Scarlet in place. He moved as swiftly as he dared down the hallway, hoping not to see anyone. As he turned the corner onto another passage, a guard approached, wearing a black uniform with the tricolor band on his arm.

"What's the matter with her?"

Clearing his throat, Matteo responded, "Drunk. Finally just passed out back there."

The guard shook his head, obviously disgusted. "Lug her down to the kitchen. Adaline will take care of her."

"Yes, sir." He continued past the guard, holding his breath.

"Hey!"

Matteo turned around.

"The kitchen is the other way." He peered closely into Matteo's face. "Who are you, anyway? I haven't seen you before, and who's this?" He moved around back, lifting up Scarlet's head so he could get a better look at her face. Whistling, he said, "She's a beauty. Maybe I'll take over from here. I'd enjoy a piece of soft flesh—"

Before he could finish his thought, Matteo's fist crashed into his jaw. While the man stepped back, catching blood falling from a gaping hole that once held a tooth, Matteo gently laid Scarlet on the stone floor and moved in on him, connecting with his stomach.

A strong punch to Matteo's eye sent him back several feet. Careful not to step on his wife, he rushed forward again, pounding his fists rapidly and with great strength on any open part of the guard's body.

Sluggish and unprepared for a fight, the guard soon tired, and Matteo's last impact at the side of his head sent him sprawling onto the ground, where he did not rise.

The man's jacket fell open, and his key ring glinted as the candlelight fell on it. Grabbing the keys and then rushing to Scarlet, Matteo walked as quickly as he could down the rest of the hallway and across an open area to the next. Now he was racing time as well as the discovery of the fallen guard. His body remained on high alert, ready for shouting or the bells to clang, signaling a problem.

Instead, he heard the shouts of a young boy. "Help! Someone, please!"

To his right, he recognized the dark corridor where he was originally held; the thought of those conditions still brought a feeling of revulsion. A girl's voice came from down that hallway. "No! Please! Leave him alone!"

Trying to turn away, knowing he didn't have any time or the means to rescue others, his feet obeyed his heart, not his mind, and carried him, rushing into the darkness toward the sounds of crying from the young ones.

Reaching their door, he hoped his keys would work. Still no sound or movement from Scarlet, he adjusted her body slightly on his shoulder.

The third key made a loud click in the door.

"Click," Scarlet mumbled.

Realization dawned. "You knew the lock was opened, didn't you, love?"

She didn't answer, but his grin spread wider than it had in weeks. "Smarter than us all, even while unconscious."

When the door fully opened, a wave of the foul air inside hit him and he stepped backward. Peering inside, he said, "Well, I haven't got all day. If you'd like to leave, now's the time."

Two sets of wide eyes approached, staring up into his face. "Really? We can leave?"

"That's what I hope. We have a lot to do between now and then, but if you follow me, there's a chance—how's that?"

The two young ones couldn't be older than seven or eight. They shared a look, and the girl nodded. "We're coming. But our pa will need some help standing."

Matteo groaned. "He'll have to walk on his own. As you can see, I've got my own load to carry." He paused. "Not that you're a load, my dear."

Other voices shouted from rooms farther down the hall. "Help! Let us out! Oh, please!"

He stepped quickly to the doors, opening them one at a time, handing the keys to another to aid with the doors, not bothering to see who was inside until he reached the end. Turning around, he stepped back in surprise. A sizable crowd stood in front of him, a good group of thirty or more, all looking at him with great expectation.

"Now what will you do, my darling?" A soft voice, muffled in his jacket, sent warmth up and down his insides.

"Scarlet! Are you awake?"

He knelt down until her feet reached the floor and then stood, helping her right herself. She leaned on him, unsteadily, but when her eyes found his, they shone with such a brilliance of life and energy that he filled with hope.

"Well?" Her mouth lifted in a shaky smile.

He pulled her into a gentle embrace, careful to leave her standing. Laughing, he asked, "Well, what?"

Eyes twinkling, gesturing to the people around them, she said, "What are you going to do with all these people?" She raised a hand to the side of his face, eyes shining with pride.

He shrugged, heart warm with her unspoken praise. "I haven't thought that far. But I do know a door that will be open, and Simon waits outside."

Her eyes sharpened. "All right, then. We go. All of us." With a huge smile, she stepped forward confidently, but her knees buckled beneath her and she would have fallen to the ground had Matteo not caught her.

"You were out for several days. Your legs are weak still. I'll carry you."

Leaning into him gratefully, she stared into his eyes. "I'm sorry to be like this. Thank you."

He felt her gaze in his center. Trying to communicate strength and constancy to her, he nodded and lifted her, this time cradling her in his arms.

His voice rang out over the group, though he spoke as quietly as possible. "We must make no noise. Not a single sound. Anyone who sees us will turn us in. We have to make it to the courtyard outside the kitchen and from there, we should be fine."

Scarlet nodded. "Let's be off then."

He walked through the group to the front at the head of the hallway and hurried them as fast as he could in the direction he had been going. Almost to the courtyard, they rushed through two more hallways, seeing no one.

Exiting the last hallway, out into the courtyard, he exhaled in relief. "We have made it." He led the group along the far-right wall, sticking to the shadows, his eyes on a small door on the opposite wall. Twenty more feet, ten; some of the children ran ahead, reaching for the handle before he could get there.

Just before the door creaked open, a voice rang across the ground. "Hold it right there."

Simon stood in full guard uniform, with a squadron behind him. "Don't move another step."

Scarlet gasped in Matteo's arms, but he shushed her. "It's all right. We need an escort through Paris."

"But—"

Simon interrupted her. "Step back away from the door and stand closer together."

The guards quickly moved into position and surrounded them, Matteo fighting a smile.

"You will follow me!" Simon barked and moved toward the door, leading their group, surrounded by men, toward freedom.

"Matteo," Scarlet whispered.

"Hmm?" He glanced down at her, but when he saw the alarmed expression in her eyes, he turned his head to see what had grabbed her attention.

"Éléonore."

"And just what is going on here?" Éléonore quickly stepped up to them, approaching from behind.

They did not have time to haggle with Éléonore. Nor did he want to draw more attention to the courtyard. Matteo decided it was time to give up their cover and stop her once and for all. Nodding at Simon, he signaled the guards to detain her.

No one moved.

Simon said, "Men. Now."

Still no one moved.

"Having a bit of trouble, my dears?" Éléonore's smug tone raised the hairs on his arms.

Scarlet whispered, "These aren't our men."

The shrill laugh Matteo had come to loathe sounded hollow as it echoed off the walls of the prison. "Do you really think, Matteo, that I would not know my own guards? Seize the one they call Simon."

Immediately the two guards nearest Simon grabbed his pistol and his sword and shoved him to the center of the group to join the others.

Matteo bore down on him. "How did you not know?" Anger brimmed below the surface and desperation filled him.

Scarlet laid a soothing hand on his cheek. "He has not met all of the league. More join every day. He couldn't have known." She tilted her head to the side, presumably to get a better view of Éléonore. "My dear! Hello. We meet again. Come closer so that I may see you better and greet you properly."

As soon as Éléonore moved into her line of sight, she exclaimed, "Oh, perfectly dreadful still. Your complexion. You look as though you never see the light of day."

"A bit peaky, yes." Matteo pulled her closer to him and whispered, "But I don't think now is the time—"

"Oh, nonsense. What is a bit of fashion advice between friends? Now, where will you be taking us?"

"You will head straight to *La Conciergerie* tonight and to the guillotine tomorrow. All of you."

A few of the children whimpered, and one lad put his arm across the shoulders of his sister.

Éléonore continued. "Unless . . ."

With raised eyebrows, Matteo shared a look with Simon.

"Unless you can produce the Pimpernel, who will stand in your place."

"Really, Miss Duplay." Scarlet's voice sounded surprisingly calm. "You will march all of us across Paris to *Île de la Cité* and *La Conciergerie*? Tonight?"

A strong voice approached from their right. "What is this, Éléonore?"

"Oh, Robespierre, darling. Just stopping a bit of an escape. Nothing for you to concern yourself with. All is in hand."

His gaze darted over their group, searching. They stopped on Scarlet. "You there, young lady. Turn your face so that I might see you."

Scarlet indicated Matteo should set her on her feet, and then her eyes searched the ground as, hair in her face, she hunched forward as if she had a bump on her back, a disfiguration. Her hands twisted in weird angles and her mouth hung open and to the side, as if she had not the ability to close it. She shuffled toward him with a twisted grimace, her tongue moving erratically in her mouth.

Robespierre stepped back in surprise. "Very well. Put them in one of our larger rooms for the night. We will take care of this in the morning."

"But I had hoped—"

"Éléonore. You will come with me."

She bowed her head; she was close enough that they could see the movement of her jaw as she ground her teeth. She looked from Scarlet to Robespierre and back, and then her face took on a calculating expression. "Of course, darling." She waved her hand to the guards, who immediately began barking orders for the prisoners to stay together and follow them.

Matteo watched Scarlet in amazement. He hardly recognized her. She kept up her new charade, walking with a twisted limp and a hunched back until they were ushered into new accommodations.

Chapter Thirty-Two

"WE HAVE MUCH TO DO before morning." Simon leaned forward, speaking to Matteo and then Scarlet in turn.

She nodded slowly; Matteo reached for her hand.

"We will have a brief window of time in the courtyard while loading carts, to win our freedom."

This time Matteo nodded.

Simon gripped his shoulder, as if trying to infuse him with energy.

A haze fell over Scarlet's mind.

Simon eyed them both and then cleared his throat. "We must get a message to our men, those impersonating Éléonore's guards, somewhere in the prison."

Scarlet focused on him. "Yes. We must. We cannot leave without them."

Simon eyed her.

She felt distant, uninvolved. Perhaps she still tried to shake the effects of her fever. She smiled weakly. "I guess we cannot wait for the Pimpernel to present himself . . ." Her laugh sounded fake, unconvincing, even to herself.

Simon's eyes narrowed. "I would never want the Pimpernel to do such a terrible thing. What good would that do? We would all die anyway, and him along with us."

Matteo interjected. "Do you not think he could negotiate for our lives before he dies?"

His question unnerved her. "Would you so casually toss his life aside?"

Simon smacked a hand on his thigh. "Robespierre does not negotiate. He barrels down everyone in his path, and if he could wipe out the Pimpernel *and* some of his accomplices all at once, more the better for him." He turned his head so that his eyes were inches from Scarlet's own. "Let us not give him that opportunity."

She swallowed. Simon need not worry. She had no intention of throwing herself onto the guillotine platform. If she could just concentrate for a moment or two, all would become clear. She felt her head fall forward and her eyes close. She jerked herself awake again. "Perhaps if I just lie here, just for a moment?" She leaned to the side, the weight of her body pulling her down to the dirt floor.

Matteo gestured for a young lady to come forward. "Would you allow her to rest her head on your skirts?"

The young lady smiled and gently lifted Scarlet's head, sliding her body beneath.

The bliss of sleep enveloped her. As she was slipping away into incoherence, a gentle thought reminded her, *But we must escape.* She countered, *Yes, yes, we have time for that later.* And Scarlet began to quietly snore.

***

"She has been ill for days and needs this rest. We can carry on without her, and she won't feel the strain of trying to assist."

Simon eyed him. "Trying to assist." He shook his head. "Without her, we are nothing." He stared at the wall for a moment. "But while she sleeps, we can try to reach our contacts here in the prison."

"Abella. She never came—just left my door unlocked. I don't know why." Not for the first time, he worried for her safety.

Simon began talking with the group, analyzing their strengths. But Matteo felt a new sharp awareness. The more he thought about their plight, the more he realized the inevitable outcome and his own part to play.

A clang sounded at their door, the metallic turning of a key in the lock. A scrawny, rat-faced young man waved a group behind him into the room. Each person carried a tankard of water for the prisoners to share. Placing them on the filthy floor, the servants filed back out.

Simon approached them. "Wait."

The rat-faced man ushered the others out and turned to Simon.

"A large group of men, impersonating soldiers. Do you know where they are being kept?"

"I might."

"Is there a way to get word as to their whereabouts or to get a message to them?"

Rat face eyed him, almost squinting. "No. And now that I know your kind of aristocratic scum is looking for them, I'll make sure no one else does either." He spat on the floor in front of Simon and then walked out and locked the door behind him.

Night passed in the longest torture possible, dragging out by the seconds, measured in drops of water falling in the corner from some moisture in the ceiling. Scarlet woke and listened then slept again. The longer the night dragged, the more certain Matteo became of his options, and his angst turned into peace.

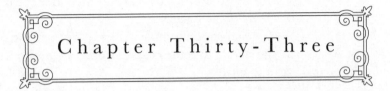

Chapter Thirty-Three

FINALLY FEELING RELIEF, ALMOST GRATITUDE even, that the night had ended and their executioners had come, Matteo stood as Éléonore and four soldiers entered the room.

"It seems that your hero is a coward. We have waited through the night to discover that he will save others but not his own friends." She made a clucking noise with her tongue and looked on them all with mock pity. "That being the situation, we will begin your executions immediately, starting with you." She grabbed the shirt of the nearest person to her—a young boy standing next to his mother.

His face pinched and he shouted, "What? No!"

The mother pleaded, "No, please! He's just a child. Surely no enemy to your republic."

"Well, there you see, evidence right here. *My* republic, is it? Why not *your* republic? You are raising the spawn of royal-loving slaves. You all must be purged." She waved her hand over their group in a nonchalant air. "You might feel honored, really. It is through your very deaths that France can be cleansed and begin a new rule." She wiped an imaginary tear from her eye and then waved to the guards to start lining people up at the door, the young boy first.

"Wait." Matteo stepped forward, his jaw firm, his countenance resolute.

"Oh, Matteo, it's you. Don't worry, you shall get your chance. We must wait a moment for Robespierre to arrive. He didn't want to miss your particular execution."

"I have news of the Pimpernel."

Pleased, a snakelike smile curled her lips. "Yes?"

"I know who he is. He's here even now." Matteo tried to stop the waver in his voice, forced it to sound calm.

Simon gasped. "You must stop this at once. Matteo, this is most assuredly not helping." His eyes bore into Matteo's with a strange intensity.

Éléonore's eyes flicked through the group hungrily. "Who is it? Tell me. Turn yourself in, I tell you, or everyone dies."

Matteo crossed his arms in front of his chest. "You must free the others. Free the group first, and then I will tell you."

"Oh no, my old friend. There is no bargaining with me. We begin the deaths immediately. And when you decide to cooperate, we stop." She held open the door, and the guards began to leave.

"Desist. It is I, Éléonore. I am the one you want. I . . . am the Pimpernel."

Scarlet stepped toward him and placed her hand on his arm. "No, Matteo. What are you doing?"

He covered her hand with his own but could not look into her face. He knew her eyes would undo him.

Éléonore scoffed. "You? The Pimpernel? Do you think I will believe that?"

He stepped forward, Scarlet at his side. "Do not let these people die. Of course it is I. Naturally he must be a Frenchman who has an understanding of the workings of this new government, with friends on the inside. You, Éléonore, have been feeding me information for years without realizing it. Things have become more complicated with my exile to England, but we have still managed to free all our old neighbors and Potier as well."

Her eyes narrowed in suspicion. "But we captured you in the foolish attempt to find him—"

"I allowed myself to be captured, with the hopes of rescuing these very people, and my wife, of course."

"She was captured after you—"

"In the act of carrying out my orders to free Her Majesty."

Laughing, Éléonore snarled, "At which she failed."

Scarlet swayed, clutching his arm. He steadied her in concern. One of the men to her left stepped forward at her other side.

"Nevertheless, I am he. And this charade of a lure and bait must end now. Let these people go, according to your word. And take me straightaway if you wish."

"No, Matteo, listen to me." Scarlet reached forward, grabbing at his hands. He pulled her into his arms.

She whispered into his ear, "Remember your jacket. If you get a chance, slit the back of Robespierre's collar."

He blinked; this was not what he expected from his fainting wife. He continued on anyway. "It is for the best, my dear." He patted her back in consolation. Then, speaking to Éléonore, he said, "I have proof. The ring itself."

He dug into his pocket and presented the ring he had found in Scarlet's bureau, with the two small flowers on its surface. It wasn't her signet, possibly was not even the pimpernel flower, but it could work.

"Could it be you?" Éléonore's face filled with a deranged aura of satisfaction, almost smiling, her mind apparently lost in thought. "Even if it isn't you, you will proclaim it is, to Robespierre and everyone. You have the ring. It *could* be you after all." She stepped up to him, her perfume irritating his nose and filling the air around them. She pressed up against him and whispered in his ear, "I am not fooled. But we will move forward with this deception. It is enough to trick that fool, Robespierre." Turning around she shouted, "Guards! Lead them away, all of them."

Matteo stepped toward her and grabbed her by the shoulders, forcing her to look into his face. "Éléonore, let them go."

"Unhand me."

The guards moved to apprehend Matteo, but he stepped away, pulling her with him. Other prisoners stepped between them.

"Let them go, Éléonore."

"Or what? You have no power here. In the Bastille prison, we kill who we like, with no trial, no reason."

He resisted shaking her in his anger and instead leaned forward until they were nose-to-nose, piercing her eyes with his own. "Or I denounce you." He glared. "I denounce you to Robespierre. Then I denounce you to the crowd. I'll denounce you to every guard I see, every other person in my path. I will spend every breath denouncing you with all my evidence."

She staggered back, hand on her heart. "What evidence?"

"All those hours wishing to be an aristo—pining away for a lovely dress— seeking my hand, my title. You are an aristo in your heart—guilty as the rest."

Her face had gone white. "Robespierre would never listen to you."

She sounded unsure and, for a moment, he thought he had won. "Let them go. Escape with us."

She turned to study him, eyes travelling over his face as if discovering his features for the first time. "I will not. We must still cleanse France, darling. And now we will be free of the Pimpernel along with the rest of you all in one morning. If I have to die too, so be it." She laughed, a maniacal, crazed noise, closer to a shriek, and then turned from him as the guards began barking orders and forcing people into a group and out the door.

He grabbed at his chest, fisting the shirt, stepping back two steps, reaching for something to steady himself. He felt soft hands holding his, loosening the fabric in his grip, cradling them.

His eyes sought Scarlet's. "I thought I could negotiate. I thought she might be reasonable. Why would she want all these people to die? Such a waste—they have done nothing." He shook his head. "And to die herself, willing to be denounced. She has lost her mind."

"You did right, Matteo." Her face shone with love. Her hand found the side of his face and she stared tenderly into his soul, infusing him with strength. He caught her into his arms and pressed his mouth to hers, blocking out everyone else for as long as he could. She had such faith in him, so much love. He would go to death a happy man. Together, they turned to face the others in the room.

Simon's face seemed pinched. "I'm not seeing a happy ending here. I can't reach the guards. Our men. I am . . . without a plan."

Scarlet turned her attention to Simon, and Matteo felt her loss.

She said, "Dear Simon. We will leave here, trying to save the people of France. Is there any better way?"

"No, I suppose not. But Franny, you know. We could have had something."

Scarlet stepped forward to embrace him. "There may still be time. Where the Pimpernel is involved, there is always hope."

Simon almost scoffed, but as his eyes travelled her face, they stopped and lit for a moment. "Hope it is. We will move forward on the merits of hope alone."

"Keep moving!" The guards had almost cleared the room, and more joined them as their large group moved down the hallway.

Éléonore rubbed her hands together in greed. "Send for Citizen Robespierre. He wished to see us before we departed. Indeed, he may even join us."

One of the guards saluted and took off at a run down the adjoining hallway while their group continued to the courtyard from yesterday. This time it was not empty. This time it held a line of cages on wheels.

Once they witnessed their conveyance to death, everyone in the group grew quiet.

Robespierre's voice carried down the hallway. "I wish to see him myself."

The head of the committee, the man who held on with such a tight fist to power in Matteo's beloved France, stepped forward.

Eerily powerful and yet unremarkable, his voice was soft, his words measured. "Who is the one who claims to be the Pimpernel?"

Matteo cleared his throat and stepped forward. "It is I."

"You?"

"Yes."

"How could it be you? One of our own? You, so understanding of our beginnings."

"The Revolution in the beginning promised peace and hope and freedom."

"You would desert your homeland? Turn traitor to your own people?"

"As soon as it became more about you and your committee than about actually freeing France, I realized you'd gone too far. I abhor your methods. Violence to stop the violence? Even a simpleton can see that you are merely grasping to cling to your tenuous hold on power. You have turned my glorious nation into a cesspool of cruelty and killing. You breed more murderers with each moment that passes."

Robespierre used a finger to loosen the cravat at his neck. "I can see you are unenlightened, but that is no matter. You will soon be dead and a frustrating bane to us no longer."

"There will be those who rise to help. The Pimpernel is but a title, a symbol for anyone who rescues those who cannot save themselves. My death will not end your bane. Where terror exists, heroes will always rise."

One of the boys from the back yelled, "*Oui!*"

With scowling eyes searching the group of prisoners, Robespierre responded, his voice low and measured, "And we will stamp them out as they come, one by one, until no one else dares. Fear, Matteo. Fear is a hefty deterrent." He stepped to the nearest guard. "I have asked for reinforcements, in the event we see anyone rising to the rescue. I want all of France to know whose head is about to fall, even should it stir up a minor insurrection. We will stamp out any who dare to interfere."

As he finished speaking, a new group of guards entered the courtyard in uniform, led by two of the prison staff. Matteo diverted his eyes before he showed any recognition of Abella. He let out a slow breath of relief. Wherever she had been, he was happy to know she lived. Walking beside her, a younger boy, maybe ten years old—her brother judging by the facial similarities—hid slightly behind her, but his eyes sought out Scarlet.

Most people would not have even noticed a response in her, but Matteo watched for it. Her shoulders relaxed, and the tightness with which she had been carrying herself seemed to loosen.

Robespierre turned to the carts. "Guards, continue as you were. I wish to witness the loading of carts myself. And never fear, unworthy traitors. I will view each slicing end to your pathetic and unremarkable lives." Robespierre gestured for them all to exit the outer doors of the prison. As some were still loading, others began the trek under a short, arched tunnel and out onto the street.

Matteo's hope to be the only death of the group crumbled around him. Desperately, he searched for an answer, some small solution, anything to prevent more from loading into those carts. The guards shoved him forward, Scarlet at his side, toward the last barred, moving prison, opening the door with a bow as if a footman on their estate.

A voice called out, carrying across the courtyard, "Wait."

Robespierre.

Everyone turned to him.

"Stop. You, miss. Come here." He studied Scarlet.

Éléonore simpered, cowering behind Robespierre. "You see, citizen, I have brought many into your hands. Even the Seamstress." She leaned into him. "She is in fact the English noble Lady Cavendish, now Comtesse Durand."

Prisoners stepped forward, watching; guards as well, curious. The carts paused in their departures.

With head high and shoulders back, she walked across the courtyard to him, passing their fellow prisoners who eyed her in sympathy, passing the guards paused in ushering prisoners toward carts, and walking right in front of Abella and her brother until she stood not two feet from Robespierre and his personal guards. She stared, unflinching, into his face.

Those first green eyes came into Matteo's mind again, courageous, shimmering. He inched closer, hoping to stand at her side in protection. A crackle fizzled in the air, tense, as if everyone stood on the balls of their feet, waiting.

"You're the Seamstress."

Scarlet pulled on her hair as if she had a braid. "I am."

"Are you also Lady Scarlet Cavendish of England?"

She smiled and curtsied. "I am."

"What can you mean, coming here, aiding the women of the Revolution and myself?" He leaned closer to her, breathing in her face. "Falsifying names, allowing hundreds to go free?" Hands clenched at his sides, he grit his teeth.

"Two hundred and sixty-two to be precise, if you are counting." She brushed the front of her prison dress, straightening it.

He raised his hands slowly toward her neck as if he meant to squeeze it. The group inched forward. He cleared his features and lowered his arms. "Then you know what is about to happen when I do this!"

He shook one arm down, grabbing at the knife handle in his right palm so fast his movements blurred, and brought his arm up in one sweeping motion toward her neck.

But a hand stopped him, a uniformed hand at his right.

Matteo had rushed forward as soon as he saw the downward shake of Robespierre's arm, recognizing it from his own practice. But now he jerked to a stop, looking from Robespierre to the guard and back.

Robespierre resisted the restraining hand, pulling his arm, twisting to loosen the grip. "What is the meaning of this? Release me at once." The veins on his neck began to swell and his face turned a deep shade of red.

The guard wrenched Robespierre's arm, squeezing at the wrist until he dropped the knife. "Not so fast, *citizen*. You have crimes to answer for, against the people of France."

Scarlet's gasp sounded small, but Matteo felt it hit his chest. Her eyes were wide, watching the guard in hopeful wonder.

Could it be him? Finally, the Pimpernel come to rescue them?

Matteo inched forward, ever closer. Whoever it was, he sensed danger could turn at any moment, so tenuous was the hold on power by either group.

The guard grabbed Robespierre by the collar and jerked his arm behind his back, reaching for the other to tie them together; but Robespierre used that moment and shook his left hand down, grasped his other knife, and whirled, cutting into the flesh on the guard's forearm.

Scarlet gasped. "No!"

Then Robespierre turned and grabbed a handful of Scarlet's hair, forcing her to her knees, knife at her throat.

Matteo ran forward, a crazed urgency filling him, his heart pounding, but the group closed in front of him. He was stopped, pushed back by a crowd of prisoners and guards all of the same mind, some with knives of their own drawn and pointed at Robespierre.

"Stop!" Robespierre shouted, wrenching Scarlet's head to the side, by her hair. "Stop it now. I would happily spill her blood right here."

They paused, everyone, in their rush to disembowel him.

Matteo only adjusted his direction and made his way slowly around behind the man.

"Stop, Matteo. I see you. Stop, or she dies!"

He froze and raised his hands.

"Drop your knives. All of you, drop your knives." Then, leaning over the top of Scarlet, he said, "Clever Seamstress. Everyone benefits from your insidious genius, do they?" He jerked her head back so that a long stretch of bare neck was visible. "But now what will you do"—he ran the cold blade along her soft, rosy skin—"knowing you will die from one of your own tricks?"

He nicked her, perhaps on accident, but a thin slice of blood welled up on her white skin. Matteo rushed forward, shoving aside the remaining few in front of him. Grabbing Robespierre's wrist, he twisted his arm, keeping the knife pointed away, and yanked him backward, jerking off-balance.

While Matteo engaged Robespierre, someone pulled Scarlet forward and out of his clutches, free from the knife.

Swinging the first fist at Robespierre's face, Matteo said, "You dare to cut her."

The man staggered from a solid hit to the jaw but rallied, laughing. He twisted his hand free of Matteo's grip and taunted, "Surely you have more strength, or did my prisons sap it out of you?" His answering fist nearly toppled Matteo to the ground.

Centering his resolve, Matteo leapt forward, both knives now in his hands, lunging.

Robespierre spun and dodged and leapt, blocking all of his forward thrusts. The man could not be contained, and his responses were lightning fast.

A searing burn sliced Matteo's upper left shoulder. Calling out, he backed up two steps, glancing at his arm. The cut seemed shallow, but blood stained his shirt and spread down his arm.

Robespierre did not wait for him to reassess; he leapt forward again, aiming for Matteo's heart.

Kicking at him, forcing the man backward, Matteo prepared himself.

Robespierre fought like a lion, lunging and retreating, not showing any signs of fatigue. In between thrusts, he called, "Guards! To the courtyard!"

Footsteps sounded down a hallway, and another group of men poured into their small space. The additional guards paused, perhaps not certain whom to engage.

Confusion reigned. Guards fought each other and prisoners.

Robespierre, caught in his own struggle, could not direct them.

Simon and the league's advantage lay in that they knew who was an enemy and who was an ally. Soon they overtook the new guards and began freeing prisoners from carts and preparing to exit.

But Matteo remained engaged in a fight for his life. They needed to head outside the courtyard gate soon to end this fight before more came to oppose them, but Robespierre did not seem to tire. Matteo spun around behind the man, finally tearing at his sleeve, making contact with skin. Circling again, he jabbed at Robespierre's thigh next, and then his arm again. He kept up his fast pace, circling behind Robespierre again, the man turning in place to attempt to face him. But Matteo was too quick, reaching in and jabbing, circling. Around and around Robespierre, he increased his speed, ever faster, not dizzy from his movements, intent only on opportunities to weaken his enemy.

The man leapt away, away from Matteo's mad dance, and struck at those in front of him, but the guards shoved him backward, almost into Matteo's knife. He maneuvered within a hair's breadth of death, avoiding a thrust of the blade.

Mind racing, searching for another strategy, Matteo spun one more time, kicking Robespierre's legs and tripping him up. Stumbling, the man spun in an effort to regain his balance. Taking advantage of that split second of weakness, Matteo lunged, knife in front of him, and thrust it into Robespierre's side. Not a direct hit to the heart, but Robespierre seemed stunned by it and slumped to the ground, eyes rolling back in his head.

Matteo searched the courtyard for Scarlet, circling again, combing the crowd. Not finding her, he became frantic.

"Matteo! No!"

He whipped around toward the sound of Scarlet's voice and was knocked to his back by a barreling Robespierre, running at him, shoulder down. Matteo blinked, trying to focus on the man now standing above him, knife in hand. He raised up on one elbow, prepared to roll and avoid a new thrust of the knife. But a guard caught in a fight with another fell across his legs, pinning him to the ground. Robespierre smiled, satisfaction and triumph darkening his features. Then they clouded, and shock and confusion marred his face.

As Robespierre started to teeter on his feet, he cried out in pain and rubbed at the back of his neck, dropping his knife, his hands slapping at his skin, spreading a thin, white powdery substance up in the air in a great cloud around him.

"Back away!" Scarlet's voice carried. "It's Hellebore. Don't breathe it or touch it."

Chapter Thirty-Four

A GREAT CHEER SHOOK THE walls of Paris as a signal from the guards indicated the start of the death processional. Callers, sent out from the committee, read decrees and with great shouts of announcement encouraged the whole city to come. A mass of people, the size of which they hadn't seen since the death of Louis XVI pressed into *La Place*, bodies and smells all blending together into one great mass. The sun shone in a great brightness and the people, glistening with sweat, chanted and cheered, knowing that today the infamous Pimpernel would finally lose his battle at the hands of the great and feared Robespierre.

"They are coming!" Guards stood at their posts, shouting.

The people, as one, strained their necks, twisting against each other from where they stood, to gain sight of the first cart as it would roll into *La Place*. Everyone attempted a guess at the identity of the clever master of disguise; many wagered they knew him. Fights broke out in the cause of discovery.

However, when the first wheels touched the cobblestone of the great square, silence rolled in, touching them one at a time, rolling through the crowd as the cart became visible to each person, blanketing all in a great wave.

Empty, pulled by a donkey, the sound of wheels on stone echoed hollowly in the great, silent square. The next cart also empty, and the next.

"*Pas encore*! Not again," someone shouted, followed by absolute quiet.

"What's this?" A guard rushed forward, checking under the nearest cart. "Empty."

Those closest checked each of the carts, responding with a similar, "Empty."

In the silence of the square, a fear developed, as cart after cart, empty, rolled toward them. The donkeys pulled up to the guillotine as they were trained to do, and stopped. The guards slapped their rumps, ordering them to exit across the back of the guillotine platform and out of the square. Cart after cart rolled in and on by.

The people shivered in angst.

"The ghosts of past victims."

"Come to haunt us all."

A slow murmur began as the processional continued. Fearful shouts sounded and then were hushed by those nearby. Women cried, confused. And then silence descended again when the last cart came into view. Stretched between two bits of a stick, a large red flower against a stark white background rode in on the top of the cart. And in it, moaning on the floor, hands and feet tied and mouth gagged, Robespierre jerked his body, writhing and grimacing. Those closest to him witnessed a red swelling on his neck and head, with the remains of a white powdery substance. Pinned to his clothing, a sign read, "A gift to the citizens of France."

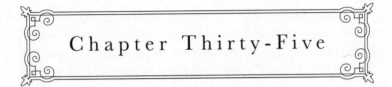

Chapter Thirty-Five

WIND RACED THROUGH THEIR HAIR, billowing their skirts, fighting against the knots of every cravat. But it carried them home to blessed England. And yet, Scarlet felt a familiar longing, a sort of homesickness for France. Not for the awful *Place de Grève* or the Bastille prison or *La Conciergerie*, but for a people she had grown to love. For dear Abelino, Abella, and for shopkeepers and their friends. Try as she did to convince them otherwise, they had refused to come to safety. And a part of her felt guilty gratitude. More would be saved because of their brave stance to help their brothers and sisters in France. But she missed them and felt their lack in the ship's celebrations.

Gathered around on deck, passengers pressed to one side of the boat, some with their first vista of England. The shopkeepers who would come, as well as some of the soldiers who had switched sides in the moment, shared the rail, pondering their new home.

And best of all, her brother, Nicholas, had joined them. When the guard stopped Robespierre's blade, saving her life, she caught his eye, recognizing him at once. No one else as yet knew who he was. Not ready to enter society, he had requested her silence. But he had agreed to return with her, and she couldn't believe the turn of her life, family near once again. Her heart flowed with warmth and love. Nicholas caught her eye, grinning as though his cheeks would crack, and then turned to respond to the woman beside him.

Breath warm and comforting in her ear, Matteo murmured, "I know he is far braver than I, stronger probably, smarter, but I guarantee I am a better dancer."

Turning to him, not trying to hide her confusion, Scarlet asked, "Who?"

He hesitated, seemed almost fearful. "The Pimpernel."

Trying to keep her grin small, she said, "You are correct on all fronts, except one. The Pimpernel is also a better dancer."

Matteo stiffened, but she faced him and placed a hand on his arm. Turning to look behind her, she called, "Simon, would you and the men come here for a moment?"

Once they had gathered, she said, "Matteo and I are having a bit of a discussion about the Pimpernel. He is of the opinion that this heroic person is stronger than Matteo himself must be." She looked around to gauge their reaction, and they all nodded their heads. "Braver?" They nodded again, some hiding smiles.

Matteo shifted beside her. "Scarlet, really, your point is made."

"Now, just a moment. We must explore your other points, equally. Is the Pimpernel also smarter?"

"Most definitely." Simon nodded.

"No thanks for that, man." Matteo's eyes narrowed farther. He adjusted his body as if preparing to leave them.

"Darling, no. Stay. You won't regret it." She turned to him apologetically.

Studying her for a moment, he resettled, hugging Scarlet from behind.

Scarlet held up a finger. "There is one more point we must discuss. It is also Matteo's belief that he is a better dancer. What say you?"

This time the league paused. Simon chimed in, "Well, now, I've never danced with him." He indicated Matteo. "As to *his* prowess, I cannot attest." He grinned. "But the Pimpernel—*she* is unmatched in her sex." He bowed to Scarlet.

"She?" Matteo turned Scarlet's body so he could see into her face. "She? You?"

This time she allowed a smile to fill her face. "What a relief that you now know. Yes, it is I, and this is a part of my league. Andrew, you see, is missing, and there are eight more in England, three in the South of France right now."

Rubbing his face, he remained silent for a moment.

"I *married* the Pimpernel?"

The men nodded in sympathy.

Lord Courtenay called out, "Best of luck, man."

A few spoke other words of condolence as they stepped away. One said, "Have the devil of a time," as they moved farther down the deck, shaking their heads and covering laughs.

Simon, the last to go, reached forward and gripped his shoulder. "We couldn't have picked a better man to join our league. Welcome, Matteo." Their eyes met, and Scarlet's heart warmed to see trust flow between them. Then Simon stepped back a pace or two.

"But there's just one thing I don't understand." Matteo's voice carried over the deck and drew a few back to them. He wrapped his arms around Scarlet as he leaned against the mast of the ship, she resting comfortably against the length of his strong body.

"Just one?" Simon quirked up his brow, and those nearest him laughed. More had left the rails of the ship and come to listen.

"And what is that, my darling?" Scarlet felt as though she might float away on the wind, so light and carefree was her heart at the moment.

"How did all of the prisoners come to have knives? And how did you know I would rescue them? It was but a whim to enter that hallway, and you were unconscious at the time." He paused for a moment. "And *how* were the guards freed and on our side in the first place?"

The men of her league laughed. Simon quipped, "So many *hows*. Unfortunately, she never answers those kinds of questions."

The others on deck joined in their laughter. One woman raised her hand and called out, "I can answer some of them. I was one that you thought you rescued." "Thought I rescued?"

Scarlet smiled with sympathy and turned to him. "Yes, my dear. You see, their doors were already unlocked. Abella saw to that. They were biding their time before they would leave their cells and release the guards, our guards, and come to the courtyard to aid us."

He ran a hand through his hair. "And so, when I opened the doors and they joined us, they then became locked in a cell with us, truly locked?"

The woman called out, "That's right. But it all worked out in the end, didn't it? And you did save a few we didn't know whose doors were truly locked, and I'll bet they're grateful."

A few cheers and claps indicated they were.

"But how did you coordinate all of this in your feverish and unconscious state?"

Clucking his tongue, Simon muttered, "More *hows*."

Matteo frowned.

"Now, darling, I will explain all; don't listen to them." She narrowed her eyes good-naturedly at Simon. "You see, these good people, and many more back in France, came to my rescue while I was trying to save Marie." Her voice faltered, and she stopped.

"I'm sorry, Scarlet. We did everything we could. My plan would have worked and she would have been saved if they had not bumped up her execution by two days."

"You had a rescue plan?" She warmed, grateful to replace previous doubts with a new pride in her husband.

"Yes, I was rather proud of it. They were to rescue Marie, replacing her with the corpse of a woman who had died in prison, carrying the deceased out to *La Guillotine* as if she had fainted, with the people of France none the wiser."

Scarlet's eyes widened, and she raised a hand to her mouth.

Nervously, he stammered, "You know, as if she had fainted . . . It is a bit gruesome, I suppose. We found a body that resembled her and everything, though a bit odiferous—"

Covering her mouth and wincing, she said, "Stop, no. It was brilliant, but I cannot stomach it right now." Eyeing him again, she said, "Brilliant." A new respect grew inside her for this man she had married.

She sighed. "Such a great loss. And now her children are alone." They both stared out at the blue water, silent for a moment. She turned her cheek against Matteo's chest. "But you were quite clever, darling. Thank you for trying." Fatigue settled, and she worked to keep her eyes open.

Matteo squeezed her in his arms. "And my question? You must know I am quite anxious to discover your methods."

She turned to him. Matteo's eyes held such boyish curiosity that she gleaned energy from them. "Oh! Yes. How it all happened. Certainly I will explain the circumstances. These good people"—she held her arm out, indicating the passengers on the ship deck—"led by our dear friend Abelino, came to my rescue once, and at that moment, we set things in motion for them to lend assistance again.

"You see, when I turned myself in at the prison for your sake, I suspected that Robespierre and certainly Éléonore would not allow me to leave. These dear souls had already agreed to put themselves in prison, risk their very lives, so that Marie would have a means of escape, and I trusted they could aid in my own rescue, notwithstanding she did not accompany."

Matteo nodded. "And your guards that Simon and I planted were also present."

"Discovered, unfortunately. We have dressed as her guards before, and she is always suspicious."

A young lad from the back called out, "Abella found them—she and Abelino."

"And led them into the square at just the right moment." Scarlet held out her hands, gesturing to include them all. Tears filled her eyes, and for a moment she couldn't speak for the gratitude that welled up inside. For the first time, as she thought of her efforts, the memory of her parents did not haunt her. "And so you see, the Pimpernel isn't any one person—just like you said, my dear husband—but instead, a feeling of selfless bravery. This strong motivation drives every one of us and those of the league who wait in France and England. We risk all." Her voice wavered, and she cleared her throat, smiling through new tears. "We risk all, to save those who cannot save themselves."

Author's Notes

As with all historical fiction, some of the elements of this story are true accounts of history and well-researched fact. I used original sources and journals whenever possible, and the setting and characters are accurate to the year 1793 as much as possible. I also made a real effort to be accurate to the original *Scarlet Pimpernel* stories told by Baroness Orczy. In addition, the following people and events deserve mention as nonfictional parts of the story:

- Prince George was soon to become the prince regent. His father showed increasing illness and mental inability. In 1793, much of this is not known and the bouts are more rare, but there is growing evidence that his mental illness was of longer duration than was originally thought possible.
- The waltz was not danced in England for many years to come, but it is not implausible that Prince George would have requested a ball with the waltz. He was known to be eccentric and shocking, both morally and otherwise.
- The description of Carlton house is mostly accurate, as are the descriptions of the ball he threw, the rose room, the artwork, and even the outdoor décor with the tents. His described plans to include a river and fountain on his next tabletop, with fish included, was in fact a reality in the next party he threw. The house was constantly under renovation and never considered finished. The renovations are not mentioned in the story. I moved forward like we all wish we could when dealing with renovations—as if they were already completed.
- Princess Elizabeth of Hungary is a fictional character, demonstrating one of the many Prince George entertained instead of accompanying his wife. Marie Antoinette was from royal lineage in Hungary, and so in my mind, they might be cousins.

- Claire Lacombe and the Society of Revolutionary Republican Women worked hard for a constitution in France, one that included women's rights. They insisted others wear the tricolor cockade, demanded the price of bread be lowered, and supported the Jacobins. I can only guess their true personalities, which may have been very different than I portray.

- Olympe de Gouges, sometimes called the world's first feminist, wrote many plays and letters and essays and other materials she spread through the city, among them *The Declaration on the Rights of Women*. She supported the king and queen, was considered a Girondist, and was executed in the year the book takes place. Some of her comments are direct quotes of her own words.

- Charlotte Corday was sent to the guillotine for murdering Jean-Paul Marat in his bathtub.

- Marie Antoinette was executed in the year 1793. An attempt to rescue her failed. She had in fact planned to travel on the ship called *The Sally* and live with the Clough family in Maine. They had some of her furniture pieces and, it is rumored, her cats. To this day, a specific breed of cat very similar to those belonging to Marie Antoinette can be found in Maine.

- Of the character and personality of Marie Antoinette, I chose to write her from the perspective of the English, Scarlet specifically. The wealthy English loved Marie and supported the nobles in France.

- The Carnation Plot is briefly highlighted as well. Someone did send in a flower to Marie, and she responded with pokes in a paper.

- I made some educated guesses with the character and personality of Robespierre. The story falls at a time when his power is not yet absolute. In my story, I write as though he has already arrived in power as the head of the Committee of Public Safety. Éléonore Duplay was his mistress. Her character, upbringing, goals, and personality in this story are all my own creation.

- The Spanish Inquisition was winding down during the time when Scarlet's parents would have travelled to Spain but was not yet finished. The disagreement over the Faulkland Islands was brief but very real and heated during the time they would have been travelling.

Also, look for brief nods, characters, and ideas found in other stories told in historical France. I have a particular fondness for *A Tale of Two Cities* and *Les Misérables*.

And finally, the premise of *Scarlet* came from the wonderful character and story of *The Scarlet Pimpernel*. I include specific references, sticking closely to the plot in some scenes, and then I deviate greatly in others. I don't follow any one particular book of Baroness Orczy's but dip into many. I may have been influenced by the film adaptations as well as the musical. I am fascinated by this story when it is told in any medium, and I am grateful to add my creativity to the others before me.

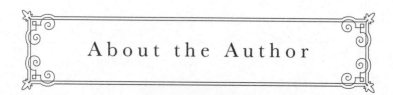

About the Author

JEN GREW UP READING *A Tale of Two Cities*, *The Scarlet Pimpernel,* and *Les Misérables.* When she discovered the character of the Scarlet Pimpernel, saving so many from the guillotine, she wished to join him. Imagining a woman doing the same seemed natural from then on. Now an award-winning author, she works to keep important moments in history vibrant and alive through her stories. Her debut novel, *The Nobleman's Daughter,* was published in November 2017. A lover of history, romance, and her husband and six children, Jen hikes, skis, and once greeted a turtle under the water by grabbing his fin. You can find her news at http://www.jengeiglejohnson.com.